Riding Hearts

Riding Hearts

Thomas Moffatt

**TOP HAT
BOOKS**

Winchester, UK
Washington, USA

First published by Top Hat Books, 2015
Top Hat Books is an imprint of John Hunt Publishing Ltd., Laurel House, Station Approach,
Alresford, Hants, SO24 9JH, UK
office1@jhpbooks.net
www.johnhuntpublishing.com

For distributor details and how to order please visit the 'Ordering' section on our website.

Text copyright: Thomas Moffatt 2014

ISBN: 978 1 78279 744 9
Library of Congress Control Number: 2014958364

A CIP catalogue record for this book is available from the British Library.

Design: Stuart Davies

Printed in the USA by Edwards Brothers Malloy

We operate a distinctive and ethical publishing philosophy in all
areas of our business, from our global network of authors to
production and worldwide distribution.

In memory of
Eric Herbert Moffatt (11.12.1909 to 15.05.2014)
A man to whom I will be eternally grateful.
My grandfather and the man who inspired me to become
an author.

Thank you to all at John Hunt Publishing and Top Hat Books.

Chapter One

The End?

The Riding Officer sat upon his horse as he gazed across the North Sea off the Lincolnshire coast. It was late March, the sun had not long set and he knew the worst of the winter weather was gone. The sea was like a millpond, the sky was clear and the air was cool. He knew the weather was too good for any smuggling or plundering; for the Riding Officer, good weather was a positive omen. Had that been the last of the Riding Officer's concerns, he would have been a content man.

He drummed his fingers on his horse's saddle as he recalled leaving London. It was too late now for dwelling on the past. He could not help but detest himself for the circumstances that had led him to reluctantly accepting the position of the much-maligned riding officer. *Exile* was the word best used to describe his residence in Upperbridge located on the North East Coast of Lincolnshire. He was employed as a coastal taxman patrolling a section of the coast on horseback, trying to catch smugglers and owlers for little or scant reward.

The year was 1797. King George the Third was on the throne of the Kingdom of Great Britain, William Pitt the Younger was Prime Minister and since 1793, Great Britain had been at war with the French Republic. In this era, smuggling was rife within the coastal communities, flooding the British market with contraband in an effort to avoid paying tax on incoming and outgoing goods. As a result, Britain and Ireland's coastlines were patrolled by customs officers on horseback, known as Riding Officers. The officers would patrol lengths of coast in all weathers looking for smugglers who were attempting to land illegal imports, owlers bidding to export goods illegally, suspicious vessels off the coast and small boats attempting to land

1

contraband.

The position of the Riding Officer was unrewarding and unforgiving. Paid between twenty and fifty pounds a year, the officer would receive no extra fees or gratuities. An officer would also have to pay for, care for and accommodate their own horse. An officer, should they have success, also had to tackle smugglers. They would often be outnumbered and out gunned; wielding just a pistol and a cutlass, they would often find themselves far more concerned about their own lives than in trying to make an arrest in the name of king and country.

* * *

The Riding Officer knew all too well the hazards of the lonely vocation he had so reluctantly taken; the 'vacancy' had arisen when his predecessor, a young, naive man, had rashly intervened on the beach during the landing of some contraband. A young man by the name of Henry Heskett had been the Riding Officer's predecessor. A farm boy, he had moved to the coast to take on a job that served king and country. He had been in the position of Riding Officer for less than six months when he tried to tackle a group of smugglers on the beach; quickly outnumbered, he was soon to fall like a leaf from a tree in autumn. His body was discovered in an isolated spot the following day. The cause of death had been noted as a fractured skull most likely caused by a heavy blunt object; the perpetrator was unknown. By all accounts there had been a considerable number of people present but surprisingly there had not been any witnesses to the fatal incident; according to those on the beach they could only vaguely remember young Heskett being present there and none of them saw him being struck. The Riding Officer knew the cruel nature of his position all too familiarly. On the occasions when he had caught a felon himself he had to finance the prosecution from his own pocket. And on every occasion bar one the felon had walked free.

Almost everyone in the local village was involved in smuggling. The justice of the peace, the magistrate, the local landowner, the innkeeper, the tailor, the tinker, the chandler, the doctor, the rector; they were all involved. The Riding Officer was a social pariah, despised by everyone in the village, often threatened, and never acknowledged, always the last in the queue and always the first to be ignored. He was disenchanted with many aspects of his life, the vices that had brought him down, the people who had brought him down, the community which despised him. He was the sole man in the village with an honest job or occupation that wasn't supported by smuggling or used as a front for smuggling. Yet it was the community of criminals which treated him like a criminal. On the times he had taken felons to court the juries were sympathetic to the smugglers or in on it themselves. Only a few families on the outskirts of the village were not involved in the smuggling.

He would spend many cold lonely nights patrolling the coast with no company except his horse and a flask of Scotch whisky he kept in his pocket. No one spoke to him so no one knew of it; he would slip off to another parish to buy the Scotch so no one knew he drank it. On occasion he would venture to the local tavern where he would drink a jug of ale and enjoy a side of roasted meat with wholemeal bread whilst reading a book in silence. He would be all alone, the silence broken only by the derogatory comments made by some patron of the inn.

* * *

The night was clear; the Riding Officer had been patrolling for around five hours. He was tired as the light had begun to fail. His feet had become cold with the tips of his toes beginning to feel numb despite his leather boots, and the chill was biting through his overcoat.

There were times he considered working against the laws he was supposed to be upholding and instead joining the local villagers in defrauding the Crown. He could carry out his duties to benefit himself. He could join them in smuggling; he could turn a blind eye to their activities for a stroke of commission or a small payment. He could falsify his records and join in league with those he was trying to track down. But he knew, no, that it would not be worth it; he could never become one of *them*. He knew he was being watched; one false move and he could be hanging at Newgate Gaol. Hanged like a common highwayman dancing the Tyburn Jig. He knew he had no one on his side, no allies, and no confidantes.

It was common for a Riding Officer to come from the community he served, but not this man. His controller had chosen to place him there for a reason. To begin with, the Riding Officer was a man for whom nobody cared about in a community whose only goal was greed. No one knew who he was; no one would care when he was gone, he would have no allies within the community. He was a purposefully selected outcast – not even a caring mother or close friend would be there to support him should something happen to him.

With the night clear, no suspicious activities were in sight and as the tip of his nose began to tingle and he could see his breath plume from his mouth, the Riding Officer decided to head for home.

* * *

The Riding Officer's stretch of the coast included the village of Upperbridge where he resided. Founded in the early twelfth century and named after a small stone bridge at the top of the village, it had quickly become a bustling fishing port on the Lincolnshire coast. However, a series of storms in the late sixteenth century had caused the river Mayne that ran through the village to burst its banks on a number of occasions, washing away villagers' homes. Over the following two centuries the population had slowly dwindled, leaving only seventy-eight homes in the village.

Upperbridge was a rotten borough. Of the seventy-eight homes, there were twelve eligible voters; twelve men whose properties were valued over forty shillings and who were of the Church of England faith. Women could not vote and many men were also disqualified on religious grounds. Upperbridge had been awarded a Royal charter in the fourteenth century when it was a flourishing port, giving it the right to elect two members to the House of Commons. It was unusual for a borough to change its boundaries as the town or city it was based on either died or expanded. Parliamentary reform was still four decades away and politicians were as corrupt as ever. Many new population centres had cropped up across Britain during the industrial revolution as particular industries took hold of certain areas. For example, the Wiltshire hamlet of Old Sarum, a once-busy cathedral city that had been abandoned when the city of Salisbury was established, had only three homes and seven eligible voters – who had the right to elect two members to the House of Parliament. Yet the rapidly expanding Lancashire town of Manchester, which had a population of over fifty thousand and a thriving economy, contributed no Members of Parliament at all.

When a rotten borough such as Upperbridge had such a small electorate it often meant that the electors could be bribed, and Upperbridge was no exception. With the amount of money that pumped through the village, from the smuggling trade and the illegal exportation of goods overseas, greed was rife in the village. The local Members of Parliament would make the smuggling communities' lives much easier if they could rely on the votes of the electorate. The Riding Officer knew this was one of the main reasons his controller had sent him to this village. Everyone important would be against him and on the side of his controller, or maybe it was everyone who his controller thought was important that would be against him. The Riding Officer's controller was a Member of Parliament for Upperbridge; he knew for a blind eye here and there with an odd concession plus the occasional gift of benevolence his controller had the electorate and the borough in the palm of his hand, along with guaranteeing his seat in the House of Commons.

* * *

Upperbridge sat on the North East Coast of Lincolnshire. To the north of the village was a rocky incline known as the north pathway, and to the south a gradual incline called the south pathway where a wooden beacon sat ready to be lit at night or during storms in order to act as a guide to passing vessels. Between the pathways a sandy beach, inhabited by old fishing boats covered in tarpaulins and the decayed ruins of other boats, ran parallel to the trail that linked the two routes. The nearest building was a wooden shack that sat just off the beach on the south pathway. He reached a small junction and after a few yards the trail was no longer dust and became cobbles lined by houses of differing size and design, the shops of the local tradesmen and business owners and a daunting church that served the small populous. In the centre of the village was a popular inn. Further down the road was another venue popular with locals; Mrs Higgins' 'Guesthouse.' Continuing up the cobbles that ran out of town lay the mighty Grantham Hall peering over the village, reminding all and sundry who was looking over them.

As the Riding Officer reached the village he noticed an old man on the beach. The old man lived in the shack by the beach whilst he kept up the pretence of being a scavenger. The Riding Officer knew better; he was one of *them*. The Riding Officer's horse pulled up slowly. The old man scowled at the Riding Officer.

"Scum!" the old man snarled, kicking sand at the Riding Officer's horse.

The Riding Officer thought nothing of it. Being a social outcast, he was used to treatment such as this. It would hurt sometimes when he was hit by a volley of verbal abuse but these were just words and they were not the types of words that could truly hurt. The only words that hurt him were the lies he had heard in the courts made by the smuggling community when they wormed out the charges brought against them, making him look like a fool and an authority figure with delusions of grandeur.

The Riding Officer rode on, his horse's hooves clattering across the cobbles. Two men were leaning against the wall of a butcher's shop. They stared at the Riding Officer with a snarl. Their brows lowered, one man shook his head before he spat into the path of the Riding Officer's horse. The other stood with his arms folded, his brow furrowed with his mouth like a small upturned smile.

At the end of the street the Riding Officer approached a heavy man he recognised as the village draper.

"Did you catch anyone, officer?" the draper asked. He tossed his greasy hair back and ran his fingers through it.

"No," replied the Riding Officer, deliberately not making eye contact.

"Better luck next time!" the draper snarled. "You'll need it!"

The draper strode off in the opposite direction with a cruel laugh as he swung a kick at a stray dog that scurried down the street and the Riding Officer proceeded home, shaking his head. He rode around to the rear of his home then dismounted and put his horse to stable. He retired to his chamber to end his day as it had begun and as it had continued: in solitude.

* * *

Anna began to clear some tankards from a table in the inn at Upperbridge. She had just begun her shift and didn't know how much more she could take of this insufferable little village. She mopped up some spilt ale with an old tattered rag that had seen better days. She sighed. Around her were drunken men with little or no future who seemed happy to waste their lives in this crooked little nothing village full of nobodies.

Two burly farm workers arm-wrestled over a table as other drinkers placed bets on who would win. She gritted her teeth at their behaviour. A man walked in leading three little children dressed in old sacks. He reached into his pocket and slammed a handful of farthings on the table.

"Him to win!" he said.

His bet was unsuccessful as the farm worker he had picked became distracted by the man, his hand crashing down to the table causing ale to spill from tankards. The man stood open mouthed. "That's all the money I had," he murmured. "I can't buy my children any food..."

Anna covered her mouth as she felt likely to vomit. *What a terrible man!* she thought, *so selfish!* She turned away from the arm-wrestlers like she wished she could walk away from Upperbridge. A picture above the hearth caught her eye. It was a beautiful painting of London Bridge, and she smiled. Her blue eyes lit up as she gazed at the monument over the most famous skyline in the world. *That's where I want to be!* she thought.

A great pair of hands wrapped around her waist. They were covered in grease and mud and were the property of a farm labourer.

"How about it, Anna?" he said. She could feel his ale-soaked breath on her cheek, and she shuddered. "How about we go out back to that old haystack?"

Anna attempted to prise the hands from her waist but it was no good. "Come on, Anna," he said, "I've heard all about you!"

Anna kicked her heel backwards, catching the man on the

shin. He screamed and hopped, and a swift elbow to his ribs saw the man release his grip and tumble to the floor.

"I think that answers your little question," she said, tossing the rag over her shoulder and making a point of treading on the man's hand as she walked over him.

Anna returned the empty tankards to the bar and headed off to clean another table.

"Not fancy a go in the haystack tonight, Anna?" said a man sitting at a nearby table, as he smiled and stroked his chin.

Anna groaned. "No." *You make one or two mistakes in your life and you are branded,* she thought as she attempted to avoid contact with the man, *so what if spend the rest of my life in hell? At least I can say I have lived.*

There was an unpleasant, stubborn stain on the table. She rubbed it hard with the rag in an attempt to shift it.

"Do you know what, Anna?" the man said. He stood up and leaned to her ear, saying, "I've got four whole shillings in my pocket. They are all yours if you fancy coming outside with me and tasting some Lincolnshire sausage!"

Anna scowled. She looked the grim brute in his eyes as he smiled at her, rubbing his hand on his crotch. He blew her a kiss. Anna threw a slap to the man's face that rang out around the inn.

"May I remind you that I am unfortunately betrothed to another?" she said, pushing him back into his seat.

"Oh, yes," said the man, his eyes looking down at the table, "to Mr Lockwood."

"Yes." Her stomach was puffing in and out in her fury. "I don't need to remind you what he might do to you!"

The man nodded. He finished his drink and quickly piled out of the door into the night. Anna sighed. She was something of a beauty, and men tried it on all the time. Sadly, those looks had hindered her. She had caught the eye of Hubert Lockwood, a local fishmonger.

As a fishmonger, Lockwood fell below par but it was well

known within the community that this was little more than a front for his smuggling empire. He was the head of the smuggling community which he ran with an iron grasp. A few years previously he had noticed the growing charms of Anna as she began to develop, and he tried to woo her with gifts of flowers and delicacies. She would have none of it. But her father, the local draper, fell into debt and to help him ease those financial issues Lockwood had welcomed him into his inner circle. Soon the debts were gone but he was now under the vice of smuggling. Within a small matter of time the two had reached an understanding, and it was a decision that Anna had not been part of.

"Where is the wonderful Mr Lockwood, then?" enquired a thin, dour-looking man who was sitting alone on a small stool by the fire.

Anna tossed the rag over her shoulders once more and folded her arms. "Who?"

"Mr Lockwood," the man said, "the wonderful patron of this community. He was saying only yesterday how he is the most important man in the village."

"I don't know who you're talking about," answered Anna, drumming her shoe on the floor.

"He worries about you," said the man. "He says he wants no wife of his going to hell if he is going to heaven."

Anna turned her back on the man and headed to the kitchen.

"He knows you'll go to hell unless you don't change your ways," the man said.

Anna stopped. "What do you mean change *my* ways?" Her head dropped, wondering what this antagonist meant.

"We've seen you," said the thin man, "swooning over *him*."

"Swooning over who?" Anna turned around to face her accuser.

"The Riding Officer."

"What about him?" said Anna, walking towards the thin man.

"We've seen you!" The man put his feet up on another stool

and slouched in his chair.

Anna kicked his feet off the stool. "Feet off the furniture," she shouted down his ear. She headed back towards the kitchen. It was funny that he should mention the Riding Officer.

He'd only attend the inn occasionally but for Anna his presence never failed to bring some pleasure into the cesspool that was the inn. He would simply enter the inn which would plunge into sudden silence. After he shut the door firmly behind him he would find a quiet corner of the inn to sit in, and enjoy a jug of ale and a side of meat plus bread whilst reading a book. He differed tremendously from the other boorish patrons of the inn. He seemed cultured amongst the crude locals, but nobody really knew who he was; or, no one was really *allowed* to know who he was. He was not local, he was not the usual naive young man who would be recruited by a corrupt official or a greed filled merchant looking to line his own pockets and out to convenience those with whom they were in league. This man was different, educated, kind but an outcast, the most loathed man in the village. But his enigmatic personality fascinated Anna. She wanted to know exactly who this man was, yet she didn't even know his name; she simply knew him as The Riding Officer.

* * *

The hour hand of the clock in the inn was a little past eight o'clock when the door opened; Anna was clearing a table when the hush descended. She didn't need to turn around to know who had entered the inn as she heard it shut firmly. His leather boots thudded distinctively across the hardwood floor, and Anna felt her heart begin to flutter.

"Not patrolling tonight, officer?" jeered a man who was playing cards.

"No..."

"Oh dear, if I performed my job like *you* perform *yours*, I would have no job!" the man said, his mouth wide and eyes narrowed as he laughed.

"I patrolled this afternoon," the Riding Officer replied in a cold voice.

"Did you see anything?" snarled a merchant who was slouched in a chair near the fire place.

"No."

"Well, if you saw even less I'd really make it worth your while!" the merchant said. "Do you know what I mean?"

"I do and I don't!" replied the Riding Officer. "You can keep your ill-gotten gains!"

The inn returned to a hush. The Riding Officer continued across the floor to a corner near the fireplace and next to the bookcase. He sat with his back partly to the room, and the murmurs began. Anna slowly made her way to the Riding Officer's table, smiling shyly and nervously; his defiant attitude impressed her so much. He sat up straight in his chair and pulled a book from his overcoat. He slowly raised his chin as he opened his literature. It was the poetry of Peter Lloyd, a romantic poet who brought a sense of manly justice to his work. Anna was an admirer of the enigmatic poet. A particular poem of a man saving a woman battered by her brutal husband appealed to her. The Riding Officer smiled kindly when he saw her beautiful face.

"You'll learn nothing from books, simpleton!" said the merchant, spitting in the direction of the Riding Officer.

"What would you like?" asked Anna, softly.

"A jug of porter and a side of roast lamb with bread, please."

"Very well," replied Anna. "I'll be as quick as I can..."

"Not a problem," said the Riding Officer. He smiled, captivated by her beauty.

Anna retreated to the kitchen, looking over her shoulder and smiling shyly. The Riding Officer began to read. The murmurs began once more but he ignored them. Anna smiled as she admired him. That was the mark of a *real* man.

The End?

* * *

Sometimes the Riding Officer felt the animosity towards him wasn't just to do with his vocation. Whenever he was spotted with a book the murmurs would begin. Could those who surrounded him simply despise him because of his education? The Riding Officer had been a fortunate man. His father was a wealthy factory owner in London, and he had worked his way up from nothing to become one of the key industrialists in the English capital. As a result of his father's wealth, the Riding Officer had been able to receive a public school education and later attended university, where he had excelled in his studies and had never failed to impress his father with his educational achievements. After he graduated the Riding Officer returned to London, his education enabling him to engage employment with a notable publisher in the capital. His earnings were good and he was able to rent fine rooms in which to live. Life was good for the Riding Officer until one fateful day when he was introduced to gambling; despite a prosperous first night, the Riding Officer was never again able to win such great amounts – he simply lost. And lost some more.

With debt beginning to affect him, the Riding Officer was approached by a man, who had once offered him a position of dubious employment, who then offered to lend him the money to cover his debts. The Riding Officer, desperate to rid himself of his debts, duly accepted and when close to having the debt paid off, he gambled rashly once more. His creditor didn't seem to mind and offered to lend him more money. So the Riding Officer gambled some more and lost more. Then he would borrow some more money which he promptly gambled away. Soon he was in a cycle he could not break. It led to his employers finding out, which resulted in his dismissal. When he was unable to repay the debt his creditor suggested he take a position as a Riding Officer in Lincolnshire as a favour to an old friend of his creditor in order to pay off the debt. The future Riding Officer declined, not wishing to take one of the worst jobs available in the whole of England.

His father summoned him one afternoon to confront him on the subject of the debt. His father had been advised of this by a business acquaintance with whom he did not get along. When the Riding Officer admitted his debt to this man, his father stated to him that because of his debts and obvious lack of financial control that any chance of him inheriting the company following his father's retirement or death had now been virtually extinguished. After a hostile exchange of words between father and son, the Riding Officer left.

That would be last time he saw his father alive; later that day his father was murdered.

He longed to know the whole story: who had done this, and why? He had his suspicions of who had done the deed though he needed further evidence but his exile to Lincolnshire would do nothing to help. Neither did his mother selling her late husband's business to a dubious character; the Riding Officer would receive no inheritance, his mother nervously insisting it would not be in his best interests. To compound matters, his creditor told him that the only way to rid his debt was to work it off as a Riding Officer. All it did was take him away from where he was a threat and kept him under the gaze of his controller.

What he did know was that his controller had selected him perfectly for this vocation he despised. He would feel alone when out on the headland gazing into the abyss that could be the North Sea. Yet, in that inn bustling with people sat around a warm fire, he never felt more lonesome.

After he finished his meal the attractive serving girl cleared his platter. She would smile at him and his heart would skip a beat. Her fair complexion and long black hair that had a hint of a wave and a curl about it made her look like a doll in Hamley's window. As she blinked slowly her eyes were such a soft blue they reminded him of a body of water in a pastel watercolour, and her lips looked soft and inviting; unlike many of the local women there was no chapping or scars. She was like a beautiful rose growing out of a barren wasteland of dirt. *Maybe, just maybe,* he thought. A smile crept onto his face when he thought about her; there was something different about her, something that made her different to the rest of the community.

But that smile quickly turned to a frown; the putrid smell of body odour and rotting fish engulfed the inn and the Riding Officer knew that Lockwood had entered. This was the man he loathed the most in the village. Originally from Scotland, he was a hunchbacked man with halitosis and a potbelly augmented by thin legs reminiscent of a sparrow. He had small hands with great long bony fingers, small pig-like eyes and his smile was grim and sinister.

The Riding Officer read his book and occasionally peered across at the foul little hunchback. He was disgusted at how the villagers continually fawned over him, how they bought him drink after drink; ale, wine, fine brandy and cognac. It was all so ill-gotten. There was one thing that really made his blood boil and that was the way he lusted after the young serving girl. The way he would leer and lust, grab and grope with his sexual advances and insinuations. The Riding Officer could easily see that she detested not just his advances, but him as well.

It was about ten o'clock when the Riding Officer decided to leave. He had tired of the antics of the villagers, repulsed as he had grown so weary of them all. The Riding Officer had not seen Lockwood put one farthing over the bar, and the fickle villagers continued to pander to him. Some to gain his pleasure, some to ensure they didn't earn his displeasure. Lockwood had driven all those not dominated by greed and those who did not subscribe to his point of view from the community. A man by the name of Cutler who had spoken out against Lockwood and his burgeoning empire of crime had mysteriously vanished when he went to chop wood in the forest. When the rumours surrounding his disappearance began, a dustman's family suddenly became rich and another man had his eyes gouged out by an unknown assailant when those rumours did not desist.

As the last drops of porter were emptied from his tankard the Riding Officer became aware of a disturbance behind him. He looked over his shoulder to see that Lockwood had the young serving girl in his grasp. As he spoke in a demonic tone, spit flew from his mouth, making the girl flinch as it hit her face.

"Let me go!" Anna wailed. There were tears in her eyes, hatred written on her face but the cruel little man whose knuckles were turning white declined to release his grip.

Lockwood's porcine eyes bored into her. *"I am your fiancé!"*

The Riding Officer stood up causing his chair to crash backwards.

"Let her be!"

Lockwood turned around as the inn suddenly hushed; he was stunned to see the Riding Officer standing up straight in front of him. His shoulders were broad as he placed a hand on his hip slightly north of his pistol. The Riding Officer, a tall man, peered down at Lockwood. He turned his head gently to the right but at no point did he take his eyes off Lockwood.

"What did you say?" asked Lockwood. His mouth trembled as he stared, wide-eyed, at the Riding Officer.

"I said: *Let her be!*"

Lockwood's claw-like hand snapped away as he released his grasp from Anna's arm. She looked deeply at her hero before she bolted to the kitchen.

"Give a man a uniform and he thinks he's the Duke of York!" sneered Lockwood.

"Give a lowlife criminal a bit of power and he acts like the King of England!" the Riding Officer retaliated.

"I am no criminal! If anyone is a criminal, it is you, officer!"

"And how do you deduce that, Lockwood?"

"You tax. You tax and tax. You steal from an honest, humble fishmonger like me. Tax is theft!" Lockwood replied through clenched teeth. He was red about the face and he began to shake.

"We need to tax," said the Riding Officer. "You might not like paying tax but we need it ... if you haven't noticed, Britain is at war with France."

"So is that how you justify your theft from me?" asked Lockwood condescendingly. "You blame the French!"

"I enforce tax on imports and exports," the Riding Officer answered. "I collect no duty on your stock because it is caught locally." His hand remained placed near his gun, as he was half expecting to have to draw it. The Riding Officer looked around. He could see men and women with expressions of guilt, but then he could also see people expressing disgust. Lockwood's expression suddenly changed to an insincere smile.

"It will be my birthday in two weeks, and I would like you to attend, officer!" he said, the oil in his greasy voice thick enough to fry a steak.

"That sounds enjoyable, Lockwood," replied the Riding Officer with a wry smile. "I have the ideal gift for you."

"And what is that, officer?"

"A bar of soap!" replied the Riding Officer.

Lockwood's evil pig-like eyes focused on the floor, his shoulders hunched and his fists clasped as he bit aggressively into his own lip. The inn descended into silence. "I always like to keep my friends close but my enemies closer!"

"I'll be leaving now," the Riding Officer announced suddenly. "As the French would say: *Au Revoir!*" He turned and headed to the door, his boots thudding across the hardwood floor. But as he opened the door, before he exited and shut the door firmly behind him, he faced the patrons of the inn with his chest still protruding and his head held high. He saw cold stares, expressions of rage, and looks of hatred but it was augmented with a few expressions of respect from those who feared Lockwood. He knew there was at least one who had been treated unfairly that respected him more, and if there was any justice she would be away from the one who made her eyes expand in fear and reduce her mouth to a scowl of hatred. He did so hate men who abused women; it struck him as being so very unmanly.

Lockwood returned to his table, his minions scattering as he sat down. He sighed and his toadies slowly returned; the silence created a tension as they saw Lockwood clasp the edge of table so hard the tips of his fingers began to turn white.

Eventually Lockwood spoke. "Landlord, where is my fiancée?"

"Gone, Mr Lockwood..." replied the landlord nervously.

Lockwood sighed loudly and angrily. He drew a pocket knife for from his pocket and unfurled the blade. "Hurley, Paine, go out and locate my fiancée. She'll be at her father's, Kitching's the draper's." His minions got up and left without argument or question, and Lockwood turned to another skivvy, saying, "Binns, I want you to take a message to Grantham that the Riding Officer must go!"

Then Lockwood scowled at the patrons of the inn. "Now somebody buy me a drink!" he bellowed as he drove the point of the knife into the table. "And for Christ's sake somebody please tell me what *Au Revoir* means!"

* * *

Anna hid in the shadows behind the inn. Her heart was pounding, for she dared not go back inside and dared not return home either. If she went back inside, Lockwood would be there, and if she went home Lockwood would find her there. As she saw the Riding Officer leave the inn she knew she had to be with him. He was the only man in the village who would not turn her over to Lockwood; even Anna knew Lockwood would not have the Riding Officer murdered in his own home.

The Riding Officer crossed the street and headed down the road. Anna emerged from the shadows and began to follow him. She would follow him to where he lived and ask to be let in. Following the events in the inn that night she knew he was fond of her, he wouldn't say no, and then she knew she would be safe if only for a while. Anna followed at a distance. The air was cold and nipped against her skin. The Riding Officer seemed to pause from time to time, aware that there was someone following him. When he reached his door, he cautiously checked before letting himself in. Anna decided to wait a moment.

Suddenly, an assailant loomed out of the darkness. He grabbed her arm and she began to struggle, screaming for help; the last thing she could remember was a blunt object striking her across the head.

Chapter Two

An Enigmatic Host

The room in which Anna began to regain consciousness was unfamiliar; she felt a cold, damp cloth being gently pressed against the throbbing bump on her head. She looked across to the person holding the cloth and smiled as she saw it was the Riding Officer.

"Where am I?"

"In my cottage," the Riding Officer replied softly.

"What happened?"

"One of Lockwood's henchmen struck you across the head. They ran away when I went outside to challenge them."

"Which one was it?" Anna asked.

"The big bloated man with curly hair and the scar below his left eye." he replied. "We have never been formally introduced..."

"Hurley," replied Anna. "A vile man!"

The Riding Officer smiled kindly as he stroked away Anna's long beautiful dark hair. "Have some water," he said, passing a wooden goblet to Anna.

"Thank you." She took a sip.

"You're very beautiful!" said the Riding Officer with a shy smile upon his face.

"Thank you, again!" Her eyes fluttered as she held her breath and blushed.

Anna began to look around the room; there were portraits of the cream of British society, and landscapes of the capital's most synonymous landmarks that brought an envious smile to her face. There were books that were battered, the leather in the covers peeled but from the way that they were placed by his chair and bed she could see that literature was important to him. The fact that he had no vases full of flowers or embroidered comforts told her he was a single man but Anna could not help to wonder who that pretty young woman with the blue eyes and head of golden blonde hair was in the portrait that sat upon his bedside table. It felt foreign to her, so unusual in this part of world – the lowlifes of Upperbridge might have had money but they were uncultured and uneducated. To them, pelting a vagrant with rotten vegetables was the height of entertainment whilst others yearned for the days when a poor woman would be subjected to the humiliating ordeal of the ducking stool for their amusement.

"I'll put a dressing on that bump," said the Riding Officer.

"Is it bad?"

"No, it should heal quickly." He smiled to reassure her. "It won't affect those beautiful looks!"

Anna smiled once again. She glanced down at the bed hoping that he wouldn't see her blushing. "Thank you..."

The Riding Officer began to rub some ointment gently onto Anna's forehead. "My mother used to be an apothecary."

"You're not from around here, are you?" Anna asked, intrigued by her enigmatic host.

"I'm from London originally."

"I've always wanted to go there. How did you end up here?" she asked.

"Do you really want to know?"

"Yes!" said Anna.

"Why?" the Riding Officer asked.

"I just do," Anna said with a smile.

"Did your fiancé send you here?" he asked, the tone in his voice became hard, direct and almost demanding.

Anna wriggled uncomfortably. "Please don't refer to him as that," she said with a clear element of distress in her voice. "I hate him!"

"That makes two of us. Why are you engaged to Lockwood if you detest him?" he asked, suddenly concerned for his beautiful guest.

Anna looked down at the floor, stroking back her long, dark locks. "I'm not. Lockwood has a business arrangement with my father," she said, sadly. "They are both driven by greed and I am simply part of that arrangement. They are rich and powerful so as part of their arrangement, my father has promised my hand to that foul, disgusting man."

"That's terrible!" He felt a pang of sympathy.

"I long to flee this hellhole," Anna said, looking up at her host. "I wish to escape the greed and corruption. I couldn't face being married to Lockwood!"

"I know how you feel," said the Riding Officer with a sad smile. "I long to leave, too."

"You should," said Anna, "and return to London. You're better than this place."

"I wish I could but I must wait for the controller to be gone or let me go," the Riding Officer explained.

"Your controller?" She was suddenly intrigued.

"The one who sent me here," the Riding Officer explained. "I have been exiled here."

"You were sent here?"

"Who would want to be a Riding Officer and who would want to come to Upperbridge?" said the Riding Officer. "The pay is poor, the hours are difficult, there's no respect, I'm continually receiving death threats and everybody hates me."

Anna slipped her hand into the Riding Officer's. "Not everyone hates you!" Anna said, smiling and gazing deeply into his eyes. "I like you!"

The Riding Officer was gobsmacked. He sat with his mouth open unable to find a word. He became concerned. He, like everyone else in Upperbridge, had heard the rumours of what Anna had done. He hoped she wasn't a lady of loose moral values out to fleece a poor sap out of every penny he had; duping a greedy fool of his ill-gotten gains he could understand but not a lowly Riding Officer with but a few pennies to his name.

"Why?" the Riding Officer asked, somewhat mystified.

"Damn it, I'll say and I don't care if I am condemned to hell. You're a handsome man," she said, stroking his hand, "and you're the only man in the village not driven by greed!"

The Riding Officer smiled wryly. "You don't know me," he said, sadly. "I had a good life in London. My father was a wealthy man, and he owned his own business. I gained a good education; I excelled in literature, art, arithmetic and archery; I went to Cambridge and earned a degree. Then it all began to go wrong..."

"What happened?" asked Anna, squeezing the Riding Officer's hand gently.

"I had a good job at a publisher's. I rented fine rooms then I began to gamble ... cards, roulette, cock fights ... anything I could ... I had a turbulent relationship with an actress ... the only woman I've shared my bed with ... I soon fell into debt! I had to borrow money and instead of working my way out of debt I gambled some more, I squandered money then borrowed some more and gambled more and squandered some more and borrowed even more ... I was greedy and I didn't know when to stop." The Riding Officer stood up and walked slowly to the window, where he gazed up at the moon, sadly, and then looked back to Anna. His mouth was agape, his eyes rolled back and forth as he aggressively rocked the heel of his boot on the floor whilst she could hear him sighing deeply as he breathed he was suffering from intense emotional pain. "The irony was because of my greed I was sent here to a community driven by greed; this is my punishment."

"My father gambled and not very well. I know what debt can do," Anna said. "Now he's addicted to another form of gambling. Can you not leave Upperbridge?"

"No," replied the Riding Officer. "My controller sent me here; when I was reluctant to come here my father died in mysterious circumstances, and if I left he would have me killed and I'd never know what happened to my father..."

"Who is your controller?" Anna asked, intrigued by enigmatic host's history.

"He's the man I'm in debt to," the Riding Officer said. "He sent me here as somebody he could control under the pretence I was helping a dear friend of his. He's a man of great power and can prevent me from doing my job – if I wanted to accept payments or align myself with the smugglers he'd have me gaoled. I earn so little, he knows he'll have me under his control for a long time but once my debt is cleared I can leave. When that is though, I do not know."

"Who is he?" asked Anna, suspecting she knew who this mysterious person was.

"Grantham!" replied the Riding Officer, his eyes wild as he mentioned his name. "The local Member of Parliament. He's the man I would simply describe as a very rotten man for a very rotten borough."

"He's in league with Lockwood," Anna advised.

"I know..." replied the Riding Officer in a hollow voice.

He turned and stared out of the window, intensely. He clutched his left hand with his right thumb, boring into the palm of his left hand, rubbing it back and forward to attempt to relieve the tension.

* * *

It was the break of dawn as Anna awoke. She was lying on the Riding Officer's bed, and she felt no pain from the bump on her head. The Riding Officer's home still felt foreign to Anna. She rolled over and climbed off the bed. Her hair was a mess, her clothes crumpled and she felt uncomfortable. *Why can't clothing be more comfortable to sleep in?* she thought.

Anna walked around the Riding Officer's cottage, studying the books he had on the shelves. What could a woman tell about a man's choice of reading matter? *Paradise Lost* nestled next to Plato's *Republic*, but she had read neither. She pulled out a slim volume of poetry by Peter Lloyd. His poetry was well thought of but little was known of the man himself. Next to that, there was a gothic romance in a frayed binding.

"You're awake," said the Riding Officer. He was sitting in a rocking chair smoking his pipe. Anna almost dropped the books. Carefully she put them all back and turned to face him. He had a curious smile on his face.

"It seems so," Anna replied.

"I wasn't a gentleman last night," the Riding Officer began.

"You were," Anna said in a reassuring voice. "You made no unwanted advances on me, and you were an absolute gentleman."

"I wasn't a gentleman," explained the Riding Officer. "I didn't ask you what your name is."

"It's Anna. Anna Kitching; what's your name?"

The Riding Officer smiled. He drew from his pipe and exhaled. "It's on that book on my table," he told her. He picked up the volume and passed it to her.

"A namesake?" she asked after she read the cover of the book.

"No," said the Riding Officer with a proud smile, "that's my work!"

Anna smiled; she was impressed. "You're a published author?"

The Riding Officer nodded. "And I'm an artist!" he added with a touch of arrogance pointing with his pipe at the art on the walls. "It's the only way I can survive; no family in the village will give me a room, and any food I try to buy costs more than anyone else's at the insistence of Lockwood. I try to hunt and grow what I can as Grantham makes a token deduction from my salary. Sometimes I don't see a farthing of my pay."

"You are an interesting man!" Anna told him as she swung her long black locks away from her eyes. The Riding Officer fascinated her. She longed to know what the world was like away from Upperbridge. She wanted to know what it was like to eat, sleep, breathe and live somewhere else. With the Riding Officer, she knew she could do that. He'd already lived a life. He could bring something different into her humdrum life, a fresh point of view, an education and a modicum of culture. Lockwood could never provide her with any of this but this strong yet vulnerable man could give her everything she had ever wished for; love, passion, reassurance and safety. Though she barely knew him she felt secure with him; he felt so different. If he was only interested in one thing he would have made his move.

"Do you think so?" His eyes darted away from her.

"I do! May I see you again?" Anna's hands interlocked as she pulled them to her chest. "I don't care what people say about you and I care even less about what they will say about me. They are just words."

The Riding Officer was hesitant. His lips trembled as he thought. It was wrong, she was betrothed to another. Then it felt right, it felt very right. For his entirety in Upperbridge he had built a wall around himself but he suddenly felt it begin to collapse. Had this beauty, this soft, delicate soul who masked herself under a hard shell to try to hide her fear of the wretched community forced that structure to collapse? "Yes..." he told her.

"I'll come around tonight." Anna's voice softened, filled with hope and fear. Hope for what lay ahead and fear for what might happen.

"Very good then." He looked away, wondering if this was the right thing to do.

"I must go," she said. "I must go home and face the music. My father will want to know where I am and I'm sure Lockwood will have been searching for me."

The Riding Officer stood up from his chair. Anna walked towards him and they embraced. Anna found herself gazing into the Riding Officer's eyes. He leaned forward and kissed her softly and gently on her lips.

"I am so sorry that I have to go..." repeated Anna softly.

"You don't have to apologise," replied the Riding Officer. "Would you like me to escort you?"

"I'll be fine!" Anna reassured him. "You'll be in more danger with me than if you remain here."

She kissed him once more before she let herself out. The Riding Officer followed. He watched her walk up the road to her own home ready to face the music. As he returned to his home and shut the door firmly behind him, he hoped there would be no severe repercussions.

* * *

About half a mile from the village of Upperbridge was Grantham Hall, the ancestral home of the Grantham family, and current home of Adam Grantham, Member of Parliament for the local borough. He was a rotten politician for a rotten borough of rotten people. It was common for a local peer to place a family member or family friend in the place of a politician in an area which he could control. Grantham's uncle Charles had been an extremely rich man and a Member of the House of Lords. Unable to vote or stand for parliament himself, Charles Grantham chose to put his nephew forward as a candidate for the borough. He was able to bribe the electorate and his nephew was elected to government. Charles Grantham had also nominated another man, an alcoholic buffoon by the name of Frederick Cheever; again he had flashed some cash and Cheever was voted in.

Whilst Cheever was a clueless, incompetent fool, Adam Grantham had excelled as a politician in Upperbridge. He had the electorate in his hand and the smuggling community were key allies. They had an understanding that if Grantham received a cut he would make life easy for them and if he could sell their contraband they would vote for him. Over the years, Lockwood had become a key ally in particular. Charles Grantham was a frail, ailing old man and the politician knew that once his uncle had passed away he would inherit his fortune, making him considerably wealthier and also giving him a seat in the Lords. Once he had secured the seat in the Lords he would need to find his own successor. And this was a position that Lockwood courted...

Corruption and Grantham were regularly used by his detractors in unison. He was also known to be involved in murder. The newspapers told England that her most violent criminal was a man named Silas Palmer. The rumour mill that operated around London often mentioned murder, linking the aforementioned Mr Palmer to Adam Grantham MP.

Grantham sat slumped in his study with a sour look on his face. Had anyone been in the same room as him they would have cringed as he slurped his tea. He drove the forefinger on his right hand up his right nostril removing a particle of mucus which he would wipe on the side of his desk. He wore foul-smelling waistcoats made from an unknown material and went days without bathing; the odour of his feet alone would overpower anybody unfortunate enough to be in his presence. He scowled at the crows in the field nearest the study; there was a sea mist that was slowly creeping its way inland. The door to the study opened and his butler, a man with skeletal features, entered.

"The Riding Officer, my lord!" he announced in a cold authoritarian voice.

Grantham scowled. "Very well, Sykes."

The Riding Officer entered, holding his hat under his right arm and bearing an expressionless look upon his face, reminiscent of a guilty man being sentenced in court.

Grantham was himself an aging man. He was rich and corrupt. Upon his desk sat a Bible placed in a holder used by booksellers that they would display their goods upon, hoping that a piece of literature opened at the right page would draw the attention of a prospective buyer. The Riding Officer noticed that the leather-bound edition was opened at verses telling the fate of Sodom and Gomorrah, and he gave a short sharp snort. The dust accumulated on the gilt edges told the keenest observer that this was a shield, a mere masking agent to cover the accusations of corruption in his business life and a personal life likely to fall foul of the church should it be revealed. The Riding Officer recalled that the volume always seemed to be placed at the point, and he doubted any other page had seen the light of day since its purchase.

Grantham continued to stare out of the window, deliberately ignoring his visitor. He growled. "Sykes! Have my rifle sent to me."

"Very good, my lord," replied the butler in his usual cold voice.

The butler left. The Riding Officer watched as he shut the door. But Grantham continued to growl. "I thought you would be on patrol." Then without warning, Grantham stood up, his chest sticking out as he placed his hands on his hips. "This mist would be a perfect cloak for smugglers!"

"I would be on patrol, my lord, but you summoned me here," replied the Riding Officer calmly.

"So I did," Grantham replied, the anger suddenly gone from his voice.

"Why was that, my lord?" asked the Riding Officer, tentatively. *Grantham was up to something. What was it? What was this game he is playing? Is this an attempt at distraction? Then again,* the Riding Officer thought, *he is an associate of Lockwood, so is this punishment for last night?*

"I don't know," said Grantham with a wicked smile upon his face. It was an expression that could regularly been seen when he was in his vault counting his fortune.

"You don't know?" The Riding Officer was beginning to feel irritated.

"No," said the politician, firmly.

Grantham began to stroke his chin. The Riding Officer noticed a few flakes of the remains of Grantham's breakfast drop. The Riding Officer closed his eyes and turned his head away. A sinister smile spread across Grantham's face, as he said, "I know why I brought you here!" He looked sly. "Your performance hasn't been up too much recently."

"My performance, my lord?"

"Your performance, the job you are supposed to be doing! You haven't arrested any smugglers for six months and even then they turned out to be fishermen." Grantham was thundering again.

"Those men were smuggling tea, my lord! You should know because you and your cronies drank the evidence," the Riding Officer replied, firmly. "And the village has been quiet. There's been no suspicious activity for months. Anyway, I can't patrol twenty-four hours a day."

"Or maybe you are not doing your job and are simply waiting for your pay to come," boomed the politician.

The Riding Officer's jaw dropped as he shook his head. He folded his arms as he stared out of the window into the distance. His line of vision snapped back to Grantham, and he slammed his hands down on the edge of the glutton's desk. As he lent forward he advised, "I've *not* received my pay for two months!"

"I know," replied Grantham, his voice suddenly tranquil without the least attempt to agitate or offend. "I have been taking it."

"Have you?" The Riding Officer felt his temper beginning to fray.

"You don't deserve to be paid," Grantham responded. "Smuggling is rife in Upperbridge and you have done nothing about it."

"The Justice of the Peace is my employer and only he has the right to adjust my salary," protested the Riding Officer.

The greedy politician picked up his tea and took another mouthful which made the Riding Officer cringe. "The Justice of the Peace is a dear, dear old friend of mine, officer," Grantham replied, "and if you recall, you owe me a *considerable* amount of money, officer! In fact I was the one who set you up this job with my dear friend when you were relieved of your duties at that publisher's."

"Yes, I do remember," admitted the Riding Officer, reluctantly, "and it was also you who made sure that I was relieved of my duties at the publisher's."

"I'm quite surprised you can survive without pay..." said Grantham in an accusing voice. "The villagers think you are a fool with delusions of grandeur but not me! You are up to something; how do you survive on next to nothing?"

"I take care of my money," replied the Riding Officer.

Grantham laughed dementedly as he sat down. "*You*, careful with money? I remember, my dear boy, when you would come grovelling for more time to repay or an extension on your loan!"

"I try to be careful now," replied the Riding Officer, firmly. "I've learnt my lesson the hard way."

"I wouldn't be surprised if you were involved in smuggling," accused Grantham in a deliberately cruel tone of voice.

"I am not!" He drove his right fist into the palm of his left hand.

"It would explain many things; no arrests, an income from nowhere!" Grantham continued. "You're nothing but a criminal!"

The Riding Officer slammed his hand from a great height onto Grantham's desk. "I, sir, am not!"

"Your father would be ashamed had he not died so suddenly from that heart attack!" The slovenly MP slouched back in his chair and placed his rotten feet upon the desk.

A wild look spread across the Riding Officer's face, his mouth quivering. "My father was murdered and you know it!"

Grantham pulled his feet off the desk and sat up straight. He reached out and grabbed a nearby paper knife. "What are you suggesting?" he said as he waved the paperknife in the general direction of the Riding Officer.

"You had my father killed!"

"That is a likely story!" Grantham replied. He lifted the paperknife up, and noticing a stain on the blade he wiped it against his trousers before he sniffed in a manner that made the Riding Officer cover his mouth.

The Riding Officer's brow furrowed as he leaned towards the depraved politician's food-stained face. "Does the name Silas Palmer mean anything to you?" he asked Grantham softly, "because people said they saw him at my father's office on that fateful day."

"Silas Palmer is a friend of one of my business associates in London," Grantham told him. "A builder by trade. His friend employs him to do a lot of contract work for me."

"Would that contract be construction work … or murder?"

"Building work, you fool!" said Grantham.

"Silas Palmer is no builder. If you picked up any newspaper you would know from the headlines that he's the most wanted man in England!" replied the Riding Officer, smiling as he thought of the crooked MP dancing the Tyburn Jig, "and if I met him I might have to demand satisfaction!"

"Do you know Silas?" asked Grantham, curiously.

"No. I've never set eyes on him," answered the Riding Officer, "but if I did … *bang!*" He shouted out, making Grantham sit up. "Just like that man in Hammersmith."

"You still duel then, officer?" asked Grantham with distinct unease.

"As a rule, no," replied the Riding Officer, calmly, "but if need be as an absolute last resort, yes."

"Interesting..." murmured Grantham, once again stroking flakes of his former breakfast from his chin. "You were quite the shot if I recall…"

The door to the study opened and the skeletal butler entered, carrying a rifle. He passed it to Grantham. Grantham rested the gun on his desk. From a drawer he removed a cloth, and he began to clean the barrel in a manner that was almost sexual. The Riding Officer began to feel uncomfortable. He hoped that Grantham was not going to make an unsettling proposition of some kind. He had heard all about what had happened to a predecessor named Pugh. Grantham pointed the rifle randomly in the Riding Officer's direction.

"Sykes!" Grantham bellowed to the skeletal butler. "Show the Riding Officer to the door before he makes a complete fool of himself! You know the man's poor mother sold her late husband's business and left him no inheritance because she was so ashamed of him?"

The Riding Officer reluctantly left, scowling at Grantham as he went out of the door. His fists were balled up as his jaw bolted shut. He was struggling to retain his composure when he really wanted to scream and bellow at Grantham and then take his rifle and wrap it around the politician's fat head.

Grantham polished his gun some more. He stood up and walked to the veranda door, opened the French windows and fired into the crows in the field. The shot rang out and the crows flew away cawing. The butler re-entered.

"Sykes, have that man at the beach sent something," he began. "His advice was correct. This mist was perfect as cover for landing contraband and my plan, too, was perfect; with that fool here, the contraband will be safely in port by now!"

* * *

Grantham knew that when he appointed a successor to his fortunes, land and title it would have to be to someone who detested the Riding Officer as much as he did. He didn't really know why he detested the Riding Officer to such a degree. Maybe it was because he was a former business rival's son; maybe it was because the Riding Officer had declined an opportunity to join Grantham's empire a few years previously, stating he did not want to become part of the criminal underworld; or maybe it was because he enjoyed tormenting him. He would pull the strings and the Riding Officer would have to dance, he could whisper a few words and have the man looking over his shoulder with fear that Grantham could have him arrested at the drop of a hat, and he could throw any accusation he wished at the Riding Officer knowing he would have little to reply with. When his offer of employment was declined by the Riding Officer, Grantham threatened to make a fool out of the university-educated man. He lured him into his trap with the enticement of more money than he could afford. When debts were nearly paid he would offer some more to which he could not resist and when he had him where he wanted he gave him an ultimatum; go up the coast to work as a Riding Officer in order to help a dear old friend of his in his constituency until all debts were paid or take up residence in Newgate Gaol where he would rot for the rest of his life, as Grantham would advise him that he had 'considerable' power. It empowered him to make a fool of this man.

* * *

Who really is the fool? The Riding Officer thought to himself as he trudged across the gravelled driveway towards the main gates of the estate. Grantham had been perfectly correct – the Riding Officer had made a complete fool out of himself. Grantham had provoked him verbally and he had bitten. To the Riding Officer, Grantham was like the perfect puppet master. He was becoming increasingly incensed by Grantham's meetings with him at the hall; Grantham had great control over him and he knew should he rebel just too much against the depraved politician then he would be on the next cart to prison. Even if he should step out of line just marginally Grantham would throw the book at him. He knew Grantham wished to make him look foolish. He was an intelligent man who had struggled with a problem; he was not the first to do so and he certainly would not be the last, but he had a vice which he knew was finally under control. Being banished to the Lincolnshire coast had done him the world of good in one way as his temptations could not be fuelled anymore despite the occasional tease by Grantham that there would be a game of cards that he would be more than welcome to join in with. The Riding Officer told himself he would never be drawn into the cycle of compulsive gambling again.

Who truly was the fool? The Riding Officer thought once more, kicking a rock away that reminded him of the MP's fat head. He knew that Grantham wished to make him look foolish by ordering one of his little interviews as a ruse to smuggle in contraband. Grantham always insisted that the Riding Officer did not bring his horse to the estate. Grantham's friends and well-wishers, better known as the electorate, simply insisted it was an eccentricity of their beloved politician. The Riding Officer just knew that it was a simple method of inconveniencing him further. On a particular type of day where the sea would be calm, some haze would be at sea and there would be a lot of fishing activity that saw no fish caught, and the Riding Officer would be summoned for an interview with Grantham or the Justice of the Peace or if he was really fortunate both of them together. During the interview he would be belittled and abused but he knew he would be away from Upperbridge and away from the coast he was supposed to control. It was then that the smuggling community would take the opportunity to bring their illegal cargoes ashore. The Riding Officer would then trudge back to the village – supposedly none the wiser.

But he *was* wise. Very quickly, the Riding Officer knew about this ruse. Grantham wanted to make him look foolish. He would simply take him out of the equation while the deed was done and once he was back in the village they could all have a laugh at his expense. The Riding Officer heard the laughs and the derogatory comments about him being a fool but who was really the fool? The Riding Officer knew it was not him; he would be away from the illegal activities of Grantham and Lockwood's cohorts, he wouldn't have to challenge anybody or put his life on the line against twenty or thirty men with just his pistol or cutlass. No, when he saw the tell-tale signs of a landing of illegal goods he would simply wait for Grantham to summon him for an interview. And once it was over he would allow Grantham and his cohorts the chance to gloat as if they had pulled the wool over his eyes, he would then let them boast like they were some kind of heroes to the downtrodden. He would ignore their comments and behaviour; he didn't have to put his life on the lines due to those common criminals. He would just let *them* act like fools.

* * *

The wind was cold as it bit through the Riding Officer's overcoat. The sea churned, the white waves frothing, the tide relentlessly pounding on the coast. From time to time he would sight a vessel, sailing to the North for coal or sailing to the South for fine fabric. He watched closely as the ships would drift past. They didn't wish to stop; none of the vessels seemed interested. What would those vessels want with Upperbridge? It was a nothing type of place filled with nothing type people. He patrolled his stretch of the coast several times. He had passed the beacon on the rocks which would be lit to make the rocks more visible to ships at night or during bad weather.

He had also passed the Herring Caller on a number of occasions. The Herring Caller was a man who watched the coastline for the tell-tale signs of herring and would duly call "Herring!" so to summon the local fishermen once the shoal was sighted.

The Herring Caller would give him the same disapproving scowl that everybody in the village, apart from Anna and an old farmer named Timms on the outskirts of the village, would give him. The Riding Officer was wise to the Herring Caller's tricks; he knew the call of "herring" not only meant the summons of the local fishermen to their boats but also the call of the privateers. He knew all too well that it was simply a front for smuggling. He hadn't been too honest with Grantham; there was suspicious activity aplenty in Upperbridge but he knew when the odds were against him. Even when he did make an arrest he stood no chance regardless of what they were doing.

* * *

Earlier, Grantham had hit a nerve with the Riding Officer in a number of ways. Bringing up his past was always uncomfortable and the jibes about his father's death were particularly painful. Grantham's continuously false tales about how the Riding Officer's father died wore at the Riding Officer's nerves. He didn't know how much more he could take before he might draw a pistol at his foe. Every comment made a fresh wound and further lead to his belief that Grantham – and Silas Palmer – were involved. Perhaps his mother sold his father's business to Grantham. It would not have surprised him. But worse than all of that was Grantham's persistent reference to two fishermen the officer had arrested.

The tale of woe behind the arrest was one that never failed to upset the Riding Officer. The farcical trial at the local court had made the Riding Officer feel like a dunce and had made him a laughing stock in the village. About six or seven months previously, the Riding Officer had stumbled across two young men who had on a calm, clear day moored their small rowing boat about a mile and a half along the coast from Upperbridge.

Noticing them by some low rocks where they were struggling to carry a wooden case ashore, he realised they had let their guard down, and that they were unarmed and had contraband.

Drawing his pistol, he arrested the two men, making them carry the contraband to the Parish Gaol. He went inland to make his way back to Upperbridge. Avoiding the coast and the main areas where he knew Lockwood's cohorts would be lying, he was able to deliver the two smugglers to the Parish Gaol where they were arrested and the contraband was confiscated, much to the chagrin of the parish constable. When opened, the case was discovered to hold fine Indian tea. The Riding Officer deduced the two smugglers to be young men inexperienced at being smugglers thus leading to them making the mistake of trying to handle a too-large load with the wrong equipment and no assistance. He added that the two men could easily have injured themselves severely on the rocks if they had fallen. The boat had been poorly moored, the rocks could have been drenched by sea water and the smugglers could have easily fallen in the sea.

As was almost customary upon hearing that two of the smuggling community had been arrested, Lockwood offered "The innocent victims of a callous bully" as he described them the services of his solicitor; his solicitor was one of Grantham's closest friends and well-wishers. Even before the trial had commenced, the insinuations of Lockwood began. The bullying comment was first, then there was the comment that rattled the Riding Officer, one Lockwood had repeated recently: "Put a man in a uniform and he thinks he's the Duke of York!"

Eventually the trial came round, and from the moment the magistrate took the bench, the Riding Officer knew he had lost the case. The magistrate was another friend and well-wisher of Grantham. He was a towering man, a retired army colonel, with a huge ginger moustache. The Riding Officer just had to glance at the lowlifes on the jury and he knew he stood no chance.

The prosecution put forward the facts: the two men had been

caught with contraband, illegally bringing it ashore and avoiding paying custom. A star witness in the shape of the Riding Officer from the neighbouring parish had testified that he saw the two men greet a ship off the coast and a case was lowered by a rope on to their rowing boat before he watched them proceed to shore. He stated that he was unable to make the arrest because they were moored outside his jurisdiction. Then the defence entered proceedings. And with that, the farce commenced.

The defence proceeded to paint the picture that the star witness for the prosecution was in fact a drunkard and frequently hallucinated as a result. A witness from his parish came forward to give an over-dramatic account of such an occasion, despite the fact that the neighbouring Riding Officer insisted he had never met the man. The Upperbridge Riding Officer felt that the defence's witness should have been on trial for overacting.

Having rubbished the prosecution's main witness, the defence then turned on the Riding Officer. No less a figure than Hubert Lockwood took the stand to tell all present that the Riding Officer was a coward, a bully and suffered from delusions of grandeur where he pretended he was the Duke of York. A man describing himself as a humble fisherman began to give evidence that the Riding Officer routinely harangued him, forcing entry to his home on an almost daily basis and challenging him on the beach when he had been "merely fishing" to earn himself a living. The Riding Officer scratched his head, trying to place the man he vaguely recognised; whoever he was he was not from this area plus he was quite the storyteller from his over-dramatic account – perhaps he was an out of work actor, perhaps he had seen him on stage in London at the theatre and that's where he knew his face from. He was certainly no fisherman, and the words and language he used sounded like those of a wordsmith. Various other members of Lockwood's close circle took the stand to fabricate tales of the Riding Officer which had him branded as a thief, a double crosser and the type of man who visited ladies of "loose moral virtues" at Mrs Higgins *guesthouse.*

The case culminated with the tale of events that led to the two smugglers' apparently false arrests; the two men had been offshore fishing, not in a rowing boat as the prosecution had falsely claimed but in a fishing boat. They were fishing for herring and also checking on their lobster pots which were what the Riding Officer from the neighbouring parish saw them handling offshore whilst he was in a drunken haze. The small fishing boat had passed close to another ship at one point; the fishermen being gentlemen had then exchanged pleasantries with their fellow seafarers. It was only once the vessel had passed them that they realised that a case had fallen over the side of the ship. Their vessel was far too small to stand any chance of catching the larger cargo vessel, so the two men pulled the case on board so that it was no longer a hazard to any other seafarers. They decided that the best thing to do was take it ashore and take it to the parish constable; as they reached the shore the Riding Officer challenged them, unwilling to listen to their catalogue of events. He marched them to the Parish Gaol where the constable had begrudgingly – at the insistence of the Riding Officer, who had physically threatened the constable causing the constable to suspect that the Riding Officer was drunk – arrested them.

In a very short period of time, the jury retired and then returned ten minutes later to give the overwhelming verdict of not guilty in favour of the fishermen. They were free. The magistrate then began summing up, delivering a thunderous verbal assault on the Riding Officer, proclaiming him a coward, a drunkard and a man of low moral fibre who, being so incompetent at his own job, targeted those who were innocent.

Outside the court, the Riding Officer witnessed Lockwood and his cohorts along with Grantham's friends and well-wishers congratulate the apparently innocent party and tell them that a serious miscarriage of justice had been avoided. The Riding Officer smiled wryly as the group who had collected outside the court taunted him and mocked him, calling him a fool and a bully. They accused him of being stupid and mostly ignorant.

The Riding Officer just smiled and said to the formerly accused fishermen, "You must be fantastic fishermen. You went out there in a rowing boat to catch fish. What is most amazing is that you didn't have a single fishing net, rod or lobster pot between you."

As he retired from the area, he heard Lockwood lead his cohorts in a rendition of "The Grand Old Duke of York." The Riding Officer headed on home with the rendition becoming increasingly louder, and he smiled. The majority of those foolish idiots had no idea what Lockwood was referring to in the slightest.

Chapter Three

The Unmistakable Odour of Trouble

Late in the afternoon, the Riding Officer passed the Herring Caller on his way south to the perimeter of his area. An hour or so later, as he returned up the coast, he could see the Herring Caller returning to the village, having finished for the day. The Riding Officer realised his patrol would end soon. The light was beginning to fade and the urge to eat was beginning to overcome him, and he had comfort in the knowledge that the smugglers' main lookout had retired for the day. The Herring Caller had vanished from sight and another figure came into view. As his horse trotted closer to the figure, he surprised when he realised it was Anna. He was not expecting to see her until the evening.

"Hello!" the Riding Officer greeted her. "What are you doing here?" He looked over his shoulders, hoping not to see one of Lockwood's lackeys. The last thing he wanted was another audience with Grantham.

"I came to see you," Anna told him.

The Riding Officer smiled. "That makes me feel special."

"I must speak to you," Anna said with a serious look upon her face.

The Riding Officer dismounted from his horse, wrapping her reins to a branch of a nearby tree. The expression on the Riding Officer's face changed to that of concern. He gently placed his hands on Anna's shoulders and lowered his face towards her. "Is there a problem? Have there been any repercussions from last night?"

"I'm fine. I just need to speak to you."

"Fire away."

"Not here, in private," Anna said. "Let's go to your cottage."

"That sounds good," said the Riding Officer. "I need to eat."

"I've taken some food to your house," Anna advised. "I've put it in the stable."

"Climb up," said the Riding Officer. He patted his horse's saddle with his left hand. "I'll give you a ride back to the village."

* * *

"How is your head?" the Riding Officer asked. It was late afternoon as he headed back to Upperbridge. Anna was sitting side saddle in front of him on the horse's saddle, with her left arm wrapped around his neck and her right arm around his torso so she did not fall. He could feel Anna's breath against his cheek. He looked across at her beautiful porcelain-like forehead where the mark was still visible.

"I'll survive," said Anna. "That ointment worked wonders."

The Riding Officer smiled. "Were there any repercussions?"

Anna sniffed. She looked away from him. "My father caught me as I walked in. He had been drinking brandy and he had a few choice words for me."

"And those words were?"

"I won't say," said Anna. She looked into the Riding Officer's eyes. "But I will say this: I don't want to be like the women around here. I don't want to be a meek woman forced into an uncaring marriage, ordered around by an uncouth brute. I want to be someone else."

The horse trotted parallel to the beach as they headed towards the village. The scavenger who lived there was loitering outside his hut, his shoulders hunched and his head stuck out as if it was on a stalk as he glared at them. The Riding Officer felt Anna squirm and her grip on his neck tighten. The old man offered his services to the smugglers for a cut. For some reason the vile old man was very protective of his hut. It was as if he was hiding something.

"I've heard the smugglers talk about his hut," said Anna.

"What did they say?"

"They wonder what he is hiding. He is very protective of that hut."

"Perhaps he has contraband."

"Why hide it from the other smugglers? He's in league with them and he has no outside contacts according to them."

"Maybe it is jewels washed ashore having been jettisoned by privateers."

"Perhaps…"

"Or gold doubloons that have gradually made their way to the beach having been sunk with a ship that was part of the Spanish Armada."

"Whatever it is, he went to great lengths to protect it. He bought an expensive lock and chain to secure the door despite he has no items of value and no one has set foot in there, other than him, in eight years."

"He must have something he shouldn't in there…"

Anna laughed. "Lockwood's crown."

"What?"

"Lockwood's crown. He had this crown he used to wear every Sunday after he had been to church. He would parade around his house with it on his head mumbling about his destiny. It went missing a while back."

The Riding Officer's head reared back as he laughed at the mere thought. "That's the funniest thing I've heard in a long while."

Anna smiled, saying, "The horrid little man must have stolen it."

As they passed some upturned fishing boats that sat at the top of the beach near the pathway, the little man, his face blackened as if he had been handling coal, appeared in front of them.

As they drew closer to the old man, the Riding Officer stared straight ahead in the direction of Upperbridge, clearly making a bid to ignore him. Anna held the Riding Officer tighter as she stared at the old man. In the Riding Officer's arms, she felt safe. He was sparking new and growing feelings in her. With him, she was secure from the cretinous little man who seemed so fundamentally wrong.

"Scum!" the old man barked at the Riding Officer. He stooped to pick up a stone.

"Don't worry," the Riding Officer murmured to Anna. "I've passed him four times today and he's said the same thing on every occasion. It's getting a bit repetitive, if you ask me."

"And a whore!" the old man barked at Anna. He tried to throw the stone but could not project it far enough. It bounced harmlessly away.

"Does he ever say that?" asked Anna. She buried her head in the Riding Officer's jacket. She didn't want him to see she was hurt but she also didn't want Samuel to see. She had a feeling of who he had been talking to.

"No," said the Riding Officer after a pause. "Anyway, who is he? He is another to whom I've never been formally introduced."

"His name is Samuel," Anna advised, "and he's trouble."

Anna looked over her shoulder back towards Samuel, who was still scowling at them as he shook a fist in their direction. Anna could tell that there would be trouble. There was something that Anna found fundamentally wrong about Samuel, though she didn't know what it was. In all honesty, she did not want to know what was so bad about him. The Riding Officer's horse made her way up the main road, and now Samuel was out of view but Anna still felt concerned.

"Are you all right, Anna?" asked the Riding Officer. He felt Anna grip his arm tightly and as she turned to look back he could feel her breath increasing rapidly.

"I'm fine!" said Anna, hesitantly.

"I hope you are; I really care about you," said the Riding Officer gently in her ear. Anna suddenly felt a reassuring warmness inside, and she smiled and slipped her hand into the Riding Officer's, around the horse's reins.

* * *

"This is good stew!" said the Riding Officer after a couple of mouthfuls of the meal that Anna had brought him. *What a risk she is taking*, he thought. *I know what they'll say about her, and though she will say it doesn't faze her, I am sure that it will.*

"Mrs Wood, the cook at the inn, made it." Anna was lying on his bed.

"She's a good cook."

"You are lucky then. That gin-soaked old witch burns the majority of the food she attempts to cook; she couldn't boil water!" Anna answered, sharply. "She has a tongue like acid and is a person who is happiest when causing mental anguish to another."

"Like a drink, does she?"

"More than her fair share," sniped Anna. "As much as she wants, it seems! I heard she is paid in gin rather than money."

Anna gazed up at the ceiling. She smiled. *May be I should come clean and admit Mrs Wood didn't cook it ... I could never inflict her cooking on someone I genuinely like ... but then again I don't want people to be aware that I've cooked him a meal – I know what they will say.* Anna sighed. *And the old witch will be unbearable if she finds out I am a better cook than her...*

The Riding Officer turned to Anna. "Anna, I know you didn't come here to talk about an old crone's drinking habits."

"No," replied Anna. She paused, then said, "Lockwood is planning something. I heard him speaking to my father today."

"What were they saying?"

"They were speaking of doing something on the coast. They said something about a storm and how they would clean up," she told him, "but that's all I can tell you."

"It helps," he replied. Now when he heard the name Lockwood, he instinctively knew that trouble was on the horizon.

"What will you do?" asked Anna.

"Well," said the Riding Officer, standing up, "I think I'll go to bed..."

"Would you like me to go?" asked Anna.

"No," replied the Riding Officer with a sparkle in his eye, "you stay there and I'll join you if you wish."

Anna smiled. She felt like she was caught up in the moment and she could not believe this was happening. She never felt this about a man before. He was everything Lockwood wasn't and he could offer her something she felt Lockwood never properly could: life outside of Upperbridge.

"You come and join me." She patted the part of the bed next to her.

He slipped off his boots and lay down next to Anna. He slipped an arm underneath and wrapped the other around her. He smiled at Anna, Anna smiled at him, and they began to kiss.

* * *

Anna and the Riding Officer had been on the bed for about ten minutes when there was a mighty pounding on the door. The Riding Officer sat up forcefully. He climbed off the bed before gently pulling Anna to her feet. The Riding Officer silently signalled to her that she should head to the back. Anna hesitated for a moment and then headed to the back room of the cottage.

The door burst open and Kitching the draper, Anna's father, entered, followed by Samuel who bared a snarl on his face.

"Where is my daughter?" thundered Kitching. He was standing about two feet in front of the doorway, blocking it as a potential exit. The Riding Officer stared him squarely in the eye.

"I don't know," replied the Riding Officer, his voice slow and steady as he tried to keep it in check. His heart pounded as he placed his thumbs on his waistline. *He may be her father,* he thought, *but if he hurts her...*

"I saw you with her!" Samuel screeched.

The Riding Officer stood tall and held his head high has he peered down at Samuel who was standing in front of the window. "You see a lot of things," the Riding Officer retaliated, "but that all depends on how much money there is going."

"She was on your horse," Samuel said.

"I took her to the inn," the Riding Officer claimed as he placed his hands on his hips. "Go and look and you should find her there."

"We had better go to the inn," said Kitching, menacingly. "My daughter is engaged to a fine man by the name of Hubert Lockwood. He wants you to know that he is the most powerful man in the parish and is a man who won't stand for any of your shenanigans."

"Lockwood does not scare me and neither do you," shouted the Riding Officer. "Anyway, if Anna wants to be with me, then that should be her choice."

"My daughter is promised to Lockwood and she will marry him," Kitching said, coldly. "If I ever see you lay a hand on her, I will have you killed."

The Riding Officer stared back firmly and showing no intimidation even as his heart began to hammer, he said, "If you were a gentleman I would demand satisfaction."

Kitching snarled and grimaced. "You, sir, have made a powerful enemy! Come on, Samuel."

Kitching turned and left with Samuel in tow. As Samuel left he pointed a bony finger at the Riding Officer and shrieked, "I'm watching you! You're up to something depraved."

The door slammed behind them. As the Riding Officer checked that the door had shut correctly, Anna emerged from the shadows.

"Have they gone?" she asked in a whisper.

"Yes," replied the Riding Officer, softly, his heart still hammering despite his calm exterior. "They're heading to the inn."

"Shall I stay?" asked Anna, hopefully.

The Riding Officer placed his arms around Anna's waist. Anna draped her arms around his neck.

"No," he said, softly. "I don't fear your father at ten paces with a pistol but I do at two inches with a pistol or a cutlass with his cohorts restraining me. You'd better go..."

Anna looked sad. "Do you not love me?"

"It's not safe here for you." He added, "You seem to have acquired a reputation of sorts."

A tear welled in the corner of Anna's eye. "That could be because I don't want to be like the meek women in the village. Bossed and bullied by men who don't care for them. People tell me I will go to hell if I don't change my ways but I don't care; it will be a change from Upperbridge."

"It's best you go to the inn where you are expected to be..." He gently stroked Anna's arm with his hand.

Anna grabbed his shirt, and looked deeply into his eyes. "Do you love me?"

"Yes ... I do..." whispered the Riding Officer without hesitation. "I must send you on your way because I love you," he added before he kissed her. "I know we're not safe here in Upperbridge..."

* * *

It was a Saturday afternoon in Upperbridge. The Riding Officer found himself by the River Mayne close by the stone bridge from where the village got its name. The weather was fine and the Riding Officer had spent the best part of the morning watching the coastline. The view out to sea was clear and the body of water itself was a rich, deep blue and as flat as a millpond. The Riding Officer knew in such fine weather the smuggling community would not strike. He knew they liked the cover of fog and haze or a wild storm in the evening. Only the foolish would try to smuggle contraband today.

Upon returning to his cottage the Riding Officer found his pantry fairly bare, so he decided to go fishing and catch some supper. Taking with him an ad-hoc rod he had made from a tree branch, discarded fishing line and an old hook made from a strong pin, he had headed to the stone bridge at the head of the village. The water was clear at that point. He felt nauseous when he saw the slovenly cohorts of Lockwood throw their waste into the village stream at a point off a grotty little side street known as Fish Row. He headed to the part of the river he knew where the water was better and the fish would be finer. In theory, he could have gone to Lockwood's shop and purchased some fish at an extortionate price, but he didn't fancy a bout of food poisoning for which Lockwood's stock was famous; *furthermore*, he thought, *why would he pay three times as much as anybody else for the displeasure?*

Upon settling on the river bank, his mind very quickly drifted away from fishing and to that of his true love, Anna. He found it hard to believe that he had rejected the opportunity to consummate his relationship with Anna a few days before, but then again, he understood why. A sexual liaison was not what she really craved – she wanted love and affection. If he and Anna were to be together it must be away from Upperbridge, he must be free of Grantham's control and Anna needed to be away from the grasp of Lockwood.

That was something else that bothered the Riding Officer. Lockwood. In one week's time, the twisted hunchback would be staging his birthday and had been adamant for the presence of the Riding Officer. The Riding Officer couldn't understand why his nemesis had been so insistent; what did Lockwood have in mind? The first thought that flashed through his mind was murder; did Lockwood and his circle of thugs plan to kill him? Would it be a message sent to Anna that she would be attached to Lockwood for a long time to come? Would they be trying to send a message to Anna that it would be Lockwood or nobody? It was a possibility but the Riding Officer began to analyse it; why would they do such a thing at an event such as that when the majority of the community would be present? Everyone would know who did it, but then again, who would speak out against Lockwood, Grantham and their associates? Would this be a message to the community in general that if you stood up to them and did not comply that you would meet your maker?

Much as the Riding Officer did not wish to attend, he was compelled to be present just to know what his fate was. As he began to think about it even more, he realised that he would be obliged to attend simply for the sake of Anna; he knew the revolting, hunchback known as Hubert Lockwood would parade her in front of his wider circle like a trophy, and he knew Anna would not be able to bear such an event and he knew he needed to be there for her even if it was just as moral support.

Suddenly something clicked in his mind – the arrangement between Lockwood and Kitching the draper had been a verbal one. Was this going to be the most torturous night of both his and Anna's lives? Was the man Anna despised going to destroy her life by announcing to all and sundry that he and Anna were formally engaged? Perhaps that was why Lockwood wanted the Riding Officer to be present – he knew there was something forging between them and he wanted to send a powerful message to the man who threatened him the most.

The Riding Officer's trail of thought was suddenly inter-rupted by the distinctive sound of a hunting horn. His stomach instantly turned as he recalled the times he had spent as a young man at the homes of the rich in the country around the South East of England. He found blood sports disgusting to start with, and he loathed himself for betting on cockfights in London. The Riding Officer had found the antics of the depraved upper classes nauseating especially the slovenly inbred nobility who gained a kick from chasing the poor beasts across country before they allowed a pack of hounds to tear the physically exhausted beast to pieces for nothing more than their twisted, depraved pleasure. That wasn't sport. That was just plain fundamentally wrong.

Curiosity gained the better of the Riding Officer. He rose to his feet and peered in the direction from where the horn had sounded. He could see a pack of horses and hounds chasing a fox; the fox ran from Grantham's land onto the farmland of a man named Timms. The fox was two hundred yards away, but the chasing pack gave no regard to Timms' land and charged on after the fox. The Riding Officer could clearly see that the creature was beginning to tire, and as he threw away his fishing rod he knew what he had to do.

Making sure that his view was not blocked he drew his pistol and fired from the road. A little over two hundred yards away, the Riding Officer saw the fox tumble dramatically to the ground in a heap where the poor beast promptly died. The pack came to halt as the hounds tore into the now-deceased fox.

"Who fired that?" demanded one of the hunters, who the Riding Officer instantly recognised as Grantham.

"I did!" admitted the Riding Officer in a calm and commanding voice.

"And why did you have to do that, you fool?" Grantham demanded, thrashing the reins of his horse. "You have ruined our enjoyment of the sport!"

"You wanted the beast dead, did you not?" the Riding Officer said coldly. He was surprised that the politician's horse had not bolted with the way he thrashed those reins.

"We did," said Grantham, "but we wanted the honour of killing it."

The Riding Officer grimaced at the politician. "You're quite depraved, aren't you, Grantham? There's no honour in tearing the beast to shreds to satisfy your own depraved pleasure."

"Just who do you think you are?" barked another familiar voice. The Riding Officer peered over his shoulder and noticed that the members of Grantham's hunting party had surrounded him. Lockwood's horse pawed the ground and snorted. Grantham stood in front of him, reminiscent of a monarch choosing to address a humble commoner. The Riding Officer glanced back to the Scot who looked at Grantham as if he was envious of the politician's regal stance.

"I'm just a lowly riding officer, Lockwood..." His hand hovered over the butt of his pistol which hung from his belt.

Grantham shook his fist. He looked to his left. "Constable, arrest this man!" His chin was wobbling like slag ready to slide down a hillside.

"What's the charge, my lord?" the constable asked, not dismounting but instead clutching at the small of his back.

The Riding Officer raised an eyebrow.

"Are you comfortable with that horse?"

"I am!" frowned the constable. He leaned forward, attempting to grab the Riding Officer, who stepped back as the constable almost pitched himself forward over the horse's head to the ground. "What's the charge, my lord?"

The Riding Officer tried not to laugh at the constable's lack of skill with the horse. *I wonder how you got the job?* he thought.

"Attempted murder," replied Grantham, pointing a finger at the Riding Officer. "He tried to shoot me!"

"I don't think so," interrupted another voice. The sound of a shotgun being cocked increased the tense atmosphere. Timms the farmer stood with his shotgun pointed in the direction of the hunters. Lockwood felt uncomfortable as he reached for his weapon, and he hoped he would not have to fire it as gunmanship was not exactly a forte of his.

"Who are you?" Grantham bellowed.

"My name is Timms," the farmer answered, "and this is my land. You are trespassing!"

"We are not trespassing. This is Grantham's land!" interrupted Lockwood. "Now, Constable, arrest that man."

The farmer shook his head, "I don't think so," Timms said, softly. "If you arrest him, then I'll have to insist you lot are arrested, too, for trespass. This is my land."

The cheeks on Grantham's bloated face began to puff aggressively. "He attempted to shoot me!" he bellowed.

Timms shook his head. "No," he answered, "he shot that fox. It was a great shot – the beast was heading to my farm. Ever seen what one of those beasts can do in a chicken coop?"

"No, I have not," answered the disgruntled politician.

"You don't want to know, Fatty!" Timms told the obese politician.

"How dare you speak to such a fine man as Mr Grantham like that?" Lockwood snapped. "He is a fine man with an elegant figure who tries to keep rich English customs alive."

"I couldn't care less!" Timms informed the hunchback.

"He, himself, has paid for a troupe of Morris dancers to perform at my birthday next week!" he informed all and sundry.

"As I said, Piggy," Timms replied, "I couldn't care less! I could not care less about him and his customs or his stupid Morris dancers."

Lockwood seethed as Timms stared at him. "I should have you arrested!" he said, "along with this fool of a Riding Officer!"

Timms laughed. "I should have you and Fatty arrested, Piggy. You're on my land. Now seeing as this lad has done me a favour and killed that fox before it got my chickens, I won't have any charges raised against you lot if you let him go."

There was an uneasy silence.

"Perhaps we could solve this another way." Timms walked up closer to Lockwood's horse and peered at the Scot's gun. "Perhaps we could solve this like gentlemen."

Lockwood gasped. "I ... erm ... I..." His jaw dropped open and he almost fumbled his weapon. "I think the man makes a good point, don't you, Adam?"

"Very well," murmured Grantham at last. "Let the fool go free."

The hunting party began to reluctantly retreat as Grantham violently cracked his crop across his mount. Over his shoulder, Lockwood could see the Riding Officer grinning as his enemies skulked away.

"I hope you enjoy the Morris Men next week, officer," Lockwood said with contempt. "You are coming, I hope?"

"Oh yes, Hubert," the Riding Officer advised him. "I wouldn't miss it for the world!"

* * *

News of Lockwood and Grantham's comeuppance spread through Upperbridge fairly quickly, and when the news hit the inn, Anna could not keep the grin from her face. Her father made her spend time in the company of the local fishmonger a couple of times a week. The stench of stale, rotting fish accompanied by the revolting hunchback's attempts at impressing her by reading poetry to her and paying musicians to play music to her made her feel all the worse. He was the only person she knew who could ruin the works of Peter Lloyd for her. The way he slobbered at the mouth and would have to pause mid-sentence to wipe his mouth upon his sleeve made her stomach turn. He would try to sing to her but his flat, out of key voice augmented by spit flying from his mouth as he attempted to sing, made her cringe. His smug announcements of his own self-importance and his gigantic, twisted ego made her loathe him further. He went as far as to make her watch him act out a mock coronation where he would declare himself the most powerful man in Britain. She enjoyed seeing him made to look like a fool and an unknown young man had drawn a caricature of Lockwood on the outside of a WC out in the street. Her father didn't see the funny side; he made sure that Anna had spent the best part of the past three days locked in her room, only being let out to work and to spend time with the revolting Lockwood. Her father was forever informing Anna what a wonderful man Lockwood was, that he was going to make an excellent husband for her, and that the Riding Officer was a glorified lowlife criminal with delusions of grandeur.

The wheelwright, something of a local gossip, had walked into the inn telling the tale he had witnessed from his workshop of the Riding Officer shooting a fox that Grantham and Lockwood were chasing stone dead at over two hundred yards. Angered by his actions, Grantham had attempted to have him arrested before Farmer Timms came to his aid and threatened to have Grantham and his hunting party arrested for trespass, leading to the corrupt politician and his pig-faced cohort leaving with their respective tails between their legs.

The Riding Officer had entered the inn a little while later. He took a seat in the corner and read a book on the works of Spinoza whilst enjoying a jug of porter. Anna gazed at him with admiration; he was a real man. He had impressed her on his own and didn't need to force anything upon her. Best of all, the Riding Officer did not smell of a mixture of body odour and rotting, stale fish. *He always smelt quite nice*, Anna thought. Anna smiled as she thought of one day escaping Upperbridge to be with him.

"I *don't* think so," said Anna as she felt a man's hands across her hips.

The Riding Officer broke from his reading and looked over his left shoulder towards Anna. "Is there a problem, Anna?"

The man's hands left her sides quickly. "Nothing that you'll need your gun for." She smiled at him, as she thought of him bringing Lockwood and his empire to an end.

"Anna!" came a bawled scream from the kitchen that broke

her thoughts and brought her crashing down to earth. "Anna! Get in here now!"

Anna reluctantly retreated to the kitchen; the voice belonged to Mrs Wood, the cook. She lived at the inn where she received, in return for cooking and preparing the food for the inn, a bed and free board plus as much gin as she wished.

"Fish pie for the man by the fire place!" she barked to Anna as she thrust a platter into Anna's hands.

"Yes, Mrs Wood," said Anna as she shoved an empty gin bottle or two out of the way before she picked up the plate.

"Nice bit of fish, that," Mrs Wood told her. Anna began to recoil at the state of Mrs Wood's rotting gnarled teeth and her permanently foul smelling breath.

"I would hope so..." she answered, weakly.

"I got it from Mr Lockwood. Some of his prime stock."

Anna had heard enough. She left the kitchen with the suspicious-smelling pie that had caused her eyes to begin streaming and placed it on the table of a bug eyed traveller.

"Your fish pie, sir!" she said to him, wondering whether she should apologise to him in advance for its coming after-effects.

The traveller stared down at the unimpressive dish in front of him as he wondered what he had got himself into. Anna paused as she retreated to the kitchen. She gazed in the direction of the Riding Officer as he sat reading at a table by the hearth. There was something quite admirable in the way he sat and ignored two men in the pay of Lockwood who sat at the neighbouring table humming the tune to the Grand Old Duke of York. Lockwood would have loved to have seen nothing more than the Riding Officer make a humiliating visit to the village stocks.

"Don't know what you see in *that*," barked Mrs Wood as she emerged suddenly as if from nowhere.

Anna attempted to ignore her as she re-entered the kitchen.

There was a sizzle as Mrs Wood threw some chopped vegetables into some fat melting in a pot on the stove. She clutched a tattered old cloth in her burnt and blistered hand as she began to shake the pot to mix up the vegetables. Anna tried to peer into the pot but Mrs Wood slammed the lid on. Anna rolled her eyes and shook her head. *What is she trying to cook?*

"You have a wonderful man in Mr Lockwood," the gin-soaked old woman told her.

"Mr Lockwood is neither a man nor wonderful," Anna replied in a blunt tone.

The old woman frowned. Her face reminded Anna of the texture of old, severely worn leather. "Mr Lockwood is a wonderful man! Kind and generous." She cracked a wooden spoon down on the kitchen table so hard it shattered.

"I don't wish to talk about him." She grabbed a stack of plates from a shelf.

"There are a lot of fine men in this village," Mrs Wood continued, wagging her finger at the unfortunate serving girl whilst oblivious to the vegetables in the pot that were beginning to blacken. "Mr Grantham, the constable, Mr Samuel, Mr Hurley and Mr Paine. They're all fine men who could treat you well but what do you do? You go chasing after the biggest lowlife and criminal in the village – that damned Riding Officer. I've seen you swooning over him like a common tart. You behave like a prostitute, no less. You should go and work for Mrs Higgins at her *guesthouse.*"

Anna curled her lips then sighed. Every day she was subjected to Mrs Wood singing the praises of the smugglers and Lockwood; every time the Riding Officer came in she had to put up with the same abuse just because of her feelings towards him. She could barely take it. Who was Mrs Wood to tell her how to live her life? She wasn't her mother or even a relative; she was an alcoholic old woman who drank herself into a drunken stupor every evening; a woman whose husband had falsely admitted to killing a man so he would be hung in order to escape her. What worried her most was that if it was clear to Mrs Wood how she felt about the Riding

Officer then it would be clear to all and this would, most certainly, include a certain fishmonger.

"Mr Lockwood is going to make a fine husband for you!" Mrs Wood proclaimed, as she poured herself a cup of gin.

"If you think he's so wonderful, you marry him then!" Anna replied, gathering up some platters and taking them to a cupboard.

"If I was younger, I would!"

"I don't think a revolting man such as Lockwood would even want a pathetic gin soaked old witch like you!"

Mrs Wood reeled back and if it hadn't been for the kitchen table behind her she would have fallen over completely and spilt her gin. "Mr Lockwood is forever telling me of my beauty," she informed Anna with a tremble in her voice.

"I think not," Anna replied, coldly. "You are as about as beautiful as a cesspit! There are lines of dog excrement on Fish Row that look better than you."

Mrs Wood picked up a wooden spoon and tried to strike Anna across the face with it. "He is a wonderful man, and more of a man than that awful Riding Officer."

"Let me tell you something about that supposed awful Riding Officer," Anna began, incensed at Mrs Wood's comments. "The Riding Officer whom everyone seems to loathe but me is the only real man in the village! He's honest and educated, he doesn't steal, he doesn't murder people plus he respects me as a woman and does not treat me like an object like so many of the supposedly wonderful men in this village do."

* * *

The Riding Officer hated to admit it but Lockwood's residence looked impressive from the outside. It was a ten bedroom house with a spacious downstairs complete with a large hall that could be used to entertain large parties. As the Riding Officer entered the residence he was announced by a small, sycophantic, effeminate man who he didn't recognise but was referred to as William Quentin.

The Riding Officer stared around at the hall. There was a large banquet table set out lengthways in front of the fire place. Two more long tables set out at the end of the main table, pointing towards it, created a horse-shoe effect; the Riding Officer suspected he would be placed at the far end of one of these tables, far away from Anna and not within view. It wouldn't be such a problem for him, for at least he would be away from the overpowering odour of Lockwood. He truly felt sorry for Anna. He knew his true love would be sitting at the side of the nauseating hunchback, suffering his atrocious personal hygiene, whilst watching him and his bloated cohorts stuff their greedy gullets with various fare.

Standing at the side of the hall in his uniform, the Riding Officer began to glance around further. There were porters carrying kegs of ale and pitchers full of wine around offering the associates of Lockwood fine beers and ales from the Trent and expensive wine from France and the Mediterranean. In fact, the wine was exquisite. The Riding Officer found it hard to comprehend that he had been offered such finery and from the same pitchers as everybody else; it appeared that his enemies weren't going to try to poison him. A traveller staying at Mrs Higgins' *guesthouse* had passed away two days previously from food poisoning, courtesy of a fish pie from the tavern, which was certainly not the way the Riding Officer would select to go.

The Riding Officer stood alone. There was a dour-faced string quartet playing the works of Mozart in a lifeless style. The host of the party, Lockwood, stood at the foot of an impressive staircase surrounded by his closest allies. Despite wearing his best clothes, he still looked a repugnant sight as his pot belly hung over his belt. There was a touch of mucus about his constantly sniffing nose. Lockwood's legs reminded the Riding Officer of young saplings as he wondered if they possessed the strength to carry the fat body they supported. Already there was a strange stain from an unknown source forming on Lockwood's jacket, and there was a particularly evil glint in his pig-like eyes that evening. The Riding Officer could see Grantham observing the sycophantic William Quentin. The slovenly politician's mouth was open with his tongue peeping out. Whenever Quentin made eye contact with Grantham, the politician would moisten his lips before rubbing his hands firmly against his trousers as if he was attempting to dry them.

"Mr Frederick Cheever, Member of Parliament!" announced Quentin as he became aware of Grantham's interest in him.

The Riding Officer looked towards the doorway. In all his time in Upperbridge, he had never set his eyes on the borough's other politician. Cheever staggered in, clearly intoxicated. He had a balding head with white fluffy hair and a purple, bulbous nose, and to the Riding Officer he cut something of a comedic looking character.

"Excuse me a moment," said Lockwood, suddenly concerned over the appearance of the borough's other politician.

The Riding Officer watched as Lockwood ordered one of his henchmen to deal with Cheever; the henchman walked over and led Cheever in the direction of an unknown room. The Riding Officer wondered what would happen to this man, but then he thought, *why should I care?*

"Scum!" was the sudden bark that interrupted the Riding Officer's thoughts as he watched the henchman re-enter the room; about a foot in front of the Riding Officer stood Samuel. The Riding Officer stared coldly at Samuel. The revolting little man made no sense to the Riding Officer. Why was he so keen to accuse others? The Riding Officer recalled the events that once led to him fighting a duel in Croydon. A man had accused him of cheating at cards but when it was all over, the accuser was the man who had been revealed as the one who was cheating. He knew from experience those with a guilty conscious were often the first to accuse others, regardless of whether they were guilty or not. Sometimes people had a habit of protesting too much.

Lockwood appeared at Samuel's side. "The Riding Officer, so very nice to see you," he said as he peered at a painting of old man on the wall.

"So kind of you to say that, Mr Lockwood," responded the Riding Officer, a frown upon his face.

"Binns?" snapped Lockwood to a henchman.

The man who had removed Cheever walked over. "Yes, Mr Lockwood?"

"Please take Samuel to the room reserved for *special* guests where he will accompany Mr Cheever," he ordered. Samuel beamed a foolish smile at his own incorrectly perceived importance.

"Very good, Mr Lockwood!" answered Binns.

The Riding Officer smirked. "Samuel, a special guest, Lockwood?" he inquired with a slight laugh.

"I don't want that revolting man around here; I find his personal hygiene quite distasteful," Lockwood informed him. "I think it is so unpleasant when people neglect basic washing."

"Do you really?" The Riding Officer covered his mouth as he attempted not to laugh.

"I'm so glad you came," said Lockwood, changing tack.

"I thought it rude to boycott."

"Well, I'm going to make sure you have an evening you'll never forget!" the hunchback informed him with a sinister glisten in his eye.

* * *

Lockwood's words rang through the mind of the Riding Officer. He had something planned for him and this would not be pleasant. Lockwood was a cruel man just like Grantham and he gained massive amounts of pleasure in tormenting others with both actions and words. Lockwood tormented Anna, the Riding Officer knew that – his ongoing boasts of their future crippled her inside on a regular basis. When once asked why he owned such a large house with so many bedrooms whilst in the presence of Anna, he proudly announced that he planned to have a large family with as many children as he could. Reports suggested that Anna left the room and vomited violently.

The Riding Officer suddenly realised that there was somebody very important missing from the event. He could see Anna nowhere. He knew there was no way that Lockwood would let her get away with not showing up that night – not even if she was dying from bubonic plague would he allow her to stay away from this party. Knowing Lockwood, Anna would almost certainly be a centre piece for him to parade in front of his followers, cohorts and enemies in a way that a trinket could be brought back from battle by a warlord.

An impressive looking long cased clock chimed to signal it was half past eight. The sycophantic, fey-voiced Quentin, who was subject to Grantham's increasing interest, walked over to the staircase.

"My lords, ladies and gentlemen!" he announced, smiling at Grantham. "May I introduce Miss Anna Kitching!"

Anna appeared at the top of the staircase in a long flowing emerald dress. Her long dark hair which complemented her fair complexion rested naturally on her shoulders. The Riding Officer's jaw almost dropped. She looked even more stunning than usual but as she began to descend the staircase he noticed she was in discomfort. The only time she managed a half smile was when she saw the Riding Officer. Lockwood grabbed Anna by the arm, causing her obvious pain, grasping at her like a possession he wished to show off to his guests. He made it clear to anyone who thought otherwise that she was his property.

"My lords, ladies and gentlemen!" announced Quentin once

more in his fey voice. "Dinner is served!"

* * *

Anna ate nothing and drank very little that evening. She did not wish to be there. She felt like a hunting trophy on the main banqueting table. She was surrounded by bloated, gluttonous, slovenly men who grunted and belched their way through the banquet of game, fish, fine meat, expensive cheese and fine wine whilst saying very little and consuming plenty. The corset that she had been forced into at the orders of Lockwood because he didn't want her looking fat had her in ever-increasing discomfort. She glanced to the left and noticed the perspiration pouring down Lockwood's face as he greedily devoured a leg of pheasant. She felt repulsed as she looked down to the end of the table and watched Grantham who, between gluttonous mouthfuls of venison, was lustfully glaring at the obnoxious Quentin whom she had been prompted to slap earlier in the day when he made suggestive comments and accusations towards her when he suggested that it may have taken hours to cram her into her dress but she would have been out of it in a matter of minutes for the Riding Officer. The aspect that disturbed her the most was the way in which Quentin seemed to enjoy being struck. She was repulsed by Grantham's greed but she hated him because he tormented the one she loved.

She switched her gaze away from the main table and out onto the tables that surrounded the main table; at the very end of the left hand side table she saw him – the Riding Officer. He had eaten a leg of roast boar and drank very little. He knew the tedium of the entertainment was to come and then there would be Lockwood's actions towards him.

* * *

His heart in his mouth, the Riding Officer fought his way through the main hall and outside into the fresh air. He fumbled for his pipe, his hands trembling so badly the tobacco spilled to the floor.

"Blast!" he said, squatting down to attempt to gather it up. He couldn't. He buried his face in his hands for a moment.

Then slowly he stood up, and his hands dropped as he tried to support his frame against the stone wall. Gazing up at the sky, he could feel the tears well in his eyes, and the Riding Officer felt as if he had been pole-axed.

He attempted to focus on the moon yet couldn't; the only image that danced through his mind was the ghastly smile that was on Lockwood's face when he rose to his feet at the end of the meal. He had announced his engagement to Anna, while she closed her eyes and her face sank. Lockwood told all present that under the eyes of the Good Lord she was to be his property and his alone.

The Riding Officer covered his mouth, shut his eyes and shuddered. "This is worse than murder..." he uttered to himself.

* * *

As the annoying entertainment had begun, the Riding Officer found himself in a secluded area of the garden. He had had to head outside to compose himself. He knew he had to speak to Anna; he knew she was no happier about Lockwood's announcement than he was, but at the moment he needed space; a rush of blood at the wrong time could be fatal. The Riding Officer found himself a secluded area of the garden near the wall of the rear of the house where he could see the light from inside Lockwood's residence illuminate a section of the garden.

The Riding Officer sighed deeply and painfully. This was one of the worst evenings of his life. There had been times in London when he had blown ridiculous amounts of money playing cards, and then there were evenings when he had engaged in brawls and found himself staring down the barrel of a gun, he had taken a kicking at the hands of a gang of thugs that left him with cracked ribs, and sometimes he had found himself isolated and alone trying to find a purpose for continuing with his life. But this was the worst feeling. There was no way he could speak to Anna in the hall, and all he could do was to sit and to listen to Lockwood when he made his announcement. He was helpless as he felt his heart shatter like poor quality porcelain from the emotional blow.

He pondered what his next move would be. He could try to flee Upperbridge with Anna but he knew that Grantham and Lockwood would track him down. On numerous occasions he had heard them boasting of the agents they had across England; the Riding Officer surmised that they were most likely vagabonds and general lowlifes augmented by a few conmen and confidence tricksters who Lockwood and Grantham had a financial or personal hold over. He knew the type of deal they would cut – *you work for me or I'll report you to the authorities*. It didn't take a genius to realise that the type of people Lockwood and Grantham would associate with liked a dance and were familiar with the actions that led to a man learning the steps to the Tyburn Jig.

He had to rescue Anna from a fate worse than death, but how?

The Riding Officer's train of thought was suddenly broken by the presence of two individuals. He recognised one as the parish constable and the other as the unmistakable Hubert Lockwood. Lockwood laughed loudly in an almost demented manner as they exited the doors leading to the garden. With Lockwood and the constable unable to see him the Riding Officer looked on.

"I must say, Mr Lockwood," the constable began, "that this has been the most wonderful of parties!"

"I do my best," bragged the hunchback.

"Did you see the look on the face of that foolish Riding Officer when you announced your engagement to Anna?" the constable asked. The Riding Officer clenched his teeth so hard that his jaw hurt.

"Yes, I did. His majesty was not amused."

"I must say, you have done well to bag a fiancée like her," the constable commented.

"There was never a doubt she would be mine," Lockwood said.

The constable frowned. "I don't understand, Mr Lockwood. She's never appeared to be particularly keen on you. She spends her time swooning over that damned Riding Officer."

Lockwood smiled evilly, his pig-like eyes glistening in the moonlight. "You see, Constable, when I see something I want, I take it! I've been in Upperbridge nineteen years. I left my native Scotland and headed south, and after six months of travelling I found the community I wanted to be in."

"What type of community is that?"

Lockwood laughed at the constable's naivety. "A rich community, my good man," he informed the constable. "I earned the trust of a fishmonger I was employed by, and then I finished him off and inherited his business. I ran the competition out of Upperbridge!"

The constable laughed softly. "You must have made a lot of money as a fishmonger, Mr Lockwood. This is a fine house you have."

Lockwood let out an evil guttural laugh that cut through the Riding Officer. "I didn't buy this property. I simply arranged for the owner to be driven out of Upperbridge and into Newgate Gaol; he was hanged and the borough gained possession of this house from where it was awarded to me. I will never pay for something unless I feel it is necessary."

"It's a good philosophy, Mr Lockwood." The constable seemed unsure of what he was being told.

"Sometimes it has its disadvantages. When I was a younger

man in Scotland I found myself fascinated by an older woman. She was beautiful and I wanted to have her, but she rejected my advances so I decided to take what I wanted anyway, and I raped her. The locals found out and I was a wanted man so I fled. It was her own damned fault if you ask me and the reaction of the locals was completely uncalled for."

"Did you really, Mr Lockwood?" he mumbled in a nervous voice. Lockwood's lack of remorse in his tone and the general flippancy over his confession left the constable stunned.

"When I saw Anna as a grown woman I decided that she would be mine. I did away with her romantic interest and gained the friendship of her father," Lockwood said. "Anna was different for me. I decided to woo her with my obvious charm and renowned good looks; I am now waiting to consummate our relationship on our wedding night like the fine Christian citizen I am. Good things come to those who wait."

"It's very noble of you."

"I have women of loose moral virtues all the time." Lockwood puffed out his chest. "Usually prostitutes; some throw themselves at me wishing to tap into my fortune. Anna is different to the whores who throw themselves at me; she plays hard to get with me! Deep down I know she truly loves me and wishes me to prove it. She wants me to finish off the loathsome Riding Officer, in reality."

The constable looked uncomfortable; this was more than he wished to know. "Very good, Mr Lockwood," he said, weakly. The Riding Officer grimaced at Lockwood's delusional comments about Anna.

The doors opened and one of the henchmen joined them in the garden, saying, "Excuse me, Mr Lockwood."

"What is it, Willis?" he snapped.

"It's Mr Cheever and Samuel," he said. "They wish to leave their room and relieve themselves."

"What do you mean? I thought their wine was drugged!"

Lockwood said, angrily. "It was supposed to knock them out."

"It seems it had no effect on them," Willis informed his employer. "Only the urge to micturate and drink some more."

Lockwood sighed loudly. "Get them an old pot or something and make sure they use it in their room. I don't need their kind wandering around my home ruining this party. And send Binns out here!"

"Yes, Mr Lockwood," answered Willis, and he returned inside.

"I think I'll head back to the party," said the constable, not sure of what to do about Lockwood's claim of rape. He knew there could be a large reward for Lockwood's capture, because there was a strong possibility it wasn't just rape that he was wanted for. He realised he could make a huge reputation for himself as well as making plenty of money for himself.

The Riding Officer watched Lockwood. The hunchback was alone and he was unaware of the Riding Officer's presence. Lockwood picked up a stick he walked over to a small stone cherub and tapped the statue gently on the shoulders as if he was knighting it. *Is he right in the head?* the Riding Officer thought. *Then again, this could be the perfect time.* He could kill Lockwood and flee Upperbridge under the cover of darkness. Dare he attack his nemesis? Lockwood's guard was down; dare he attack Lockwood like a coward?

Suddenly, the door opened and Binns joined Lockwood. "You requested my presence, Mr Lockwood?"

"Where is Grantham?"

"Upstairs with that Quentin character," Binns said.

"Disgusting!" snapped Lockwood. "I don't know where he found that William Quentin but I wish he would take him away!"

"I couldn't say," answered Binns in a dour voice.

"I wasn't asking!" Lockwood barked. "There are times that Grantham angers me; I know he enjoys tormenting that Riding Officer but I need to rid myself of that wretch! If I am to wed my beloved Anna, I need the Riding Officer disposed of. I'm concerned that he could corrupt her mind against me."

"That is a possibility."

"And watch the constable, Binns!" Lockwood advised. "I believe he could be up to no good. I dare say he's a man who cannot be trusted. I truly despair at some people's greed…"

Lockwood walked back into the house. The Riding Officer made a fist of his right hand and began to grind it into the palm of his left once more. The misery he had had inflicted on him that evening by Lockwood was purely mental but the thought of doing away with Lockwood ran through his mind constantly. If he killed Lockwood and even if he was killed himself as a result at least he knew Anna would be safe and would be away from Lockwood's grasp for good. It was a tempting thought. He reached for his pistol.

"Great minds think alike!" said a soft voice.

The Riding Officer turned to face the voice. He smiled as he saw it was Anna.

"What do you mean, Anna?" he asked, wondering if she was aware of what he had considered doing to Lockwood.

"Coming out here to escape that horrid party; I couldn't take another minute of those wretched Morris men!" she told him, sadly. Before he could respond she kissed him on the mouth. "I need you to do me a favour," she added. "Come down to the stables with me."

* * *

The Riding Officer could hardly believe it. Anna had asked him to go with her to the stables at Lockwood's residence whilst the hunchback was throwing a party.

"We could get into a lot of trouble," he warned Anna as she sat down on the hay in the stable. "Lockwood would have me killed on the spot if he found us together."

"Help me undo my gown," Anna said to him, almost oblivious to his comments.

"Didn't you hear me?" he asked Anna. "If he catches us making love, he will kill me!"

Anna shook her head. "Typical man!" she said to him. "I don't want to make love. I just need to loosen this damned corset he had me forced into!"

"Oh," said the Riding Officer, tamely.

Anna wiped a tear from the corner of her left eye. "Lockwood told me I looked fat ... he told me I was fat."

He sat down next to Anna on the hay and began helping her with the gown. She pulled it down to her waist, exposing the corset. The Riding Officer began to unlace the corset, fumbling at first. Eventually Anna exhaled heavily. She seemed relieved that the corset was now looser. The Riding Officer wrapped his arms around her waist and he felt Anna slip her hands into his. He rested his head on her back. Her fair skin felt cool. He began to gently kiss her neck.

"You're not fat, Anna," said the Riding Officer, softly.

"We can't stay too long," Anna said to him. "Lockwood will have noticed I'm gone."

The Riding Officer began to lace the corset back up, but he kept it loose in order not to cause Anna any further discomfort. The Riding Officer had reached a decision – he knew he had to remain in Upperbridge, for Anna's sake. Only he could protect her from the fate known as Lockwood.

"I heard them discussing something again," Anna told him. "Something to do with the beacon on the south pathway..."

* * *

About a week had passed since Lockwood's party and the Riding Officer was cleaning out his horse's stable. He had laid down fresh hay and had just endured abuse from some passing boys from Fish Row, most likely paid by Lockwood, who indulged in an extremely boisterous rendition of the "Grand Old Duke of York" and hurled a few stray pebbles at him. He was proud of himself though, as he resisted temptation to hurl horse muck at the boys. *Oh, how Lockwood would string me up for bullying a couple of young boys!*

The atmosphere felt stuffy. The Riding Officer initially thought nothing of it, as cleaning out a horse's stable could be heavy work that left him sweating. He stood up to straighten his back and somewhat instinctively looked to the coast.

It was there and then that the Riding Officer noticed the unmistakable form of a storm brewing. He thought back to the previous week when Anna had informed him of Lockwood planning something. It could have taken years for it to come into fruition but it was only going to take a week. *This was Lockwood,* he thought, *this will be evil.* He turned to his horse, stroked her mane and said, "We're in for a long night, girl!"

Chapter Four

Heroes and Villains

The wind howled and the rain whipped down relentlessly on the Lincolnshire coast. The Riding Officer had patrolled this stretch of coast for what seemed like a lifetime. He was soaked to the bone, his hat had blown away in the wind and his eyes were red and stung mercilessly from the rain that pounded and whipped into his face. He had covered his four miles to the south and the three and a half to the north of the village repeatedly, trying to find evidence of any wrong doing. The pathway had turned to mud, and the conditions were so bad that he had become fearful his horse would slip and throw him. But he continued with dedication; he hated this job and right now he hated the rain lashing into his face but he detested Lockwood even more than those elements combined. He would not let the vile fishmonger get away with whatever he had planned.

The Riding Officer rode his horse down the north pathway that led to the stretch of road that ran parallel to the beach. He could feel her hooves begin to slip as they headed down the gradient. In a bid to gain some shelter he headed into the village behind the houses. Not a person seemed to stir, and all the houses and shops were shut up tight. Soon he was onto the beach and back into the unrelenting weather.

From in between two boats that sat upturned at the head of the beach, Samuel lunged out at him. He barraged the Riding Officer with a tirade of unintelligible abuse, and grabbed at the Riding Officer's leg in an attempt to drag him from his horse. The Riding Officer kicked back before striking him with the butt of his pistol across the head, finally kicking him clean away. It was then the Riding Officer knew there was something planned on the south pathway. Why else would Samuel be there to hinder him?

His horse galloped up the slight gradient towards the beacon. It was a pile of kindling packed together in a cone that sat on the site where a stone tower that, Grantham claimed, was 'destroyed' in a storm once sat. Many areas around Britain had purpose-built lighthouses but for some reason the authorities in Upperbridge had prevented such a structure being built. Grantham had gone as far as to say that it would be a blight on the coastline. The Riding Officer had never believed his comments and suddenly it became evident why when he heard the Herring Caller who dramatically screamed "Herring!" and within seconds the beacon was alight. But there was something amiss. The beacon was not in its usual place – it was a hundred yards inland. Lockwood and his conspirators were going to deliberately run a ship aground on the reefs off the headland in order to plunder the cargo.

Despite the howling wind and cold unforgiving rain, the Riding Officer could smell burning fuel. Whoever had lit the false beacon had doused it in a flammable substance to help it burn in the atrocious weather. He pulled up his horse a yard from the beacon, and he stared at the burning kindling and then to the coast. He could see a vessel close by, trying to shelter from the storm as it made its way to the North of England and beyond. On the tip of the headland he could see the real beacon. He knew what he had to do.

Suddenly a hulking figure loomed out of the gloom and struck his horse across the rump with a branch. His mare whinnied in pain and she reared up, throwing the Riding Officer backwards and he landed heavily in some mud.

The wind was knocked out of him but he desperately tried to climb to his feet. The figure appeared once more, along with a smaller figure. They both tried to grab him.

"Throw him into the sea!" he heard the smaller man bellow over the howling wind.

Instinctively, the Riding Officer struck the smaller man in the stomach then punched him in the jaw; the hulking man tried to smother him from behind but the Riding Officer kicked him in the shin with the heel of his boot then struck him in the temple causing the man to fall to the ground. Without thinking the Riding Officer booted the man in the head, rendering him unconscious. As the flames of the false beacon lit up his face, the Riding Officer recognised him as Hurley, the man who had assaulted Anna a couple of weeks earlier.

"Serves you right!" snarled the Riding Officer, recalling what Hurley had done to Anna.

His attention was now back on the vessel. The Riding Officer knew he had to act quickly. He kicked mud on the beacon to no avail; he tore Hurley's overcoat from his torso and beat at the blaze desperately; nothing seemed to work. The Riding Officer had one last desperate solution. He grabbed a piece of kindling from the fake beacon and began to scramble towards the true beacon. He slipped, slid and staggered, desperate to keep the kindling alight. He fell to his knees as he reached the beacon.

"Burn! Burn! Please burn!" he pleaded as he thrust the kindling into the beacon, hoping it would catch ablaze.

The beacon was wet and the kindling was slow to light; slowly the beacon began to ignite but it was too late. Just as the Riding Officer rose to his feet he was horrified to see the shape of the vessel only a hundred or so yards away from him. He watched aghast, helpless as the port side of the vessel crashed into the reef. As the wooden vessel pressed hard against the rocks, the hull shattered with ear-splitting horror.

The Riding Officer fell once more to his knees. He held his head and began to weep, shutting his eyes and telling himself that the screams, howls and wailing he heard was the wind and not the cries of dying men whom he was powerless to help.

Eventually, the cries, wails and screams subsided and the Riding Officer pulled himself to his feet. He was emotionless, devastated inside; he felt like a shell of a man having witnessed life cancelled out in front of him. Slowly, he staggered to the pathway. He began to wonder where his horse had bolted to. He paused. As he stood in shock at what he had witnessed, a figure lashed out, but the Riding Officer did not see where he came from. All he knew was that a man wielding a large stick hit him in the head and knocked him to the ground, sending him sliding towards the edge of the cliff. The Riding Officer looked up and saw Hurley's accomplice.

"You bastard!" snarled the man, "trying to ruin our plans!" He kicked the Riding Officer powerfully in the gut, knocking him over the cliff.

"That's the last of him, Paine!" said Hurley with a callous laugh.

"Let's head back, Hurley, let Mr Lockwood know!" Paine replied with a remorseless smirk.

"He'll be pleased, will Mr Lockwood!"

"The Riding Officer is no more!" Paine said. "And *we* can expect an excellent bonus!"

The Riding Officer reached out as he fell and grabbed a rock to prevent his descent into the North Sea. He pulled himself onto a ledge as the wind howled around his frozen ears. "I knew this would be a long night..."

* * *

The wind and rain had begun to finally relent just as day was breaking. The Riding Officer was cold and exhausted, soaked through to the skin. His head swirled and he could barely move. He looked to his left and saw the body of a sailor floating face down in the sea.

Miraculously, he had been able to lie there all night waiting; waiting to be rescued; waiting to summon the energy to pull himself to safety; or waiting to die; whichever came first. His lips were chapped, his uniform torn, his boots full of water and his feet were numb. He barely managed to remain conscious. He recited poetry and wondered if he would see his beloved Anna again.

Morning had not long broken when the Riding Officer heard voices – was he being rescued? Or was it the case that Lockwood's men had been sent back to finish him off?

"He's down here, father!" cried a voice.

Minutes later, the Riding Officer saw a face peering down at him. "Grab onto the rope, officer!" shouted another voice.

The rope dropped down and the Riding Officer secured it around his waist. "Use your legs to walk up the cliff, officer!" advised the voice.

The Riding Officer lumbered up the cliff face and eventually spilled over the top. He collapsed face first, completely exhausted, clutching his stomach. The rope had driven the air out of him completely and he felt like he had been struck repeatedly about the mid-section by a blacksmith's hammer.

"Help him up, boys!" instructed the voice.

Two men sat the Riding Officer up as held his stomach. He felt his head begin to clear and his breath return.

"Help me up..." he said, his mouth dropping open.

The Riding Officer could feel himself being lifted to his feet by two men. When he was finally upright, he recognised his rescuers as Farmer Timms and two of his sons.

"Are you all right, lad?" asked Timms.

"Just about, Mr Timms..." slurred the Riding Officer.

"We'll get you home, lad!" Timms told him. "A nice warm bed and a bite to eat will do you the world of good."

Timms led the way towards the village and his sons carried the Riding Officer, his feet slipping in the still-waterlogged south pathway. They had tried to lift him onto the back of a horse but his exhausted state coupled with his big frame had made this too difficult.

"Where's my horse?" murmured the Riding Officer after a

while.

"Gregory the blacksmith has her," advised Timms. "He saw you head out to stop the wreckers, as did a lot of villagers."

"Did they?"

"You're a hero, lad!" said Timms. "There's one thing smuggling – the king might lose a few shillings here and there – but wrecking is another; men lost their lives."

"Me, a hero?" asked the Riding Officer in disbelief.

"Three men survived last night, made it to shore!" Timms said. "My boys headed down to the beach when the ship was wrecked and helped to rescue them."

"There's a man's body in the cove," said the Riding Officer.

"We'll pick him up later. He's not going anywhere at the present," said Timms' younger son.

The Riding Officer staggered on towards the village aided by Timms' sons. "Herring!" was the sudden violent, angry and aggressive shriek from the Herring Caller who snarled at the group of men.

"It was strange that the Herring Caller was out last night, wasn't it, Father?" said Timms' younger son. "In that weather, there was no way they could have launched their boats and gone out fishing."

"I'd watch it if I was you, Dixon!" warned Timms' eldest son. "We know you're part of this!"

The Timms brothers helped the Riding Officer down the slight gradient towards the beach. He saw a group of villagers had gathered. In fact almost the whole village was there. The Riding Officer stopped.

"I'll be all right from here!" he told the Timms brothers.

The Timms brothers gently let go of him and the Riding Officer staggered forward with trepidation towards the crowd. The man the Riding Officer knew as the blacksmith stepped forward. The Riding Officer stopped. His frame was exhausted and he was in no mood for hostility; he looked the blacksmith in the eye. The blacksmith smiled and began to applaud. Then the crowd began to applaud. And cheer. Anna burst forward from the crowd, ran up to her exhausted hero and embraced him, almost knocking him off his feet. She held him tight before kissing him on the mouth. There were a few gasps from the villagers at Anna's open display of affection though most put her actions down to high spirits. Their argument to Lockwood would be that she was in the presence of a bona fide hero.

"Where are the survivors?" he asked Anna.

"They're at Mrs Higgins' *guesthouse*," Anna told him. "They've been given clean clothes and something to eat. They're resting. And they are sailors so they want to make use of *certain services*."

"That's good," the Riding Officer whispered with an exhausted smile.

But the happiness was short-lived. There was a clatter of horses' hooves and carriage wheels on the cobbles. A carriage pulled by two horses drew up at the bottom of the road leading to the beach. It suddenly became surrounded by the parish constable and his men. The carriage door swung open and Lockwood emerged. He held the door open and Grantham climbed out. He had a fearsome look on his face.

"Constable, have that man arrested!" Grantham bellowed. "The Riding Officer! Arrest him!"

"On what charges?" asked the constable.

"Three accounts of assault, one of damaging property and finally for the heinous crime of wrecking with intent to plunder!"

"But he's innocent!" cried the blacksmith.

"The lad's a hero," added Timms. "He tried to save that vessel and the men aboard."

The crowd began to cry and jeer, and there were murmurs of dissent as they realised that Grantham was trying to falsely and deliberately accuse the Riding Officer of a crime he had not committed.

"Silence!" demanded the vile politician. "Lockwood's men witnessed him."

"It's true," declared Lockwood in a false, insincere voice, his clammy hands clasped in front of his chest whilst his pig-like eyes darting back and forth. "Two of my finest men, Hurley and Paine, caught the Riding Officer lighting the false beacon. He proceeded to assault them when they attempted to stop him, then tried to destroy Hurley's overcoat!"

"A likely story!" shouted a fisherman, sensing an injustice about to be done.

"It was them who lit the true beacon; *they* are *your* heroes," Lockwood answered in a condescending tone.

"Who exactly saw them?" asked the blacksmith, not buying into the words Lockwood was spouting.

"Ask Samuel!" said Lockwood, patronisingly. "Old kind, gentle Samuel. He saw the ghastly Riding Officer go to the headland to commit the deed and tried to stop him; but what did that coward do? He attacked him! Poor old Samuel, he was attacked by a gutless coward!"

Samuel slipped around from behind the coach. He nodded and smiled hideously, displaying the last few remaining teeth in his mouth. His demeanour was anything but kind and gentle. It was more of a dark and sinister nature.

"I wouldn't trust him," barked a labourer, obviously familiar with Samuel. "Him and that wretched little shack he's so protective of."

"And Dixon," Lockwood said. "He saw him assault Samuel and light the beacon, too! And you people want to treat this scoundrel as a hero? Constable, please arrest that man."

The constable's men descended on the Riding Officer. The villagers tried to protect him, but the constable's men drew their rifles. The crowd was silenced and then dispersed slowly. They knew Lockwood all too well. The constabulary burst forward and shackled the Riding Officer. As they began to drag him away,

Samuel approached him and spat in his face.

"You're scum!" Samuel shrieked. "You're a crook! Hanging is too good for you!"

Lockwood turned to one of his men who had been in the coach. "Binns," he said. "My fiancée," he nodded in Anna's direction, "Go and retrieve her! My property has been a very disobedient girl and I have some urges that need to be dealt with."

* * *

The full sherry glasses of Grantham and Lockwood clinked together at Grantham Hall. A mighty fire roared in the drawing room, and the worn leather covers of books that were once the volumes of the romance poet Peter Lloyd were scattered forlornly on the floor. The pages had been removed to fuel the fire.

"This really is fine sherry, Lockwood!" Grantham said, and he beamed.

"It is, my lord!" Lockwood gloated with a grin. "All the way duty free from Spain!" His reflection could be seen in the face of a grandfather clock. Drool in the corner of his mouth, his hair reminiscent of bird's nest. His waistline had slipped free of his shirt and hung over his belt.

"A wonderful country is Spain, I went there with my late mother," Grantham proclaimed, flapping his hand in the direction of a portrait that hung on the wall.

Lockwood gazed up at the picture. Grantham's mother looked unhappy, angry to be fair, and looked like Grantham as if he had been attired as a woman. "A charming lady," Lockwood said with a smile, baring his gnarled yellow teeth.

"I particularly enjoyed the bullfighting," Grantham sniffed. He took a handkerchief from his jacket pocket and mopped his brow.

"Bullfighting, my lord? What is that?"

"A man goes into a ring and fights a bull," Grantham explained, waving his glass of sherry in the air, droplets spilling onto his hand and running down his arm. "He has to try to kill the bull but sometimes the man will be gored by the bull. Either way, it is excellent entertainment." His head rocked back as he laughed, the shadow of his bloated chin juddering on the wall.

Lockwood smiled in a sinister fashion. "Type of career that would suit our dear friend the Riding Officer to the ground!" Lockwood picked up a hat, similar to that worn by the Riding Officer.

"Well, thanks to our good work I think we can finally say goodbye to our friend, the Riding Officer!" Grantham roared with delight as Lockwood cast the hat onto the fire.

"Absolutely, he'll be rotting within the prison walls by this time next week. And I will finally be free to wed the lovely Anna."

"Did you deal with your *urges*?"

"I did indeed, Adam, I gave the disobedient wench a mighty bruise or two upon her arms and back."

"That is excellent, my dear Hubert, excellent!" Grantham laughed. He peered over at the door that led outside into the grounds of his home. It was open and the mangy drapes fluttered in the evening breeze.

"Are you not concerned about the debt he has with you?" questioned Lockwood, his attention became diverted following Grantham's line of vision wondering what had caught his eye.

Grantham laughed again. It was a loud booming sound he had made earlier that day in the same room when he gouged out the eyes of a young serving girl he caught admiring his late mother's pearl necklace that sat under her portrait for far too long. "I don't care about that piffling debt!" he announced. "The joy of being able to control a man like a marionette puppet is reward enough for me." He laughed once more, this time reminiscent of the sound he made when he had the hands of a young gardener chopped off for trying to prevent the eye gouging.

"He's a pugnacious character is the Riding Officer," Lockwood rubbed his hand on the arm of the chair he was sitting in. "He might escape..."

"Do not worry, Hubert." Grantham's chins wobbled as he laughed. "If he does there will be someone waiting for him." Grantham peered to the open door once more. Lockwood could not help but wonder who was there.

Lockwood laughed, too. "Very good, my lord."

The two men had retired along with Lockwood's conspirators to Grantham Hall following their work the previous evening and although they had not been able to finish him off, the Riding Officer was now incarcerated in the Parish Gaol awaiting trial. It was a trial that promised to be greatly one-sided and with only one eventual outcome. Grantham began to smile. It was meant to be a kind, warm smile but as these emotions were a foreign concept to the crooked politician he could only harness the look of a man suffering from a severe case of haemorrhoids. "Are your men all right?" he asked, nodding to Hurley and Paine.

Hurley and Paine had been sitting in the corner greedily clawing at a platter of roast poultry, meat, vegetables and pie.

"Very good, my lord!" said Hurley with his mouthful of chicken.

"Your generosity is greatly appreciated, my lord!" added Paine.

"Hubert, my dear man," Grantham said. "I believe you may be the man to succeed me."

"As the local Member of Parliament?" asked the hunchback as he drummed his fingers together, his sense of greed suddenly stimulated.

"Possibly, but I meant mainly as my heir apparent."

Lockwood's evil face beamed into a smile, and he grovelled to his knees, saying, "My lord! I cannot believe that you can deem me so worthy of such an honour."

"As you know, I have no heirs. My two brothers died, one in childhood, the other in the North American Colonies prior to the disgraceful acts of the colonists in 1776. I had one nephew who vanished mysteriously and whose current whereabouts are unknown, so I sent word to my solicitor to have you named as my successor."

"Why, my lord?"

"A close, loyal and trusted friend is whom I need to succeed me, not some ungrateful flesh and blood," Grantham informed him.

"Bless you, my lord!"

"You have been a loyal subject, Hubert; we are both rich men in many ways."

"What happens if your nephew reappears?" asked Lockwood, sensing a possible threat. "He could be anywhere, ready to return."

"Oh, that is highly unlikely!" Grantham laughed, maniacally. "I know for a fact where he is. He's lying in a sack full of stone in the middle of the North Sea!"

* * *

It was about midday. The Riding Officer had spent the past day shivering feverishly in the cell of the Parish Gaol. Exhausted from his exploits the day before and having not changed from his cold, saturated clothing, he had begun to suffer from the initial stages of flu that might possibly degenerate into fatal pneumonia. Huddled on the bunk under a tatty blanket his feet were still numb and he was burning hot yet shivering. He had been given a jug of water and a stale crust of bread that seemed inedible. The Riding Officer longed for a simple bowl of broth and a clean warm bed where he could rest properly.

An unpleasant smell overcame the Riding Officer. Initially he thought it was from his drying clothes but he realised it was coming from outside the cell. The Riding Officer shivered. He heard the sound of a knife cutting onto a platter followed by the sound of a man chewing. He could not see into the central area but he knew that Grantham and Lockwood would have him under constant surveillance. He heard the creak of a door opening, and scowled when he did not hear it shut properly.

"Nice piece of fish, constable?" asked the guard.

"Lovely, Johnson!" said the constable. "Mr Lockwood in person brought it around especially for me."

"Why was that?"

"Our guest!" The constable laughed. "He's been after him for a while; Mr Grantham suspects he's been up to no good for some time. Apparently he's wanted for a lot of crimes."

"What's he done?" asked Johnson.

"For a start," said the constable, "Mr Grantham believes he was the one who did Cutler in! And he suspects that this man is the most wanted man in England, the infamous Silas Palmer who is wanted in six counties."

"How is his majesty today?" asked Johnson, condescendingly, as he walked over to the cell that held the Riding Officer. He thumped the iron bars of the cell.

"I feel as bad as that fish smells!" slurred the Riding Officer.

"Somebody got out of bed the wrong side today!" snarled Johnson. He smirked as he stared at the Riding Officer as he lay shivering under the blanket in his torn and ripped clothing that were starting to smell. His hair was a mattered mess and dirt was smeared on his face.

"He hasn't left his bunk since we threw him in there," said the constable. "The lazy sod!"

"He doesn't do anything anyway. When was the last time he arrested anyone?"

"Couple of fishermen, weren't it? A couple of men fishing. If I was him, I would put more into my job or I'd be looking for a new one."

"If I was you," slurred the Riding Officer, angrily, "I'd be heading to an apothecary for a cure from the horrific food poisoning that you will suffer as a result of eating that fish."

The constable stood up and walked over to the cell. "Watch it!" he said. "You'll be heading to the gallows a lot sooner than you're supposed to if you're not careful."

"And you'll be heading to the latrine very shortly because of that fish," snapped the Riding Officer as he rolled over in the bunk so he could look at the constable as he addressed him.

"That fish was wonderful," said the constable. "That was some of Mr Lockwood's prime stock."

"If that is dear Mr Lockwood's prime stock, sir, then I would hate to smell what he throws out," replied the Riding Officer, turning on his side so he no longer faced the constable.

"Mr Lockwood has been the finest fishmonger in this village for years."

"He is the *only* fishmonger in the village," the Riding Officer retaliated, "and from what I heard he fought off all the competition by giving them his stock."

"Hubert Lockwood is a fine tradesman!"

"Well, I wouldn't buy fish from him," the Riding Officer replied. "I catch my own."

The constable snarled. "Well, not everybody has time to go fishing – some of us have jobs to do."

"Like who?" asked the Riding Officer, sarcastically.

"Like me!" shouted the constable. "I have highwaymen to catch as well as vagabonds, scoundrels and burglars! All dangerous criminals whilst you can't handle a few smugglers."

"Oh, I can handle smugglers. It's just corrupt public figures I can't handle," said the Riding Officer. "Like you..." he added under his breath.

* * *

For about two hours the Riding Officer had been drifting in and out of a feverish sleep. He was suddenly awakened by a loud unfamiliar voice.

He heard a hand slap down on to the constable's desk. "Who is that man?" demanded the voice.

"In the ledger!" answered the constable, pointing to the principal book on his desk with an outstretched finger, its nail clogged with dirt.

A fist thumped loudly on the desk. "Why has he been arrested?"

The Riding Officer heard the constable's boots hit the desk as he decided to rest his feet. "Wrecking with intent to plunder!" said the constable.

"This man is innocent!" the voice said.

"Says who?"

"Says I..."

"And who might you be?" asked the constable, tossing his head back and folding his arms across his chest.

"I am the Earl of Lincoln," answered the man. He opened his watch, checked the time, smiled politely before he closed the watch and slipped it back into his waistcoat pocket.

The constable became wild eyed. He unfolded his arms and dragged his feet off the desk as quickly as he could and leapt to his feet. "I c-can't let him go!" he said. "I am just a c-constable!"

The Earl stood up straight and looked down at the constable, asking, "Who *does* have the authority to release him?"

"The J-justice of the P-peace," the constable said, "and there's bail... fifty guineas..."

"Fetch the Justice of the Peace," the Earl said to the constable, "and *I* will pay this man's bail."

* * *

The Justice of the Peace was a bizarre looking cove. He was thin, bony and gaunt, with fair red hair which had receded dramatically and a large hooked nose, whilst also lacking a chin. He was an effeminate bachelor and there were rumours rife about his personal life. The rumours were indeed true; he had in fact been involved sexually with Grantham for many years but in a time when homosexuality was a crime, their affair was repressed by Grantham. This, however, had not stopped the two from travelling across Europe and indulging in acts together that would be considered by the church to be depraved whilst Grantham, often in Parliament, would condemn those of loose morals and liken their alleged crimes to those from Sodom and Gomorrah. When Grantham's nephew had discovered the two men's activities, driven by greed like all the Granthams before him, he attempted to blackmail them both. It would be a move he would come to regret in particular when he drowned in a stone-laden sack in the middle of the North Sea.

The Riding Officer lay on the bunk as he listened to the heated debate between the Earl and the Justice of the Peace. From what he could gather, two further survivors of the shipwreck had been picked up by a vessel owned by the Earl of Lincoln off the coast in the neighbouring parish. The two men had given an account of a heroic man whose description matched that of a riding officer. The Justice of the Peace threw the argument back that no one could confirm that nonsense he was spouting because of the distance from the coast and the fact it was night. The problem was exacerbated further by the arrival of Grantham.

"Who is this fool?" Grantham thundered, as he slammed the door.

"I am the Earl of Lincoln. Who, I ask, are you?"

"Adam Grantham," Grantham replied. "I'm the local Member of Parliament."

"Oh, the rotten man from the rotten borough," the Earl said, scornfully. "I have heard plenty about you, I'm afraid to say!"

Grantham balled up his fist and shook it wildly at the Earl.

"What brings a petty elitist like you here?" he said as he stamped his foot.

"This man, Adam," the Justice of the Peace said, "has come here with a cock and bull story that the Riding Officer is innocent of the heinous crime he committed."

"It isn't a cock and bull story – I have witnesses," the Earl said as he checked his fingertips to make sure his nails were clean. The constable was still fiddling with his fingers as he hid behind the Justice of the Peace.

"Balderdash!" shouted Grantham.

"Witnesses who have reported the Riding Officer innocent and that the true perpetrators are two men named Hurley and Paine under the pay of a local fishmonger," said the Earl. "And they are witnesses from within this village, I must add."

The expression on the faces of Grantham and the Justice of the Peace were no longer angry and aggressive. They were scared and fearful as their mouths dropped and their eyes were wide as they realised they could very easily be implicated in the wrecking and any retaliation against the witnesses would point directly at them.

"Very well," said the Justice of the Peace, meekly. "Release him."

"I will pay the bail, and should he be taken to court I will provide a lawyer," the Earl added. "And if I have heard you have done anything to him, I will return to Upperbridge with entire regiment of the County of Lincoln."

* * *

Within an hour the Riding Officer was at home in bed. The Timms family had helped him. Mrs Timms had provided him with some broth. He fell into a deep feverish sleep. From time to time Anna would drop in when she was not working and could slip away from Lockwood's grasp; she would mop his brow, keep him comfortable and reassure him. She was glad he was too feverish to know that she, herself, was covered in bruises inflicted by the brutal hand of Lockwood.

On the fifth day, his fever broke and the Riding Officer began to rebuild the events of the past week.

When Anna dropped in she found the Riding Officer sitting up in bed. She smiled as she saw him sitting up; the Riding Officer returned the smile, wriggling his toes from under the blanket to show they were fine.

"You're looking better," said Anna with a smile.

"I'm feeling it," he replied. He peered in the direction of the door. "Did you shut that firmly?"

"Of course I did. You've been through a bit of an ordeal." Anna placed a small loaf of bread and a few slices of roasted ham wrapped in a cloth onto a platter that sat on a table beside his bed.

"I can remember very little about the past few days," the Riding Officer said, turning down the cover on his bed. "I remember being kicked over a cliff and clinging on all night but after that it's a blur."

Anna sat down on the bed beside him. "You were arrested. Grantham and Lockwood tried to frame you for the plundering; but it's all right, because the Earl of Lincoln bailed you out and the charges have been dropped. Hurley and Paine have been charged. Apparently they've confessed that they are the sole conspirators although everyone knows that isn't true."

"The Earl of Lincoln? I wonder what this all has to do with him. How did I get home?"

"The Timms family helped you," Anna explained. She threw her arm around the Riding Officer and lifted her legs on to the bed so she was lying next to him. She looked into his eyes and moved her mouth towards his ear. "Don't be alarmed. You know I am not a conventional girl..."

The Riding Officer bit his lip and smiled nervously. "Good. It's good about the Timms family. They are good people which is a rarity around here. My horse!" he said suddenly. "What's happened to her?"

"Gregory the blacksmith has her," Anna reassured him and rested her forehead against his head. "She's safe and well."

"That's good," said the Riding Officer with relief. He stroked Anna's cheek softly with the back of his finger. "I am feeling so much better already."

Anna smiled and laughed. "You're in a better state than the constable," she informed him. "He's at death's door after eating some fish."

* * *

In the week following his recovery the Riding Officer discovered a new-found respect from the people of the village. He was no longer a victim of scorn apart from Lockwood and his cohorts; he no longer found himself a complete outcast; when he walked into the inn there was no longer a strangled silence. But despite the change in attitude, the Riding Officer was still not happy, and he knew this was a passing phase. The smuggling had stopped for a brief while but the villagers would miss the income and it would restart along with the abuse, with the villagers conveniently forgetting about his heroics on that fateful night. That said, there was one man had vowed to turn his back on smuggling and that man was Gregory the Blacksmith. The Riding Officer found himself gradually warming to the local blacksmith and was compelled to stand his ground for the tradesman when Lockwood and associates challenged the man over his new stance. He had enjoyed watching Lockwood squirm when he pointed a pistol at his foe offering to fight a duel on behalf of the blacksmith if the fishmonger continued to harass him.

The Riding Officer was sitting under a tree on the north

pathway. The sun was shining down on the deep blue glistening sea. *If I had a canvas, some oil paints and a few brushes that would make a glorious landscape*, he thought. The Riding Officer was watching a small vessel off the coast through a small telescope he had been given as a child by a favourite uncle which he had taken with him to Lincolnshire with his personal belongings. The vessel resembled a herring boat but from what he could see the occupants of the boat were not fishing. When Dixon had raised the call of herring there were no tell-tale signs of any herring and when a small boat met the herring boat the Riding Officer knew instantaneously that they were smuggling.

As blatant as it was, there was nothing he could do. He could try to arrest them but they would fight back with possible fatal consequences. He knew the tale of a Riding Officer in Kent who attempted an arrest and was shot dead on the spot; the people who became Riding Officers always struck him as incredible fools, and he still felt shocked he had ended up becoming one.

He would occasionally see Samuel wandering around on the beach clearly keeping an eye out for him. The Riding Officer just sat in the shade of the tree his boots and socks off, the grass cool on his feet. The wretched scavenger was oblivious to where he was sitting. He recalled the previous night in the inn when the fisherman who voiced his dislike of Samuel called the scavenger "a revolting little shit" in the packed hostelry in front of Lockwood and associates. What amused him the most was neither Lockwood nor his associates said or did anything to defend Samuel.

He wondered what they were smuggling; perhaps it was fabric from France or maybe fortified wine from the Iberian Peninsula. Maybe it was tea from India and beyond or maybe gold from darkest Africa.

In the past, the Riding Officer might have sent a message to the local barracks to assist in the arrests but he knew by the time the soldiers had arrived the smugglers would be long gone, along with their contraband. Even if the Riding Officer did successfully make an arrest it would be pointless. With the constable now deceased from eating Lockwood's fish, the Riding Officer knew no action would possibly be taken, and an attempt to prosecute would be even more pointless as Grantham and the Justice of the Peace would prevent any action from being taken simply so they could line their own filthy pockets of their own filthy britches. *Then again,* he thought, *what if they were an outside threat?*

From time to time, the settlement of Upperbridge would be threatened by smugglers from outside the community trying to muscle in on their territory. The Riding Officer smiled wryly as he recalled the time he had his sole successful arrest when he caught outsiders and how he was a 'hero' for the day to the hypocritical figures of Lockwood, Grantham and the Justice of the Peace. They paraded him as a hero for tackling the outsiders and then treated him as a pathetic lowlife less than twenty-four hours later for trying to uphold the law he had been employed to enforce. He knew that the contraband was kept as 'evidence' and always found its way into the market place. *Maybe I should tackle them,* thought the Riding Officer, *I could be a hero.* Once more, the Riding Officer shook his head as he deceived himself, as he knew his efforts would be futile. There was no way they could be outsiders as it was clear that Samuel and Dixon were in on it.

Instead the Riding Officer sat in the shade as his horse grazed. He would have the occasional sip of water from his flask and would gaze upon the sea. He found it so inspiring – whether it was blue and glistening on a summer's day or grey and roaring in the middle of winter, it would fuel his creativity.

The Riding Officer dozed off. When he awoke, the herring boat was gone. He could see Samuel pottering around by the shack where he lived near the beach. There was some ground next to the hut where Samuel had been attempting to keep a garden in which he could grow vegetables. Instead, there was tangled mess of non-descript greenery.

Then the Riding Officer noticed that a man was approaching Samuel's hut. The man had, the Riding Officer deduced, been sent with a message for Samuel, most likely from Lockwood. The man's approach was sending the vile little man into a frenzied state. His hands, in particular, were wild. He waved them frantically when somebody got too close before forcing them out towards the messenger as if he was pushing them away and, finally, he would place his arm over the door to the hut like his limb was a bar on a gate. The Riding Officer couldn't help but wonder what the obnoxious Samuel was hiding. *It must be contraband,* he thought. He could go down there and arrest Samuel on suspicion of smuggling and holding contraband just to satisfy his curiosity but then again, he thought, *what was the point?* Lockwood would just use it as ammunition against him, painting the picture of Samuel being an innocent victim with the Riding Officer holding a grudge against him over the wrecking incident.

The Riding Officer gazed out to sea. He wished he had a pencil and some paper so he could capture the inspiration of the sea, but it was time to head home.

As the Riding Officer began to pull his boots back on, he saw the biggest inspiration of his life. Anna walked up the pathway with a look of purpose, and a sudden gust of wind blew her long black hair in the wind. She walked up to the Riding Officer with a confident smile on her face, and before the Riding Officer could even say "hello", Anna simply told him, "I want us to elope!"

Chapter Five

Murder

Joseph Bell was a simple young man. A ploughboy who was mentally challenged, he had no enemies and was cared for by the community in general bar the likes of Lockwood and Grantham, the latter branding the boy "one of God's embarrassing mistakes". He never broke any laws, he never insulted anybody and always went to church; he was an increasingly rare exception in a far from glorious community. Why anyone would want to kill him was a mystery. But somebody did.

A man named Eustace Hogg had emerged in the village about a week earlier. Hogg was an exceptionally ugly man with thick lips and a gargoyle-like face. His head was completely bald and an inverted pear shape, with a distinctive scar on his chin. He had issues with his temper, as an opium addiction had left him quick to anger and when he did get angry his face and head would turn a hideous purple colour that some would find humorous. Should anyone dare laugh at him when he did this they would often find this would be the penultimate action of their lives.

He was a man the Riding Officer unwittingly knew from his past. Hogg was an ex-Bow Street Runner, a violent and corrupt man who had become a success in London because he would arrest criminals. Unfortunately, these criminals were usually innocent people in the wrong place at the wrong time that would be set up for a crime, that or they would be beaten or black-mailed into making a false confession. On one evening, years before in London, the Riding Officer had nearly been one of those people. He just happened to walk down the right road at the right time and avoid the wrath of Hogg for the time being; instead the wrath of Hogg would be projected onto some poor unfortunate soul who did not deserve it.

Hogg's fall from grace had come about as a result of him shooting a man in cold blooded murder. When he was unable to pin anything on the innocent man or even provide a reason for shooting the man he was discharged from the Runners. He subsequently set up his own private illegal enterprise as an assassin. He used his knowledge of the underworld to tap up victims. One of his major centres of business was the Houses of Parliament. The Riding Officer heard a rumour buzzing around that Hogg was an associate of the brutal Silas Palmer, a man wanted in no less than six counties for theft, assault, rape and murder.

When the Riding Officer first saw Hogg in the village he was suspicious. The Riding Officer recognised his face but could not remember where he knew him from. It put some concern in his head. *Who was this man and why was he in Upperbridge?*

The appearance of Hogg wasn't the Riding Officer's only concern. The woman he loved had asked him to elope and he felt conflicted. He loved Anna and wanted to spend his life with her. He knew if he tried to flee, Grantham would surely have him tracked down and killed which would leave to Anna being forced to marry the revolting Lockwood but he also knew that if he fled and he was killed that he would never find out who had murdered his father. Suddenly the Riding Officer had found another reason, alongside Anna, for him to stay in Lincolnshire. The Riding Officer later hated himself for thinking it but at one point he even suspected that Anna might be working with Grantham and Lockwood in a bid to set a trap for him.

On a Thursday afternoon the Riding Officer was sitting once more under the tree on the north pathway smoking his pipe staring into the North Sea. The weather was overcast, reflecting a grey colour on the sea, when a shotgun went off. The Riding Officer thought nothing of it. *Someone was hunting or shooting vermin.*

The Riding Officer heard the church bell ringing two o'clock.

Samuel was pottering around by his shack looking guilty about something and Dixon the herring caller was sitting in the south pathway staring at the sea. Suddenly he heard a commotion from the village.

The local wheelwright ran into the village.

"There's been a murder!" he screamed hysterically, perspiration streaming down his forehead. "There's been a murder!"

"Where?" asked a villager.

The wheelwright's face was white with shock and his bottom lips trembled. "Outside the village on the Gainsborough turnpike!"

* * *

A deputation was gathered before they made their way out to the turnpike. A little over half an hour later they found the murdered corpse at the side of the road. The local brewer was the man who had the grim task of identifying the deceased.

"It's Joseph Bell!" he told everyone as he peered over the corpse, taking off his hat and holding it over his heart. "The poor lad, he's been shot in the face."

For the following few days there was a sombre feeling about the village. Nobody could understand why Joseph Bell had been killed. He didn't harbour any grudges and never wished any harm upon anyone. The wheelwright kept recalling the tale. He lived on the outskirts of the village and as he was working in his workshop that afternoon he heard a gunshot. He looked towards the fields opposite his home when he saw a man running across the field, then a second man followed about fifty yards behind him, carrying a shotgun. The second man fired twice. One of the bullets wounded the first man and he hobbled towards the turnpike. As he reached the road he tripped and fell. The second man caught him before shooting him in the face at point blank range. When asked who did it, the wheelwright's head would drop, he would say he didn't know who did it and added that he didn't recognise the man who shot him.

It was in the dampened mood that followed Joseph Bell's murder that the Riding Officer realised that he was an individual who bore him no hatred. Joseph was an innocent in an area full of greed and corruption, and he wasn't involved in smuggling; he was too simple to understand why people smuggled and why people hated the Riding Officer. In fact, the Riding Officer could not recall Joseph Bell utter a single bad word toward or against him.

Throughout the village there was the continuing utterance of why and who would do what they did to Joseph. However, within three days it all came into fruition.

On the day after Joseph's murder the mumbling began. When the Riding Officer turned around there would be Samuel or Dixon ready to whisper to whoever was passing. By the next day neither Samuel nor Dixon was required for the mumbling to start. It was quite obvious what had happened. An innocent like Joseph Bell had been murdered to frame and vilify the Riding Officer.

It was confirmed later that day when the blacksmith turned up on the Riding Officer's doorstep. He knew it was another set up.

"Rumours around the village say you shot Joe!" Gregory told him, "but I know you didn't. I saw you heading down from the north pathway when the wheelwright ran into town and neither Dixon nor Samuel could have seen you like they claim, as they didn't leave the beach."

The Riding Officer nodded as he flexed his fingers and grasped the butt of his pistol. "Thank you, Gregory, for your support," he told the blacksmith, calmly. "Now I have to see a group of men about some business."

* * *

Lockwood and his associates sat around a table in the inn. They laughed and jeered at the expense of the Riding Officer. Kitching rocked back in his chair, his hands resting behind his head, the damp stains under his armpits on display to all. Hogg placed his boots on the table, kicking away an almost empty tankard, and Dixon laughed as it hit the floor and broke. Samuel grinned broadly, the rotting stumps in his mouth clenched together. Lockwood sighed, a content look on his face, as he took out a handkerchief and blew his nose loudly before wiping his hand on his leg. Despite his brief popularity, Lockwood felt the tide of change was now against the Riding Officer.

"Just think," Lockwood began. "All it took was the murder of a useless retard! People have sympathy for the likes of Joseph Bell and don't take kindly to people victimising him. The simpletons of the village will finish off the Riding Officer whether he is innocent or not."

Lockwood cackled evilly as his eyes darted back and forward with glee as his cohorts took immense joy from the misfortune of Joseph Bell and the effort they had made to frame the Riding Officer.

"People have long memories," Kitching told him. "Stigmas attach themselves to people; it can take years for them to fully subside. Even when people realise he didn't murder that boy there will still be people who insist that the Riding Officer is guilty."

The door opened and the inn fell into silence. The door was shut firmly before there was distinctive thud as the Riding Officer swaggered across the floor. He stood tall and proud, his chin raised. The expression on his face was cold and unforgiving, and his dashing looks were complimented by this demeanour. A young lady uttered a flustered gasp at his appearance. The Riding Officer strutted across the floor at a methodical pace towards Lockwood. The flats of his hands hit the table with a slam as he glared into the face of his foe.

"Mr Lockwood!" said the Riding Officer in a strong, commanding voice, his face inches from his nemesis. "I need to speak to you."

"Ah, the Riding Officer," said Lockwood in a sharp voice as he folded his arms across his waist. "Just the man Mr Hogg will need to speak to."

"Who is Hogg?" asked the Riding Officer.

"This man," said Lockwood with a mean look, pointing towards the former Bow Street Runner with a long claw like finger.

The Riding Officer stared hard at the hideously ugly man sat next to Lockwood. "And why would I need to speak to Hogg?"

"I am the new constable," said Hogg as he stood up.

"Is that true?" The Riding Officer, ready to reach for his pistol, studied Hogg's face trying to desperately place where he knew this man from.

"Mr Hogg has just moved from London," Lockwood explained. "He used to be a Bow Street Runner."

"Good for him!" replied the Riding Officer.

"Dixon saw you in the field killing Joseph Bell," accused Lockwood with a cruel smile that he used when he kicked stray dogs.

"Did he hell!" barked the Riding Officer. He pounded his fist onto the table causing the ale to spill from the tankards.

"And Samuel saw you with a pistol," added Lockwood, lounging back in his chair like a sloth in his seat, his arms still folded and a pout on his mouth. "I think it's quite obvious what you did. But why did you do it, officer? Why did you kill Joseph Bell?"

A platter clattered to the floor spreading the remains of a meal across the surface. There were a series of dramatic gasps at the revelation, people sat with open mouths, and others covered their faces. The drinkers on a nearby table edged away from Lockwood. One man grabbed his coat and hat and ran out of the door. A heavy silence hung in the air, the patrons wondering what was about to unfold as the Riding Officer stared a hole through Hubert Lockwood. He stood up straight. The patrons began to murmur as the thumb on his right hand came to a rest atop his belt. The Riding Officer's nostrils flared.

"Will you stop this bullshit?" When the Riding Officer spoke, the inn fell silent once more. "I did not kill Joseph Bell and you know it!"

Kitching stood and glared into the Riding Officer's face. "You were seen, officer," he snarled.

"You're scum," snapped Samuel before spitting on the Riding Officer. "A damned murderer, no less!"

The Riding Officer's head turned away, and a minute passed before he slowly returned his focus to Samuel. The Riding Officer snarled, and he grabbed Samuel by the wretched man's shirt. He pulled him violently towards him before throwing the scavenger to the floor. The Riding Officer snatched a napkin from under Kitching's elbow that was resting on the table, wiped the spittle from his jacket and dropped it into the drink he presumed was Kitching's. "It's a lie! How could Dixon have seen me? He was on the coast gawping into the sea like the gormless halfwit that he is."

"I saw your pistol," Samuel accused. As he tried to make it to his feet, he looked pathetic as his legs buckled and he fell on his decrepit face.

"I always carry a pistol," the Riding Officer responded. "Anyway, it was impossible to see that field or the turnpike from where you were. You were on the beach protecting the contents of your damned shack, you wretched little man."

"I saw you looking guilty running from the turnpike," Samuel said, spit from his mouth spraying across the floor as he lay on his belly.

The Riding Officer shook his head slowly. "You saw nothing. I was on the north pathway when the murder was committed, and the blacksmith saw me. And he saw you, too, Samuel."

"Did he?" asked Samuel, burying his face on the floor. He attempted to pick himself up once more but the Riding Officer drove him back to the floor courtesy of the flat of his boot.

"And the wheelwright confirmed he saw a man chase Joe with a shotgun, not a pistol!" said the Riding Officer. "And the brewer confirmed he had been shot with a shotgun."

"You sound like you might possibly have a valid argument," said Lockwood, his head turning away as he pretended to look at a picture above the hearth.

"I have a very good argument!"

"I'll collect a couple of statements tomorrow," said Hogg with an unpleasant smile as he flexed his right hand.

"You better had!" said the Riding Officer. "There are laws against false accusations, don't forget."

The Riding Officer turned and headed towards the door. When he reached it, he paused and turned around. He thought he could sense an element of respect from the patrons for standing up against Lockwood. "I bid you farewell!" he said, and left.

The door slammed shut and suddenly the murmured buzz began about the inn. Glances of contempt were passed at Lockwood and his associates. The general consensus of Lockwood was changing. The villagers had finally begun to see the vile hunchback for what he was.

"Silence!" thundered Lockwood, and the inn descended into an uncomfortable quiet. "Binns!" Lockwood bellowed to one of his minions, "fetch my carriage – I wish to see Grantham!"

* * *

Anna's heart pounded as she saw the man she loved stand up bravely to the man she loathed. Earlier that day Lockwood had tried to force himself upon her. His words had been that once the annoying Riding Officer was gone they would be consummating their relationship. His vile breath on her cheek and appalling personal hygiene had almost made her vomit. There were times she feared that she might no longer be able to shake off his advances, and if she were to wed to him she would have no option than to comply whether she wanted to or not.

When the Riding Officer left the inn, Anna followed. She arrived at his door minutes later, and he scooped her into his arms whispering to her, "There's something I've always wanted to do." He gazed deeply into her beautiful blue eyes. "I wish to draw you!"

Anna was surprised. Her mouth dropped and her eyes spread like saucers. *What a request!* she thought. *I've had some 'requests' in my life but no man has ever asked* this *of me...*

Anna sat as still as she could, as his kind eyes darted between her and the paper in front of him. All she could hear was the scratching of his pencil and the flickering candlelight. She found it all very erotic, and she could sense the shape of things to come.

Anna smiled at the Riding Officer.

"You look very beautiful by candlelight!" the Riding Officer said to Anna. She was captivating and alluring. Her heart pounded, and she couldn't stop her eyes fixing on the Riding Officer.

There was no sound but the scratching of his pencil and her own hammering heart.

As the strokes of his pencil increased so did the amount of time his eyes spent on her. He would half smile before his eyes returned to the paper. Anna, for the first time in her life, was very self-conscious of her looks. She had always been told of her beauty and Lockwood's only interest in her was her looks but she had never seen a portrait of herself. She was curious. How did her lover truly see her?

"You don't look too bad yourself," Anna whispered.

"I've never noticed quite how beautiful your eyes are until now," said the Riding Officer with a shy smile before his eyes darted back to the paper.

"Thank you," said Anna, sweeping a stray hair or two away from her face. What else could she say? Her heart was so full yet there were no words to express her longing for this strong, brave man. She watched how tenderly he held the narrow wooden pencil. His fingers could snap it without a thought. But he caressed the paper and made her feel quite hot as she thought about how his touch would feel on her own skin.

"What shall we do once you've finished my portrait?" Anna asked with a sparkle in her eye.

* * *

The silence at Grantham's estate was uncomfortable, and the expression on the greedy politician's face was one of extreme displeasure.

"What's the issue with this Riding Officer?" Hogg asked, his hunched body moving forward in his chair.

"He's a threat!" Grantham explained, his chin wobbling as he spoke. "He's the one I had to remove from London when what was done was done. He's not a fool, he's an intelligent young man and could have easily got to the bottom of his father's death and I could be dancing the Tyburn Jig at Newgate Gaol."

Hogg smiled cruelly. He was a man who was happiest when he was spreading fear into people's hearts for his own demented needs. "I could speak to my old friend Silas Palmer. I'm sure he could make another appearance if need be. He's staying around this area for the present. Dropped round one night after that horrific storm but you were busy with someone."

"No, not yet, Eustace," Grantham said, stroking his chin. "I need to keep him here where I can watch him. It would be unwise to gun him down, anyway, because everyone would know it was us. How is Mr Palmer?"

"He's well but he's been a bit bored recently." Hogg cracked his knuckles.

Grantham puffed his bloated cheeks, "You know, for all the work he did for me, I have never actually met him. Now, how will we deal with the scourge that is the Riding Officer?"

"We could frame someone..." said Kitching.

"We tried that!" said Lockwood, striking his own leg with his fist. "Hogg shot that retarded plough boy in an attempt to frame him and the damned Riding Officer is still walking."

Grantham scowled. He locked the fingers on each hand and rested them on his bloated waist.

"He has friends in high places," the politician explained. "The Earl of Lincoln would be onto us like Lord Byron onto a rent boy!"

Dixon sniggered at the analogy.

"And what is your problem?" the Justice of the Peace asked sharply.

"Nothing!" said Dixon. The lowly herring caller was desperate for respect but he looked away from the Justice of the Peace. He knew there were subjects best not discussed in his presence.

Kitching held his finger to his mouth, then dropped it. "Why not find someone to murder him? We could get a third party to do it," the draper explained. "Surely someone down in London hates him; we know his past as a gambler and duellist, so someone must want to exact revenge on him." Kitching was convinced that a wager of such proportions was viable.

There was silence for a short while.

"That's a good idea..." said the Justice of the Peace, at last. His motives were never clear.

"Very good," added Lockwood, a plan forming in his power-obsessed psyche.

"What are you thinking of, Hubert?" Grantham asked.

"I suggest a trip to London, Adam," said Lockwood. "We could dig some dirt on him; let a few unsavoury characters know his whereabouts."

"A good idea, Hubert," exclaimed Grantham. "I'm due a visit to parliament; a good five months since I attended."

"We have that business with your solicitor to resolve," said Lockwood, slyly, his agenda evolving by the second.

Grantham smiled unpleasantly, reminiscent of someone suffering from a burst ulcer. "Don't worry, my dear Hubert," he told Lockwood. "That matter is resolved."

Lockwood smiled greedily. "Excellent," he said. "May I raise a toast – to Adam Grantham!"

"To Grantham!" toasted his cohorts.

What no one had noticed was the smile on Lockwood's face, the same smile he had expressed a day or so earlier when he kicked a crippled man's crutch away. He smiled as there was a new plot beginning to evolve in his mind and he began to edge closer to his ultimate goal; absolute power.

* * *

The Riding Officer completed the portrait of his lady love. He smiled as he passed the portrait to her.

"What do you think?" he asked. He smiled nervously. He felt a tingling in his fluttering heart as he waited for Anna's response.

"It makes me look beautiful!" said Anna.

"That wasn't hard; you are beautiful!" the Riding Officer told her, captivated and relieved by her soft, sensual smile. "Now tell me, was I professional in my work?"

"You were an utmost professional," she replied.

Anna leaned over slowly. The Riding Officer bent forward to meet her and they kissed. She broke away, and said, "But seeing as you are no longer working and having to be a professional, I advise that we should retire to your bed with haste!"

Chapter Six

Death, Dishonesty and Dishonour

Lockwood's carriage clattered across the village cobbles. Inside the carriage were Lockwood, Kitching and Hogg.

"I better get out here!" snarled Kitching. "I fear my daughter may once again be in the hands of that loathsome Riding Officer."

"Watch your temper, Jeremiah," warned Lockwood. "I don't need to lose my business partner."

"I've been thinking," added Kitching, sticking his right index finger in the air as an idea came to him.

"And what's that, Jeremiah?" asked Lockwood.

"A duel," suggested Kitching, a compulsive gambler of many years.

"No!" said Lockwood, firmly.

"Why not?" asked Hogg.

"The Riding Officer is an excellent shot; I'd never take him on myself," Lockwood informed them. "I've witnessed him myself. I saw him shoot a fox we were hunting. Shot dead at two hundred yards!"

Lockwood would never admit it but he was completely hopeless with a pistol. He could never let his cohorts know this as it would make him vulnerable. They would think less of him if they knew he could not hit a barn door at ten paces.

"Lucky shot!" Hogg sneered in a callous fashion.

"I've also witnessed him in a duel, about four years ago in London," Lockwood recalled. "He was sleeping with the daughter of the Swedish ambassador, a very beautiful young woman with blonde hair. Her name was Malin. The woman's fiancé took exception and the Riding Officer shot the gun clean out of his hand!"

"He shot his hand?" asked Kitching.

"No," Lockwood replied, "he shot the *gun*. The bullet struck the gun – an incredible shot!"

"You would say the odds were against me?" Kitching asked.

Lockwood frowned. "Definitely." He drummed his fingers upon the seat, and glared into Kitching's eyes. "And I don't want *you* doing anything foolish. *I* have far too much to lose if you get yourself killed!"

The carriage ground to a halt. "I better get out," said Kitching in a disappointed fashion as he reached for the latch on the door. He was disappointed that he could not demand satisfaction.

* * *

Anna led the Riding Officer towards the bed, pulling him by his belt. They kissed and caressed and it looked as if they would finally consummate their relationship. Anna didn't care what the naysayers would say for they did not care for what she truly wanted. All she ever wanted was an education and the chance to embrace some culture instead of being like the women of the time who were trained for a life of servitude to a husband who would not care for them.

They were interrupted by a clatter of carriage wheels outside. Anna sat down on the edge of the bed and ignored the sound. Instead, she began to unbuckle his belt.

Suddenly there was a pounding at the door. "Open up!" bawled a voice.

"I don't believe this," murmured the Riding Officer as he began to redo the work his lady love had undone. "Who is it?"

"Jeremiah Kitching!" shouted the voice.

Anna froze where she sat. Her jaw dropped as she gasped and she could hear nothing but her own heart begin to pound. The Riding Officer looked her in the eyes and stood up.

"Just a moment!" the Riding Officer told him. *"To the back,"* he mouthed to Anna.

The Riding Officer walked to the door, drew the bolt and opened it. "Yes, Mr Kitching? I was just going to bed."

"Where is my daughter?" The draper barged the Riding Officer out of the way, huffing and puffing as he looked for his daughter. His desire for Anna to marry Lockwood was purely financial.

"She's not here," said the Riding Officer. He stood with his chin held high but his stomach rumbled nervously, and he hoped that Kitching was too intoxicated to notice.

"Where is she, then?"

"Home?" suggested the Riding Officer as bluntly as he could. "You know? That big building you reside in."

Kitching looked down his nose at the Riding Officer and scowled, saying, "A fine home of wealth and comfort awaits her with Lockwood."

The Riding Officer uttered a short nasal snort. "I doubt it with that cretin!"

"How dare you!" retorted the draper, poking the Riding Officer in the chest with a pudgy finger. "An excellent businessman, wealthy, dashing; he'll make a wonderful husband for my daughter! Unlike a lowly, corrupt Riding Officer like you, a man who willingly breaks the law and has got away with murder."

"Go away, Kitching! If Lockwood heard what you just said about him, he could take you to court for defamation of character," shouted the Riding Officer. "I am going to bed!"

* * *

The Riding Officer watched from the doorway as Kitching stormed off down the street to his shop. The Riding Officer slipped back into his home, shutting the door firmly behind him. Anna was waiting for him.

"Has he gone?" she asked quietly.

"Yes," said the Riding Officer. "I think he may be losing his sanity. He referred to Lockwood as dashing!"

"Lockwood is anything but dashing," Anna replied, incensed at the mere thought. "The man is more disgusting than the rotten carcass of a dead whale!"

"Indeed," agreed the Riding Officer. "I recall the carcass that washed ashore last summer. Even Samuel thought it was putrid."

"Shall we go to bed?" Anna changed the subject. She didn't want to think about dead whales or Samuel.

"No. I think you better go, too; if he doesn't find you at your home, he'll come back and shove a cutlass into my abdomen."

Anna clung to the Riding Officer's shirt. He rested his head against hers, and he wrapped his arms around her as he felt her breath on his chest. His heart pounded as Anna turned her head against his chest and she could feel every beat.

Anna looked up at the Riding Officer, and her lip trembled as a tear formed in her eye. "Do you not want to make love to me?" she asked.

He smiled and gently stroked her cheek. "I do!" he advised her, "but away from here, away from Upperbridge. I do want to elope." He lifted his head, narrowed his eyes and sighed. "The problem is I can't figure a way out. When contraband lands, Grantham wastes my time and if you spend too much time away Lockwood or your father come looking." He rubbed Anna gently on the shoulder. "But if I could whisk you away right in front of Lockwood's eyes... well..."

* * *

Lockwood's carriage continued onto the Parish Gaol and Hogg's residence. Inside the carriage, Hogg sat alongside Lockwood. The carriage jolted and Lockwood rubbed his shoulder from the impact. Lockwood glanced at Hogg. He rubbed his chin covered in food particles with his hand.

"So, Mr Hogg," Lockwood began, looking his travelling companion in the eye, "what do you think about our dear friend Adam Grantham?"

Hogg rubbed his hands together then used his tongue to clear particles of food from between his teeth. "He pays well," said the ex-Bow Street Runner.

"Does he have any other qualities?" Lockwood probed.

"Not really. He makes me want to vomit at times."

Lockwood smiled evilly. "Do you think it's time our dearly beloved Member of Parliament stepped aside?"

"Could be," said Hogg, nonchalantly, "but politics isn't my thing."

"At the moment he has a tendency to be in the way. I'm due to come into a lot of wealth soon," Lockwood told Hogg. "I wonder if you would be interested in undertaking some private business for me."

"If the money's right then yes, I will."

"Not only will it lead to increasing my wealth but Grantham will be forced to step down as the Member of Parliament which means we should finally be able to get rid of that damned Riding Officer." Lockwood sucked in his stomach and sat up. He flicked a few hairs away from his perspiration-etched face as he raised his head in the air. "Grantham has had more than enough fun with him. It is my turn with him now and I don't intend for it to last very long."

"You're not keen on that man, are you?" Hogg asked with a snarl. "Do you know Grantham deliberately rigged card games so he lost more money?"

"No, I did not! And yes, I am not keen on him," said Lockwood. "He's a threat. *I* run this borough, *I'm* the most powerful man in this area – even more than Grantham – but my popularity is dwindling which is not good for the most powerful man in the county and I need to be shut of the Riding Officer. I need the villagers to hate him even more than I do."

"What about Kitching?"

"Kitching has his uses!" Lockwood told him. "Such as that beautiful daughter; my fiancée. It is very important that the most powerful man in the county has an attractive wife."

"You mean that dark haired girl who works at the inn?"

"That's the one; her name's Anna. I have plans for her. But you see, once I'm married to his daughter and she is under my control, Kitching will be of no use to me and will have to be disposed of."

Hogg drummed his fingers against the window frame of the carriage door. "I like the way you think, Mr Lockwood!"

"But to marry Anna *he* must be gone – the Riding Officer!" Lockwood explained. "I feel they might try to elope but I have agents all over England and I will catch them. He has infected her mind. Anna speaks as if she is now above me and does not want to marry me. The girl needs to learn to be more subservient to her master."

"Maybe we should send him for a swim or something," jeered Hogg as he clapped his hands together. "I'll make some inquiries to my old friend Silas Palmer."

"Tell me, Hogg," Lockwood said, "how did you get to know such an infamous figure like Silas Palmer?"

"We were in the Runners together," Hogg informed him. "We were thrown out on trumped up charges at the same time. Some stupid shit got himself killed when he shouldn't have."

Lockwood laughed heartlessly. "We could make a fine team!" the hunchback said. "When our beloved Member of Parliament returns from London he will have an incident with that other friend of ours, the Riding Officer. I know all about his history with Adam Grantham, and it's time to wind up the rumour mill and let a few cats out of the bag!"

* * *

A few days had passed since Kitching had been to pay him a visit. The Riding Officer was on the south pathway during a patrol. He had just passed the beacon when he gazed out to sea and the setting sun. "Time for home, girl!" he said to his horse. He wondered how Lockwood and associates would taunt him today. Their latest line of hostility was to accuse him of being out to get Adam Grantham because "the foolish Riding Officer wrongly believed him to have masterminded a murder" and "the man dropped dead of a heart attack so he could not have been murdered."

He continued on towards the village. From the corner of his eye he noticed Dixon the herring caller.

"Don't say it, Dixon!" warned the Riding Officer. "You'll see no herring now!"

Instead of calling, Dixon began to whistle the "Grand Old Duke of York." The Riding Officer halted his horse and turned to Dixon, and said, "Do you have any idea why you whistle that incessant tune?"

Dixon shrugged as he picked up a stick. "Mr Lockwood likened you to him."

"Do you have any idea who he is?" the Riding Officer asked him, bluntly, taking the reins in his left hand.

"He is the Duke of York!" laughed Dixon, his mouth open wide as he looked away from the Riding Officer. He struck the ground aggressively with the stick. "Everyone knows that!"

"So you have no idea what position Prince Frederick holds, Dixon?"

"He's a Duke!" answered Dixon, sarcastically, "of the city of York! Any fool knows that. Except maybe you..." He cast the stick in the direction of the Riding Officer's horse.

"Oh, is he?" replied the Riding Officer with equal sarcasm as he watch the projectile fail to reach his mount. "I thought he might be the Commander-in-Chief of the British Army or something, but I wouldn't expect you to know that."

The Riding Officer rode on down the gradient and past the shoreline; he could hear the church bell sound seven. Samuel was on the beach collecting debris. Samuel noticed the Riding Officer, and shouted out, "Scum!" in his customary fashion. "*I've heard* what you are planning to do to Mr Grantham."

"Tell me, Samuel," began the Riding Officer, "how can a man like you who spends so much time near water be so disgustingly filthy?"

The wretched little man's face contorted. "I don't know what you mean," Samuel said. "Mr Lockwood tells me I'm one of the best dressed men in the village."

The Riding Officer shook his head. "What's in your shack, Samuel?" He was feeling a sudden urge to rile Samuel.

"You stay away from my shack!" Samuel bellowed. "Or I'll have you killed like you did to Simple Joe Bell!"

"Stop trying to pretend you are important, you awful little man. If you were a building you would have been levelled by now."

I truly do hate this place, the Riding Officer thought to himself as his horse continued up the road towards his home. He had thought Joe Bell was cared for but it was clear that certain elements did not care at all for him – though it did not surprise him who those elements were.

"Evening, officer!" said the blacksmith as he passed him.

"Evening, Gregory!" replied the Riding Officer.

The Riding Officer dismounted from his horse and led her around to the stable. It was there that he saw his lady love.

"What are you doing here?" he asked Anna.

"Waiting for you!" she replied with a glint in her eye. "Where have you been?"

"On patrol," the Riding Officer replied.

"Is that true?" asked Anna. She was worried. She'd heard some unpleasant hearsay earlier in the inn having heard the rumours that the Riding Officer was out to 'get' Grantham.

"Why are you here?" asked the Riding Officer.

Anna moved up closer to him. She put her arms around him, and he embraced her in return. Anna looked at the hay that was packed into stable.

"I fancied a roll in the hay," she whispered in his ear, "so I came here."

"I didn't know you knew about things such as that." His hands worked down her fine figure.

"I'm a woman of hidden talents," Anna told him as she felt his hands upon her rear.

The Riding Officer kissed her and they fell onto the hay. "You are so beautiful!" he said as he looked into her beautiful blue eyes and gazed at her captivating smile.

"I think tonight is the night!" Anna whispered. "And damn it if I get sent to hell!"

All of a sudden the moment was broken when there was a loud explosive sound. It was a shotgun being fired. Then it fired once more. A cold shiver went up the spine of the Riding Officer as he sat bolt upright. He had an ominous feeling.

* * *

The coach rattled and bumped along, making Grantham's stomach churn. He'd already vomited at least three times in the journey from London. That was hardly surprising. He'd spent a few days of debauchery – drugs, gambling and sexual liaisons – and was now on his way back to Lincolnshire.

Lockwood had accompanied him but had left earlier. Grantham was alone in the coach, trying not to think about the thousand pounds he'd wasted. Was it worth it? Certainly, the uncomfortable journey was making him regret some of the more gluttonous excesses.

He fell into an uneasy slumber.

The coach was in its final stretch of the journey when

Grantham awoke. Through the window he could see the sun setting and he could hear the church bell ringing seven o'clock. The coach continued a little further and then stopped. He heard the coachman murmuring to somebody. Curious, he looked out of a window and saw a small crowd of unfamiliar people; they were not from Upperbridge. Grantham was confused as to why the coach was stopped. The bloated politician was just about to shout at the coachman when the coach door swung open.

A masked figure in a riding officer's uniform stood at the door holding a shotgun.

"Who are you? You're not the Riding Officer!" said Grantham angrily. "Oh, it's you!" He recognised the masked man's true identity. "What are doing dressed like that? And watch what you are doing with that gun – I could get hurt!"

The masked man did not answer. Instead, he fired the gun at Grantham's stomach. He groaned in horrendous agony as the cartridge passed straight through him.

"Why?" he hissed.

The gun went off again, this time taking off half of Grantham's face.

* * *

The Riding Officer held Anna close to him as a feeling of tremendous uncertainty overcame him. Suddenly he felt that he would be threatened imminently, and he was almost paralysed by the fear. There was an almighty crash as the front door was knocked off its hinges and about twenty men led by Lockwood and Kitching swarmed in.

"There he is!" thundered Lockwood. "That's the man who murdered Adam Grantham!"

"Get him!" roared the mob.

Anna clutched the Riding Officer tight. "I didn't murder anybody!" he protested.

"We saw you!" raged the mob.

"When did this happen? I've been at work all day, riding the coast," he shouted. "Ask Dixon, he saw me pass him countless times!"

"I never saw you on the coast!" said Dixon, emerging from the crowd with a smirk on his face.

"Or Samuel!" added the Riding Officer, desperately.

"Murderer!" screeched Samuel, having fought his way to the head of the crowd.

The Riding Officer's heart began to pound, and his head was swimming unclearly as he began to fear for his life. He stood up tall, attempting to dismiss the fear he was feeling. He pondered momentarily, as he recalled his route home. "Gregory the black-smith, he saw me!"

Lockwood smiled cruelly. "As we speak, Mr Gregory is being arrested by Constable Hogg for handling contraband."

"I killed nobody!" the Riding Officer insisted, shaking his fist at his accuser.

"A masked man in a riding officer's uniform murdered our beloved MP Adam Grantham with a shotgun just after seven tonight!" announced Lockwood with an air of authority.

"I didn't shoot Grantham. I was with Anna," he shouted, realising he was being set up once more. "Tell them, Anna!"

"Binns! Edwards! Retrieve my property – my fiancée!" Lockwood barked. "I will not have her lie for this criminal!"

"I'm no criminal," the Riding Officer bellowed, incensed by the injustice that was about to be done. "Why would I shoot Grantham?"

"You owed him money," Lockwood replied, coldly. "And you believe that he had your father killed."

"He *did* have my father killed," the Riding Officer retorted, "and it was Silas Palmer who did it at Grantham's expense."

"Very original, officer, blame the most wanted man in England for a crime that you can't prove was ever committed. If

Dick Turpin had not been hung in 1739 you would probably try to blame him, too!" Lockwood shouted. "But that does not give you the right to kill a wonderful, kind and benevolent man such as Adam Grantham! You'll probably blame that on Silas Palmer, too."

"I didn't kill Grantham," said the Riding Officer. He was red in the face at the fury caused by the accusations, and he stamped his foot powerfully to the floor as if to taunt those who accused him. "Why would I wear a uniform to kill someone? It would be like suicide."

"That's what you did because you are a fool," Lockwood answered. His head snapped in the direction of Anna as he glared at the beauty. "This idiot has always struck *me* as having no intelligence. A very unattractive quality, don't you think, Anna, stupidity?"

"I, sir, am no fool!" The Riding Officer balled his fist and threw a mighty right hook that caught Lockwood square on the side of the jaw causing him to fall backwards into the hands of the mob members.

"Murderer!" screamed Samuel, once more. The Riding Officer lunged forward trying to grab the repulsive little man by the throat. Four members of the mob broke free seizing him by the limbs so he struggled to move.

"I heard a rumour today, officer," Lockwood said, his tone cruel and sinister. "I heard that *you* are in fact none other than Silas Palmer!"

"I am not, Lockwood!" the Riding Officer snapped, shaking his fist that he had broken free at Lockwood as if he was fighting the urge to strike him once more.

"Gentlemen," Lockwood sneered, "do as you wish with this pathetic excuse for a human."

Lockwood's minions grabbed hold of Anna and dragged her away from the Riding Officer's arms. The mob pounced onto the Riding Officer, clawing him to the floor.

* * *

Anna struggled as the men dragged her from the house towards the waiting carriage. Lockwood strutted out of the house with a proud smile on his face.

Anna's shoes bounced off the cobbles. One man had her gripped by the arm to the point she felt it would be wrenched from its socket. Another man had a great clutch of her hair, her neck was hurting tremendously and she had never been so petrified in her life. "What are you doing to him?" she called out hysterically as she lashed out at one of the men.

Lockwood sniffed, making a disgusting sound. "Hanging him," he said.

"You bastard!" shouted Anna. She was trying to keep control but felt on the verge of breaking down in tears, and Lockwood slapped her hard across the face. She lashed out a kick catching the brutal man in the groin.

Lockwood doubled over grasping at his nether regions. "Binns, Edwards! Take my fiancée home!" he told his men. "I'll be along later with my belt to remind her she is to be *my wife* and not the Riding Officer's *whore*."

The two minions violently shoved Anna into Lockwood's carriage, where she landed atop the corpse of Grantham. As she landed his blood spoiled her dress, and she looked her hands which were now coated in the bodily fluid and screamed. The henchmen jumped up and followed her into the carriage. Lockwood reached into his pocket and passed a five pound note to the coachman.

"Make sure my fiancée gets to my home," advised the vile hunchback, "then take Grantham's corpse to the undertakers."

"Very good, sir," said the coachman.

"And here's another five pounds for your part tonight," Lockwood explained. "You did the correct thing during the shooting; we wouldn't want you to get hurt in the process."

* * *

The Riding Officer was bound and gagged. The mob dragged him along the ground, his head banging on every bump, striking him with continuous kicks and punches up and down his legs and torso.

Somewhere on the outskirts of the village, the Riding Officer found himself thrust against a tree. He gazed up at the sky as the light was fading, and he could see he was in a wooded area. Suddenly, the mob descended upon him; a noose was thrown around his neck and a bag went over his head. He was hauled up onto the back of a horse.

"Go ahead and hang him!" was one scream he heard.

"Throw it over the branch!" was the next.

He felt the horse move beneath him causing the noose to contract around his neck, leaving his body hanging in mid-air. The air was expelled from him and he could no longer breathe. He began to fade.

He heard a pistol fire three times. The rope gave way and the Riding Officer hit the ground gasping for breath; he struggled with his ropes and freed his hands. He heard the pistol fire again, and he heard a groan and a scream. A man dropped dead in front of him as the Riding Officer threw the bag from his head. A stranger rode up on a horse and pulled him to safety.

As the mystery horseperson turned to him and smiled he was completely shocked. So shocked he nearly fell off.

"I told you I was a woman of hidden talents!" said Anna with a smile.

* * *

A light from outside shone into the gaol casting the shadow of the bars across the main floor. A candle flickered on the constable's desk and a gentle breeze caused some papers to ripple.

Lockwood turned his head to one side as he gazed at Hogg with a sole beady eye. "You did a good job tonight, Hogg!"

The big-headed crook puffed out his chest and straightened the buttons on his jacket. "Thank you, Mr Lockwood!"

Lockwood rubbed his grimy, dirt-laden hands together. "Grantham is gone and your idea for a lynch mob will terminate the infernal nuisance known as the Riding Officer from his employment within this parish."

"I'll tell Palmer to have the uniform burnt," snarled Hogg. "He'll be laying low at this moment. Do you know there are disgusting lowlifes who would turn him in for the reward money?"

Lockwood smiled and stroked his chin with his hand as Hogg mentioned the reward money. "Where is he? I'd like to shake that man's hand."

"Only I know where he is," advised Hogg. "That way he can remain safe from anyone who might want to grass him in for their own benefit! The greed of some people sickens me."

"Can I ask a question?" asked Lockwood

"Go ahead..."

"Where did you find that mob?"

"Here and there," said Hogg with a dismissive swagger. He walked up to the bars of the gaol cell, and pointed to the blacksmith, saying, "What shall we do about him?"

"Leave him," replied Lockwood heartlessly. "By the time this has blown over, he'll have starved to death. He knows too much by now, anyway, so we're better off with him dead."

The blacksmith stared, gobsmacked. The disregard for his wellbeing shocked him, and suddenly he realised if he could somehow get out of the gaol then he needed to get out of Upperbridge as well.

"And what will we do about our friend, the Riding Officer?" Hogg asked.

"We'll send a search party in the morning to retrieve his

body," Lockwood said. "There was so little we could do about that mob incensed by him murdering our beloved MP! And it would be of advantage to our friend Mr Palmer if we lead all and sundry to believe that the man who will very shortly become the former Riding Officer is Palmer! There will be a nice reward for us, too."

"Very good, Lockwood," laughed Hogg. "Silas will be pleased to hear he is off the hook for a while."

"We'll make haste to my home," Lockwood said. "I have some fine brandy for us to enjoy. It was recently imported from France – duty free, of course."

The two men laughed as they headed to the door, but as they reached it, it opened to reveal Binns and Edwards. Their shoulders were hunched and their heads were down as they looked at the ground. They entered, their feet dragging and their hands hanging so low they could have grazed the floor.

"Binns, Edwards! What are you doing here?"

"Your fiancée, Mr Lockwood..." began Binns.

"What about her?" Lockwood asked, angrily.

"She's escaped!" said Edwards, petrified.

"She did what?" Lockwood stamped his foot on the floor.

"Escaped!" reiterated Edwards, avoiding eye contact with Lockwood.

"Go and find her!" Lockwood thumped his fist down on the nearest surface.

Before Binns and Edwards could scuttle across to the exit away from the wrath of Lockwood and Hogg, the door opened once more and a man who had been a prominent member of the lynch mob entered, cautiously.

"What is it, John?" asked Hogg. "You're *supposed* to be at the green, supervising the execution..."

"The Riding Officer, Eustace..." John stuttered.

"John, what is it?" asked Hogg, his voice growing louder. The tensions of the past few days were beginning to stretch him thin, and he could feel a vein throb painfully in his forehead. *Any much more of this....*

* * *

Anna and the Riding Officer had ridden five or six miles into the Lincolnshire countryside. Some hours had passed since the attempted lynching, and she was tired, he was tired – even the horse was tired.

Somewhere on the road to Nottingham they passed a small farmhouse, with smoke rising from the chimney and a light in the window. The Riding Officer dismounted and led the horse up the dusty driveway towards the door. The Riding Officer rapped on the door with his knuckles. He felt exhausted, his body was still sore from when he fell from the noose, and in particular his neck hurt. He lent against the doorframe fearing he would collapse if he stood unaided.

Eventually the door opened. It was answered by a farmer who was about sixty with a bald head and a beard. "Yes?"

"The young lady and myself," the Riding Officer began, "we would like something to eat and a place to sleep if we may."

The farmer nodded. "You can have the loft in the barn. We have some pie and vegetables, cold."

"You're very kind," said the Riding Officer.

The farmer noticed that Anna was shivering from the cold. "I'll get you a blanket, my dear."

Anna smiled. "Thank you."

"Your horse must be tired. Take some water from the well for her," the farmer added.

* * *

They sat in the farmhouse kitchen eating the food in silence, while the farmer watched them like two animals in the zoo, intrigued by his impromptu guests.

"Where are you two from?" the farmer asked after a while.

"The Lincolnshire coast," said the Riding Officer. "A village by the name of Upperbridge."

"Upperbridge?" the farmer repeated. "What brings you this way?"

"We're eloping!" Anna told him.

"Eloping?"

"We're heading north to Gretna," Anna said.

"Are we?" the Riding Officer asked her, turning to her with a smile on his face.

"We are heading to Gretna, then onto Liverpool, then onto America for a new life!" Anna continued, firmly.

"Sounds good!" said the farmer. "Why are you eloping?"

"Anna was engaged to repulsive man, name of Lockwood," the Riding Officer explained.

The farmer scowled. "Only man named Lockwood I knew was a fishmonger! His fish killed my brother ten years ago. He's probably a different bloke altogether."

"Sounds like the same man to me!" muttered the Riding Officer, as his memory caused him to recoil.

"Horrible little man, he was!" the farmer continued. "Hunched back, legs like saplings and tiny hands with great long fingers that were clogged with dirt. He stank to high heaven as well!"

"Definitely the same man," concluded the Riding Officer.

There was a brief silence while the farmer stroked his chin. He viewed the Riding Officer's uniform. "What was your line of work then, lad?"

The Riding Officer wriggled uncomfortably, and his shoulder in particular undulated quite significantly. He lifted his hand and rested his chin upon it. He sighed. "I was the Riding Officer in Upperbridge."

"Dear, dear!" sighed the farmer, shaking his head. "Why did

you want to do that in an area like that?"

"Wasn't really my choice," the Riding Officer answered, "but at least something good eventually came out of it!" He smiled at Anna and slipped his hand into hers.

"My nephew was the riding officer out that way," the farmer said. "Henry Heskett was his name; a politician tried to bribe him into turning a blind eye to the smuggling. He didn't comply, so they had him killed – fractured skull they said."

"It's a sad tale," said the Riding Officer, familiar with his predecessor's passing.

"Didn't want a farm job," the farmer continued, "went to Upperbridge full of himself, wanting to serve King and country, wanted to be respected and people to look up to him but ended up in a wooden box."

"I think we'll retire now," the Riding Officer said, not wishing to enter into a morbid conversation, "but thank you for your hospitality, Mr Heskett."

"Help yourself to water," the farmer told him. "I won't disturb you!"

* * *

The Riding Officer soaked down his horse with some cold well water. He made sure she had some water in a trough and headed to the barn to rest. His fatigue had subsided, and the pain in his neck and back was eased.

After moving some old pots of paint out of the way for his horse he climbed the steps to the hay loft, where he expected to find Anna asleep. Instead he found her lying on a blanket in the hay. Her beautiful blue eyes sparkled sensually, her black hair complementing her fair skin so perfectly and the smile on her lifting and inspiring. When she smiled at him it made him feel like the most important person in the world.

It was that night in the barn Anna and the Riding Officer

consummated their relationship. It felt so beautiful, so natural, and so right. They lay on the hay for a while, entwined in silence as they reflected on their act of intimacy.

"Was I your first?" asked the Riding Officer after a while.

"No," replied Anna, "there have been others." She sighed deeply. "They were all stupid, stupid mistakes. The last was killed by Lockwood..."

"I won't ask," replied the Riding Officer.

"It's all right," Anna told him. "The first man I ever fell in love with – and Lockwood had him killed."

The Riding Officer propped himself up on one elbow, in his mouth he chewed on a piece of straw. "Who was he?"

Anna lay on her back, her head fully back as she gazed at a moth fluttering about the rafters. "His name was Morton," she said. "He was a farm labourer. There was talk of marriage but we parted as a couple when he slept with a local whore."

"How did you find out?" asked the Riding Officer. He pulled the chewed straw from his mouth and cast it away.

"I caught him," Anna said with a slight laugh. "Walked into the stables behind the inn and caught his bare backside bobbing up and down on top of her in the middle of a stall. Lockwood did him in for that reason, some act of bravado to impress me. It failed ... I always suspect it was Lockwood who paid the whore to do the deed with Morton..."

"Terrible..." The Riding Officer looked up to the rafters and the flight of the moth. He remembered the whole affair with young Morton not long after he had arrived in Upperbridge and wondered, *Dare I tell her she is indeed correct?*

Anna looked at the Riding Officer, and she smiled. "I'm sure you heard what they used to say about me..."

The Riding Officer sat up and pulled a few pieces of straw from his shirt. "What did they say?"

Anna laughed. "Don't play the fool; it doesn't suit an intelligent man like you," she said. "You know they called me a whore, told me I would go to hell. But I don't care. At least I won't have to put up with the church types who have spent my life telling me how to live it!"

"Amen to that," said the Riding Officer as he lay back down.

"What about you?" Anna asked. "Am I your first?"

"My third," the Riding Officer confessed. "I had a difficult relationship with an actress in London and I fell in love with the Swedish ambassador's daughter, but both ended in heartbreak, with the second almost ending in tragedy."

The Riding Officer held Anna closer. By the moonlight, her captivatingly beautiful blue eyes looked even more so. "You need not worry, Anna, they are both now history." Anna smiled; in the Riding Officer's eyes her face was a picture of perfect beauty, and he kissed her. A short while later they descended into a peaceful sleep.

* * *

The farmer had left a simple breakfast in the kitchen. The Riding Officer was very keen to find him before they set off on their proposed trip to Scotland. He was frantic and kept reminding Anna it was important they find him and warn him what could happen. The Riding Officer snapped his fingers, muttered something about pots of paint and taking Anna by the hand they headed back to the barn.

Anna wrapped her arms around the Riding Officer's waist and rested her head against his back; it was amazing that on that highway away from her home with nowhere to live that she felt much safer with the Riding Officer than she ever had in the village of Upperbridge where she had lived her whole life.

The Riding Officer was relieved when they stopped and she released her grip from his waist. He loved her but it had hurt when she bolted her hands round his still-sore torso. They had found a secluded area off the main road to Nottingham. The

Riding Officer took out a couple of woodpigeons with a few shots of his pistol.

"Where are we?" asked Anna. She was sitting upon a log plucking the wood pigeons as the Riding Officer began to set a fire.

He gently blew onto the kindling as it began to burn. "I'd say we were a few miles north east of Gainsborough."

"Why don't we head north, then?" Anna asked. She kicked her heel into the ground as she plucked the feathers from the pigeons. *Ugly creatures!* she thought. She found them the creepiest of beasts.

The Riding Officer stood up. "Lockwood will have headed south towards Lincoln."

"So why didn't we head north?" Anna was agitated, continually looking over both shoulders. She would see a twitch in the bushes and stare intensely at them.

The Riding Officer rubbed his hands together as the fire came to life. "Lockwood will then try north." He stood up tall and placed his hands on his hips as he admired his handiwork.

"I hope you are right..." said Anna, her faced creased with worry as she watched something in the bushes.

"We'll be fine. I'm off to the river to get some water."

Anna dropped the pigeon, her brow furrowed and her lip trembling. "You are not going to leave me?"

"No, just to get some water." He smiled. "I'll be back."

Anna got up and walked over to her love. "What happens if somebody comes?"

"Will they?"

Anna looked over her shoulders. "Lockwood has agents..."

The Riding Officer shrugged. "I know all about them and what is more, I can tackle them."

Anna grabbed his jacket. "I've been thinking. Let's go to Lincoln. To the Earl. He spoke highly of you."

"How do you know?"

"He told Mr Timms. Apparently, you can head there whenever you like."

"I hardly know him, Anna..."

"It's somewhere to go..."

"Let us marry first," he said, slipping his hand into his hers.

"Then we go to Lincoln?"

"No, I like your original idea!" laughed the Riding Officer. "To America for you and me! Away from England and far from the threat of Lockwood. He could trace us to Lincoln but not to America!"

Anna smiled, as she nodded her head her mouth was tight and nervous. "If you say so... you make a modicum of sense," she said, "but where will we sail from?"

"I was thinking Liverpool." The Riding Officer wrapped his arms around Anna.

She raised her eyebrows. "Are you suggesting that we ride all the way to Scotland to then return to England?"

"I don't think my horse will make it to Scotland," the Riding Officer said.

"What are you saying?" asked Anna with slight concern. *Had he changed his mind about marrying her already?*

"Let's get married at the nearest church we can find," he announced.

Anna felt her heart skip, "Won't that be expensive?" she asked.

"I have some sovereigns on my person!" he advised. "We can get married today."

* * *

Anna sat on the horse as she watched the Riding Officer talk to the rector of the small church they had passed in the hamlet of Lesser Neston. It was early evening and the sun was setting. The rector was a towering man with a grim, grey complexion. He shook his fist violently and shouted loudly though unintelligibly at the Riding Officer.

The Riding Officer stomped back to the horse with a look on his face that could kill. He turned back to the rector. "Philistine!" he scowled as the rector shook his fist at him once more.

"What did he say?" Anna peered down at her love.

"Words a rector should not use!"

"What did he say about us marrying?"

The Riding Officer took a few paces away and kicked some dirt. "He said that the banns need to be read three times."

"Oh!"

"So I offered to make a generous donation to the church if he would turn a blind eye to this."

"Oh!"

"Then he shouts at me and said he hoped that God would send me straight to hell where I will burn for all enternity. I said that was fine as I have lived in Upperbridge and hell would be a casual stroll through the countryside in the middle of spring compared to that *place*."

"Where now?" Anna asked. She wanted to be wed as soon as she could. This man would provide her with the safety and security that she yearned for. If Lockwood caught up with them she would have a safety net for him to contend with.

The Riding Officer walked back to the horse and pulled himself back on. An ugly fat man on horseback came trotting along beside them. Anna recognised him. As his horse stopped the stranger stared on.

"We'll head to Clay Cross," the Riding Officer said. He took his flask from his belt and sipped some water before passing it to Anna. "Mr Heskett, the farmer, he said that there was a good rector there who was accommodating in such matters…"

"Where is that?"

"Derbyshire." The Riding Officer took the flask from Anna as she handed it back. "We can get there tomorrow dinner time."

"Let us find an inn then." Anna closed her eyes. "I am tired and need rest."

"Separate rooms then..." mumbled the Riding Officer.

"Yes," Anna said, firmly.

The Riding Officer sighed deeply. He looked up and noticed the stranger. "What are you looking at?"

The stranger didn't say a word and rode off. Anna rested her head against her man's back and wrapped her arms around him. "I know him..."

The Riding Officer squeezed his mount with his legs and she trotted on. "I have to ask, Anna, how did you rescue me from that mob?"

Anna suddenly gripped him tight, her arms driving the air out of him. "I know that man!" The Riding Officer felt her begin to tremble. "He's an agent of Lockwood!"

* * *

The church clock in the Derbyshire village of Clay Cross struck midday. The elderly rector watered the flowers in the boxes outside his home. It had been a pleasant day so far. He had awoken very early in the day, everything had breezed along gently, his paperwork was complete and he was now able to tend to his garden before he had a light lunch. A slight breeze picked up which wisped through his white curly hair.

"Good day, reverend!" said a voice behind him.

The rector turned around. He saw a young man in an unfamiliar looking uniform who was leading a horse carrying an attractive young woman with long black hair.

"Good day to you, too!" said the rector, politely.

"I was wondering if you could help," said the young man.

"Certainly. What can I do?"

"The young lady and I would like to get married," the young man told him. "Today if possible."

The rector smiled. He locked the fingers on each hand together and held them to his chest. "You're not from this parish, are you, young man?"

The Riding Officer looked away then back, and he winced. "No, we are not, sir…"

"You do realise that the banns need to be read three times?"

The Riding Officer coughed, he looked to his left and then his right. He took a purse from his belt and opened it showing it to the rector. "I *am* willing to make a *donation* to your church…"

The rector put his hand to his mouth. "It would be *quite* expensive!"

"That isn't a problem, sir," the young man replied.

"I can wed you this afternoon at three o'clock; there is an opening," the rector replied. He smiled once more. *I am sure the Lord will understand.* "You will need to provide witnesses though."

"I can do that."

"That's an unusual uniform," said the rector.

He knew he looked out of place so far inland. "I am – or I was – a Riding Officer," explained the young man.

* * *

At a little after quarter past three that afternoon, the Riding Officer and Anna were pronounced man and wife. The ceremony was simple; the rector's housekeeper played the organ, a couple of hymns were sung, and then the vows were read. The Riding Officer had found four people at the village inn and after paying them half a sovereign each they had agreed to be witnesses.

Shortly after the ceremony concluded, the rector left the church to walk in the grounds. At the side of the church he found the newlyweds sitting on a stone bench. They had their arms around one another, and the Riding Officer smoked a pipe.

"You're still here!" said the rector with a smile. He stopped and placed his hands on his hips.

"We ... wanted to speak to you..." the Riding Officer began, as he stood up and approached the rector.

"This is a beautiful land," he said, turning from the Riding Officer to admire the countryside.

"We need to talk to you," said the Riding Officer, hoping to engage the rector.

"When I see this country I cannot help but think of the works of the poet Peter Lloyd. He paints the beauty of our land so well in his volumes." The rector spread his arms before dropping them to his side, and he turned around. "Do you read Lloyd?"

"Yes," said Anna. She looked admirably at her husband. "I think *everything* he does is amazing!"

"Wonderful!" said the rector as he clasped his hands together in front of his chest.

"My husband is a poet," said Anna.

"Are you really?" asked the rector, covering his mouth with his hands.

"I am indeed. It was the only way to survive. Out there on the Lincolnshire coast the pay was poor and selling poetry was the only thing I could do. It prevented me from starving to death. I used to paint a few pictures but materials out there were both scarce and expensive."

"You have made good money from your poetry," the rector told him. "Your *donation* to the church was most generous."

"I've made some honest money," the Riding Officer explained. "I've just left a community of greed and corruption; I've learnt that money simply corrupts people."

"Where are you heading from here?"

"The inn for some rest," he said with a twinkle in his eye as he gazed at his wife lovingly.

"I meant from Clay Cross," the rector clarified.

"To Liverpool then onto America," Anna replied. "We're off to begin a new life, away from the place we both grew to detest."

"Well, may God take care of you both," said the rector.

"We *need* to speak to you." The Riding Officer tried to reach out and grab the rector's arm but he walked away.

"I wish you all the success in the future and a safe journey across the Atlantic!" he said with a cheerful wave.

* * *

Anna was awoken by a scratching noise. Initially she was concerned; was it a mouse? Or had Lockwood caught them? She slowly sat up in the bed and looked across to a desk in the corner of their room at the inn. She breathed a sigh of relief as she saw her husband was sitting, writing by candlelight. It was the early hours of the morning and the scratching she could hear was his quill on the paper.

"What are you doing?" Anna got out of bed.

"Writing," replied her husband, his eyes not leaving the paper. "I couldn't sleep."

"What is it?" Anna asked as she padded barefoot across the floor to the desk. "Is it poetry?"

"No," he replied, "it's for you."

"It's for me?" Anna said in a confused tone. She was tired, having had her deepest sleep for days if not weeks. "Is it poetry?"

"For you," he replied, "and again it's not poetry; it's a letter to the Earl of Lincoln."

"Why?"

"If we ever get parted, please take this to the Earl of Lincoln," he explained. "You know I'm highly thought of by him; I think he will be able to protect you if I cannot."

"But we will never be parted," Anna reassured him.

The Riding Officer stood up and embraced his wife. "I have an awful feeling after seeing that man in Lesser Neston," he confided to her. "Something tells me we haven't escaped Lockwood. I remember times when Lockwood and Grantham would threaten me by telling me if I fled Upperbridge that they have a network of agents across the whole of England who would locate me. He could still get us!"

He held Anna tight, gently rubbing her back. Then he stroked her long black hair away from her eyes and gazed deeply at her. "If something happens to me I want you to be safe; somewhere where Lockwood and his cohorts can't get you."

Chapter Seven

The Flying Man at Warrington

A few days had passed and the farmer could not help to think of what had happened to the young couple who had stopped at his farm a handful of nights before. Why were they affecting him so much? He wondered where they were; they were possibly in Cumberland by now, heading towards Scotland. What he found to be so odd was that the man they were fleeing was the man who was responsible for the indirect deaths of his brother and nephew.

It couldn't be the same man, could it? he thought. *No!*

He told himself, it couldn't be – most likely his aging mind was playing games with him.

He was collecting hen and duck eggs at the farm when he heard the distinctive sound of horses' hooves. He saw a group of men on horseback, trailed by a coach and horses pulling up the driveway. The lead horse rider was dressed in a parish constable's uniform; he was an exceptionally ugly man with a violent purple face, bald head and a scar on his chin. He said nothing to the farmer. Instead, he simply stared a burning hole through the farmer when he sighted him; he climbed off his horse and walked to the coach.

He opened the door and the farmer was horrified to see Hubert Lockwood emerge. The vile hunchback climbed out and inhaled deeply then exhaled, mumbling something about farms smelling terrible. He strutted over to the farmer, scowling. The farmer simply stared back, undaunted by Lockwood's presence.

"Tell me, my man," Lockwood barked. "Have you seen a couple go past?"

"Can't say that I have," said the farmer, firmly.

"A man and a woman," snapped Lockwood.

"Not today," Heskett replied.

"A young woman, attractive, long black hair," Lockwood informed him. "And a man in a riding officer's uniform."

"It doesn't ring any bells," Heskett answered.

"Look, my man," Lockwood said, clapping his hands together and interlocking his long phalanges. "That man is a dangerous, wanted criminal. He murdered a dear friend of mine before he kidnapped my beloved fiancée and is currently corrupting her mind against me."

"Who did he kill?" asked Heskett, not believing Lockwood's information. He was a man known across the parish for his lies.

"Adam Grantham, the Member of Parliament for Upperbridge, a devoted Christian citizen and a fine all-round human being."

Heskett's eyes narrowed. The name of the rotten man from the rotten borough was one he knew all too well. "I told you, I haven't seen anyone today."

Lockwood pulled his pocketknife from his pocket. He unfurled the blade and ran his thumb across it. "I'm willing to pay you for any information. We believe the man we are looking for is the notorious Silas Palmer, the most wanted man in England."

Heskett scowled. "Don't you understand me when I say I haven't seen anybody?"

"I can't expect a damn inbred like you to have seen a thing anyway," Lockwood replied, venomously. "You country bumpkins are all the same! So inbred you can't see a thing."

"My eyes are fine," Heskett told him, coldly. "I haven't seen anybody today except you."

"Very well!" Lockwood growled, and turned to walk towards his coach. He took a few paces towards it before spinning back to the farmer. "Your face looks familiar," he told the farmer in a sinister tone. "What's your name?"

"Heskett," the farmer replied. "Dick Heskett."

"Any relation to Henry Heskett?" asked Lockwood.

"I had a great-uncle Henry," the farmer replied. The muscles in his aging frame tensed and he was half expecting Lockwood and his men to pounce on him. "I've no family left since my wife died."

Lockwood smiled a twisted smile. "Wrong man!" the hunchback said. "I heard the boy Heskett's family had sworn revenge."

"Why's that?"

"Had him killed, didn't I," the hunchback answered with evil glee, his eyes wild at the mere thought. Lockwood turned and he laughed manically as his head reared back and returned to his coach. His procession headed down the dusty driveway and followed the road to Clay Cross. *If I had been a younger man and he didn't have that army of thugs with him,* the farmer thought, *I would have knocked his block off.*

The farmer stared up at the sky. Though it was blue and clear with a few clouds, the farmer sensed an awful impending fear.

"May God have mercy on their souls!" he mumbled.

* * *

Early that morning Anna had once more witnessed her new husband's prowess with a pistol as he shot a rabbit in a field just outside of Lymm. By no means a bad shot herself, Anna was suitably impressed by his display and felt reassured by his actions. To Anna, the Riding Officer was the perfect combination of manliness and sensitivity.

On the third full day of marriage the first port of call for the Riding Officer and his beautiful wife was Warrington in Lancashire. There was buzz about the town that morning. When they arrived everyone seemed to be heading to the town centre.

"What do you think all the fuss is about?" the Riding Officer asked Anna.

"Perhaps it's market day."

"No," the Riding Officer replied. "It feels much more important than that. It feels like there is an event about to take place."

"It could be the circus or the carnival," Anna replied, resting her chin upon her husband's shoulder.

The young couple continued on, and discovered a lot of people surrounding a church.

"What's going on?" the Riding Officer asked a young man who was wearing a leather apron.

"It's the Amazing Anthony!" the young man answered.

"Who?"

"The Amazing Anthony!" The young man grinned. "He's a flying man!"

"A flying man?" said the Riding Officer with bemusement; it had been many years since he witnessed such a person.

"He's grand, he is," the young man said, jovially. "He came here last year."

Anna leant forward. "What's a flying man?"

The Riding Officer pondered for a minute. "A flying man, you ask? Some say entertainers, some say daredevils, I say a complete and utter lunatic!"

The horse trotted on and as the young couple reached the town square, they saw a crowd gathered by a church. There was a rope tied from the church bell tower to some iron bars on the ground outside a nearby inn. A man appeared on the parapet of the bell tower causing the crowd burst into a spontaneous round of applause and a rapturous cheer.

The man, who was obviously the Amazing Anthony, posed one hundred feet high above the square. He raised his arms, shook his fists and blew kisses to the crowd.

"What's he going to do?" asked Anna.

"Fly down on the rope, dear," replied a woman standing nearby with a pipe.

Anthony climbed over the parapet of the bell tower and secured himself to the rope. He supported himself on the rope with his knee. He gave a signal to his assistants and launched himself into the wild blue yonder as he slid down the rope face first. The crowd was euphoric as he shot down the rope. There was also an element in the crowd that seemed to want to see him fall.

But the ghoulish contingent of the crowd was to be disappointed. He judged his run perfectly and smoothly. He reached the cobbles and dismounted. Using his momentum as he reached the ground, he ran into the nearby inn amidst further cheers to claim a free tankard of ale.

After a while the crowd began to disperse. The Riding Officer dismounted from his horse and led her to a nearby water trough. He helped Anna down from the horse. As the mare refreshed herself at the trough, the young couple ate a simple lunch of wholemeal bread and roasted beef, with some fruit from a nearby grocer and a jug of ale from the inn.

A little while later, the Amazing Anthony emerged from the inn. His assistants were packing his rigging into a wagon.

"That was some show you put on today!" the Riding Officer told Anthony.

Anthony laughed. "I am a professional showman!" he announced. "I always entertain. I am the only professional flying man in the North of England."

The Riding Officer was stunned. He had always thought of flying men as fools. "You risk your life to make a living?" he asked in complete amazement. Flying men were usually naval men who performed just the once for a large sum of money. The Riding Officer had never heard of a professional flying man before that day.

"There's plenty of money in it," said Anthony. "I've been doing this for years."

"How much money is involved?" the Riding Officer asked,

intrigued by the flying man's comment.

"*Plenty!*" said Anthony with a confident smile. "I only have to perform a dozen times a year – only in the summer months, mind you, and I live in luxury."

"When are you performing next?" the Riding Officer asked.

Anna did not like the look in her husband's eyes.

"I'll be performing tomorrow afternoon in Widnes," Anthony told him.

"No, you're not," the Riding Officer replied.

"Why won't I be doing that?"

"Because I will be taking your place!" announced the Riding Officer.

* * *

There was an unnervingly tense atmosphere spreading across the village of Clay Cross. A group of men in search of a young couple who had passed through the village had begun a brawl in a local inn. They had assaulted the patrons and the landlord, they had torn out parts of the upholstery; smashed tables, chairs and windows, and destroyed one of the rooms upstairs. They had threatened a number of drinkers before heading to the church and then the vicarage.

Shortly after the group of men had burst into the rector's home. There was an exchange of abuse, then a bullet was fired. The men had left, led by a hideously ugly man with a bald head and a scar on his chin. After speaking to an unknown individual in a carriage, they left in the direction of Lancashire. Once the men had left, the rector's housekeeper emerged from the house crying hysterically and the local constable was sent for. As the villagers waited for the constable there were murmurs, mainly referring to one of England's most wanted men: *Palmer*.

The Clay Cross constable approached the rector's doorway with great trepidation. The unnerving silence from the crowd gathered outside the vicarage that preceded his entrance to the building seemed to intensify the matter. Using the butt of the pistol, the constable tentatively pushed the door open. He was a young man, the Clay Cross constable; the occasional drunk, a stray vagrant and every so often a highwayman foolish enough to get caught, that's what he was used to dealing with. That's how bad crime was in this area – they were not used to serious crime like this. He hoped they were all gone; it didn't take a genius to realise that the men who had done this were very dangerous men.

After a matter of minutes the Clay Cross constable re-emerged. He staggered out of the door, gasping for his breath. His complexion was as white as a cooked chicken breast, sweat was pouring from his forehead and he was clearly in shock. He fell to his knees and began to crawl up the path towards the gate like a baby.

"Muh..." he stumbled. "Muh..." He hiccupped and vomited. "Muh... muh... murder!" he eventually screamed. "Summon the guards!"

"What's happened?" a man asked anxiously.

"The rector ... he's been shot ... his face ... a big hole in it..."

* * *

Anna felt uncomfortable as she saw the rigging being set up in the town square in Widnes. She didn't wish to be made a widow so soon. There was a breeze building up and a shiver went down her spine. She glanced at her husband, but he was unnervingly calm. She was uncomfortable at the way he seemed to be proceeding, as if he was on his way to the inn and not risking his life in such an alarming manner. It was shocking how he could hardly have a care in the world for her feelings. She slowly walked over, still confused at his reasoning for such an act of foolishness.

"Why are you doing this?" she whispered, her voice consumed with concern. "Why are you risking your life like this?"

"We need the money. We need it for tickets to America and for property out there; if we are going to begin a new life away from Lockwood we need money. I hate money and the vices that come with it but in this case it is a necessity."

"Does that involve you risking your life?" Anna asked, her voice trembling with fear. "Didn't you say that only a complete lunatic would try this? I'm really scared that something bad will happen to you!"

The Riding Officer draped his arms gently around his wife's beautiful neck. "I'll be fine!" he reassured her with a kind smile whilst gently rubbing the back of her head in a comforting manner.

* * *

A suitably sized crowd had gathered outside the church bell-tower. The breeze had picked up slightly. Suddenly, the Riding Officer began to feel nervous about what he was about to do. He made his way to the bell-tower, and heard the crowd begin to murmur. He took off his jacket and passed it to one of Anthony's assistants. From his pocket he took his trusty hipflask and took a nip of scotch whiskey to calm his nerves. He took a deep breath and began to climb the bell-tower steps.

From his mind he tried to banish thoughts of Anna; for the first time since he had first laid eyes upon her he tried to expel the thoughts of his beautiful wife from his mind, his inspiration, his passion, his love, his everything. If he thought too much of her, he could become nervous and fall. As he slowly made his way up the bell-tower he could hear every step echo around the spiral stone stairwell. Much as he tried, he couldn't push the comments made from outside away from his pattern of thought;

he'll bottle it, was one; *he'll fall,* was another; *he'll die,* was one particularly grim comment. Over and over he remembered Anthony's words: *secure yourself to the rope, head down, push off clearly and think of England.* He knew he had to trust Anthony. *I would have to make the flight myself if you lost your bottle,* he told the Riding Officer, *that rig is strong and steady. I wouldn't send anyone up there if I wasn't prepared to use that rig myself.*

A little while later he was a hundred feet high on the bell-tower. He could see the whole of Widnes from his point of view plus a fair amount of Lancashire. He could feel the breeze against his face as it slowly picked up and he looked down to the flagstones below. Anthony was there, standing on a box giving him an enthusiastic introduction. The cheers of the onlookers were unnerving – all he could think of was the day before at Warrington and the ghoulish comments of the minority who came to see an accident.

He recalled the first time he ever saw a flying man. It was at Gillingham, seven years before, when he was young and impressionable. A sailor from the Navy performed the stunt at the dockside. The roar of the crowd, coupled with the respect and adulation of the onlookers as he flew down the rope a victor, had made a lasting impression on him. The Riding Officer thought it wonderful. The following year, when he was visiting friends on the Suffolk coast in the town of Hastings, a young red haired boy of seventeen years signed up to be a flying man; the screams of the onlookers as he fell from the rope to his premature death still haunted the Riding Officer to this day.

When Anna heard her husband's name called out by Anthony to the crowd it became all too unbearable. She ran into the church and up to the pulpit. She got down on her knees and began to pray. She did not want to become a widow in her first week of marriage. How had Anthony allowed her husband to talk himself into doing this?

The Riding Officer could still feel the breeze against his cheek;

he closed his eyes and fell into a trance-like state. Suddenly, he was back in the village of Upperbridge, being sent to the gallows for the murder of Adam Grantham. Those who knew he was innocent were either gagged or dead unless they were in league with Lockwood, and the man himself was sitting gleefully on the back of a cart, his arm bolted uncomfortably around Anna's arm as he forced her to view the Riding Officer's execution. When the rope went around his neck he saw that the gallows were manned by a hideous purple-faced gargoyle named Hogg. The gargoyle then kicked the ladder away and the Riding Officer was suspended by his neck, much to Anna's horror and Lockwood's delight as the cart slowly drew away.

There was a white flash and suddenly the Riding Officer found himself back on the bell-tower of the church in Widnes. He recalled Warrington the previous day. As he heard Anthony call his name he raised his arms and blew the crowd kisses. His heart was pounding. He made sure that he had secured himself to the rope once he had climbed over the parapet. It felt tight as he draped his leg over and tried to balance his knee on the rope. The thick hemp felt strong but the Riding Officer could not help thinking, *I hope it takes the strain of my size, don't let me end up like that boy in Suffolk*. Feeling the sweat upon his palms he pulled his leg away and stepped back. A few members of the crowd began to jeer him. It was a mighty drop down to the ground, and he knew of mountains that were not as steep. He took a deep breath and exhaled slowly, finally allowing a thought of his beloved Anna into his mind. If he could pull this off, he and Anna would be set for their new life in America, away from Lockwood, away from Upperbridge, away from their pasts – he was doing this for *her*. He draped his leg once more and rested his knee on the rope. He wiped his hands on his trousers before he gripped the rope in his hands as he lay on top of it. *I can do this*, he thought as he peered down the rope. He kicked away with his other leg and launched himself.

Anna held her herself in prayer, hoping the Riding Officer would be safe. Her heart was beating erratically and she could barely breathe through the panic that was overwhelming her. She heard a roar from the crowd followed by an even more tremendous roar. Were they cheering because he was safe? Or were they cheering because he had fallen?

Anna stood up. She walked slowly and nervously towards the door of the church with her heart thumping with every step, and stepped out fearing for the worst. But her fear was unfounded. As she looked across the town square she was overcome with relief as she saw her husband held high above the shoulders of four men clasping a tankard of ale in his hand and a satisfied smile upon his face.

* * *

"What's that commotion?" snapped Lockwood from inside his coach, barely three hundred yards away from the church. "Have they heard the most powerful man in Britain is on their doorsteps?"

"Flying man, Johnson says," replied Hogg before he sniffed and spat on the floor.

"Has anyone seen them?" Lockwood asked. He peered out upon the masses with contempt.

"Not a peep!"

"We best head on to Liverpool," Lockwood said. He coughed and a chunk of phlegm flew out of his mouth onto the doorframe of his carriage. "These people look uncouth!"

"Are you sure that's where they'll be?" asked Hogg, his head slowly filling with unprovoked acts of violence against the citizens of Widnes.

"I've had a tip-off from our agent in this area. They were sighted in Warrington, talking of fleeing to America, so we'll target the shipping offices," Lockwood told him. "By the way, I have plans for our dear friend the Riding Officer."

* * *

"I've never been so scared in my whole life!" the Riding Officer confessed later in bed. "Even when I was hanging off that cliff back in Lincolnshire! But the money was worth it."

"How much do we have?" asked Anna. There had been plenty of people in attendance more than happy to put their money over to see the death defying stunt.

"Fifty pounds," he told her with a proud smile. "I'm putting a few sovereigns in my purse, just in case of any emergencies."

"Fifty pounds!" Anna said in amazement. "Yes, you keep some money, my love, just in case..."

"Yes," he replied. "And tomorrow we'll go to Liverpool, we'll buy tickets and relocate to America, maybe Massachusetts, maybe New York, maybe Philadelphia, who cares! Now Grantham is gone, we'll be away, away from Lincolnshire, away from the greed and corruption and most importantly – away from Lockwood."

* * *

Dick Heskett had been bugged by the trail of events that occurred a few days earlier when a man responsible for his brother's death had made his presence felt. Heskett did not trust Lockwood. He knew he was an evil man and he couldn't help but be concerned about the young couple. He tried to put it from his mind. He had to head to Clay Cross to visit a relative who was keen for him to relocate there. He was getting old now, and he considered selling his farm and maybe buying a small cottage where he could grow a few vegetables to support himself. A place like the Derbyshire town could be ideal for this.

He arrived at Clay Cross a little after ten o'clock in the

morning. It was a bustling little market town. There was always an upbeat and pro-active feeling about the town but for some reason the town felt different. The mood was sombre, and it didn't take Heskett long to learn the horrific tale of the fate of the rector. Heskett visited his relative but did not stay for very long because the sombre mood was beginning to affect him and he soon longed to get out of Clay Cross as quickly as possible.

As he exited Clay Cross, Heskett noticed a poster on the wall outside the Parish Gaol and he instantly recognised the face on the poster as the gargoyle-faced constable who was with Lockwood the previous day. It fell into place – Lockwood had ordered the killing of the rector. A man in the market had said the rector had married a young couple the day before he was murdered. A group of militiamen led by a hideous looking beast had arrived in the town. They destroyed a local inn because some of the locals who they severely wounded had acted as witnesses at the wedding, and from there they had headed to the church where they had read the parish records and as a result of the marriage one member of the group had murdered the rector in cold blood. The name *Palmer* reverberated around the town.

It was early evening when Heskett returned to his farm. He felt numb from the news of the murder of the rector. There was no honour in murder and he found it hard to justify, even that of a murderer being killed. He had witnessed the hanging of a highwayman a number of years earlier at Tyburn, and the depraved pandering of the mob cut him up inside.

Heskett felt cold. He didn't often feel it but tonight he did. He searched for a blanket but remembered he had given it to the young lady a few days previously. *It must be in the hay loft in the barn.* He took a lamp with him. He climbed the ladder, and began to gaze around at where the young couple had spent the night. Suddenly he saw something on the wall – it was a message written in paint. He slowly read it.

"Head to the Earl of Lincoln."

Heskett froze on the spot. *Who had written this?* It wasn't Lockwood. They didn't go near his barn, so it must have been the young couple. Had they warned him of the danger he might be in if Lockwood did not get his own way? Could he be in danger like the old rector at Clay Cross? Suddenly, Heskett did not feel safe. He decided the next morning he would leave, after he had sold his ducks and chickens along with his remaining produce. If he was to remain alive he had to flee.

* * *

Liverpool was bustling. Thousands of tons of cargo were arriving from all over the known world. The port reminded the Riding Officer of London. The memories it stirred were both positive and negative but they were mainly bad, and he wished to get in and out of Liverpool as quickly as he could before any of his old vices reared their ugly heads and took control of him.

To Anna it was a completely foreign environment. After all, she had grown up in a small village on the Lincolnshire coast. The bustling Lancashire port amazed her. She was used to a few greedy smugglers and small herring boats steered by local men, but Liverpool was full of ships of different sizes with cargos of goods she had never heard of from places she did not recognise manned by people from all over the world. She clutched her husband's arm as he strolled carefree through the streets of Liverpool towards the docks, his horse led by the reins.

"I don't like the look of those men!" said Anna. She was nervously aware of some dockworkers staring at her like she was a piece of steak on a butcher's slab.

"I'm a crack shot with a pistol," her husband replied. "They wouldn't stand a chance!"

Anna noticed a woman with four children, their faces smeared with dirt and clothes made from tatty old sacks. The woman's hand was outstretched as she begged for money. "That poor woman and those poor children." Her bottom lip tremored. "Could we spare some coins?"

"Watch out," her husband said. "There are a lot of professional pickpockets about, like those children." He could sense a trap. He knew about women who would beg for money whilst their children picked the pockets of a sympathetic person.

They continued on towards the shipping offices near the docks. "We'll be on a packet to America within a day," the Riding Officer reassured his wife. "We'll soon be away from our pasts."

"I don't think so!" barked a familiar voice.

The Riding Officer turned.

"Lockwood!" he snarled. He was shocked to see his nemesis in front of his naked eyes. "How did you find us?"

"My agents told me you were heading here," he told the Riding Officer, his eyes glistening with demented glee. "We heard you had a wee journey planned!"

"Yes we did, you twisted bastard," the Riding Officer shouted, angrily. "We wanted to get as far away from you as we could."

"You have something of mine, officer!" he shouted menacingly, his teeth bared, his brow furrowed deeply and his eyes wild. He balled up his right fist and pounded it into his left palm, the impact making a loud crack. "Guards! Seize my fiancée!"

"I'm his wife not your whore!" shouted Anna proudly as she tossed her locks backwards. She noticed how she made the hunchback squint with anger at her announcement.

"Get them!" Lockwood screamed. He was beginning to froth at the mouth.

In the packed streets of Liverpool six guards suddenly pounced from the side streets. Two men grabbed Anna and the other four pounced on top of the Riding Officer; dockworkers, sailors, vendors and passers-by simply stood and watched as the young couple struggled with Lockwood's men. The onlookers were unwilling to help – some were too scared, some had been paid not to help, and some simply did not care. The Riding Officer's faith in mankind had been tested once more. A blunt object struck the Riding Officer about the back of the head, his vision suddenly began to fade and he crumpled unconsciously to the floor.

Chapter Eight

Separated

As he began to come around, the Riding Officer became aware he wasn't in Liverpool anymore. In fact, he suspected that he wasn't in England. Or even on dry land. The rhythmic undulations coupled with the continuous creaking of wet rope and wooden decking led him to believe he was on a ship, and his head was throbbing from the blow he had received. He stretched his arm out and felt it bang against an iron bar. He found that he was in a small holding cell in the hold of a ship. It was a tiny area of about two by two feet. The bars were made of iron and the Riding Officer guessed he could fit his arm through the gap in the bars. There was a smell of wet sacking. It was musty and irritated his nose. He could see the outline of barrels and crates plus a rope or two against the side of the hull. Something squeaked, and he hoped it was a floorboard but he knew most likely a rodent.

"It lives!" said a crewman's voice. The voice had an accent associated with the area surrounding the River Mersey.

"Where am I?"

A candle lit up in front of him and a figure moved closer. He did not recognise the man, who was stocky, with a bald head and a moustache. "On a ship," replied the crewman. "You are on the Wandering Star, the pride of the Monarch Packet Line."

"Where are we heading?" asked the Riding Officer as he began to sit up, fighting the grogginess that seized him.

"The ship's going to America."

"Who are you?" the Riding Officer asked.

"The name's Malachi," the crewman informed him. "I'm the ship's storekeeper. I'd ask your name but it would be a bit pointless."

"Oh, wonderful!" said the Riding Officer, sarcastically, "all the way to America with a rude Liverpudlian!"

"How dare you," said Malachi. "I'm from Birkenhead!"

"Well, I've always wanted to go to America," said the Riding Officer, glumly. "Ironically, it was where I was headed when I arrived in Liverpool..."

"You're not going to America," Malachi snapped, still clearly offended by the Riding Officer's accusation of him being from Liverpool.

"You said we were going to America," the Riding Officer replied.

"No, I didn't!"

"You did!" insisted the Riding Officer. "You said the ship is going to America."

"Yes, I said the ship's going to America," Malachi clarified. "But you're not!"

The Riding Officer stood up suddenly. "What do you mean, I'm not going to America?" he said in a panic. "Where am I going?"

Malachi grinned. "Well, after we've stopped off at Cobh in Ireland," he said, "you get thrown overboard halfway across the Atlantic."

"What? I'll drown!"

"No," said Malachi, shaking his head. "The sharks will eat you before you drown."

"Sharks?" said the Riding Office, weakly, shock beginning to overcome him. For a moment the Riding Officer paused in silence, before saying, "You're lying!" Anger was beginning to take over him. "This is some cruel joke!"

"I wish it was," Malachi told him, coldly, "but you're getting chucked over the side of the boat when we reached halfway, most likely on the back of a mountainous wave."

"Says who?" demanded the Riding Officer. He thumped his hand against the bars of the cell.

"The captain!" said Malachi.

"Why does the captain want to throw me overboard?" He was beginning to shake with adrenalin. "I've done nothing to him."

"Some bloke paid him," Malachi responded.

"What *bloke*?" He already suspected he knew the truth.

"He was a horrible little hunchback who stank of fish and body odour and had pig-like eyes," Malachi said. "And a fair bit of money he gave the captain, by all accounts!"

"I should have known," seethed the Riding Officer. He slammed his hands violently against the bars of the cell, causing them to vibrate viciously. "Damn you, Lockwood! Damn you!"

* * *

The undulations of the ship increased and the Riding Officer felt nauseous. He sat bitterly in his cell kicking at the bars. The jug of water he had been given, out of pity more than necessity, had spilt and his head still throbbed – the rocking motion of the ship and his increasing seasickness did not help the matter.

Malachi was securing some barrels with some ropes. "Looks like a storm is picking up!" he said with unnerving happiness.

"Lovely!" said the Riding Officer. *Another thing to look forward to,* he thought; *my wife's been kidnapped by my mortal nemesis, I'm going for a swim with some sharks and now we have a storm on the way! What else will go wrong?* He felt that he would never see his beloved Anna once again.

"Who's this Lockwood?" Malachi asked all of a sudden.

"What?"

"You shouted *Lockwood* when I said you were going in the ocean."

"He was a dirty little fishmonger back where I lived in Lincolnshire," the Riding Officer explained, his spirit beginning to wane.

"Lincolnshire? What are you doing out this way?"

"You've already explained," the Riding Officer said.

"Apparently, I'm going for a swim."

"I meant in Liverpool," Malachi responded as he secured some barrels with a vigorously applied knot. "What were you doing in Liverpool?"

The Riding Officer's eyes grew wide with alarm. No matter how severe the weather could get there was no way those barrels would break loose. "I was eloping."

"Eloping? What led you to do that?"

"I was a riding officer in Lincolnshire," the Riding Officer began to explain.

Malachi groaned and shook his head. "Why would you want do that? My brother's lad is one out Southport way."

"Is he really?" The Riding Officer buried his face in his hands.

"Complete outcast, he is!" Malachi told him. "The pay's rubbish, no one likes him and he gets his life threatened all the time. Some git bashed him on the head the other week and robbed all his money, the lousy sod!"

The Riding Officer sighed. He folded his arms and dropped his head. "Tell me something I don't know! I was, like your nephew, an outcast. Everyone hated me; except one! The woman I love - she is the most beautiful woman on the face of the planet."

"Who is she, then?"

"Her name was Anna, and she worked at the local inn," the Riding Officer said, a smile on his face as he began to think of his beloved. "She, for some reason, loves me! We fell in love very easily."

"So why did you elope?"

"Anna's father was a prominent member of the smuggling community. He promised Lockwood Anna's hand in marriage. When she didn't want to comply, we escaped."

"And that's the reason he wants you killed?"

"Lockwood despises me," he responded. "He tried to frame me for wrecking and then for two cases of murder! He knows that once I am gone, Anna will be at his disposal."

"So where is your wife now?"

The Riding Officer sighed. He raised his head high, staring up at the decking above him. "Most likely back in Lincolnshire with Lockwood!"

* * *

The Riding Officer looked pathetic as he sat uncomfortably in his cell suffering from seasickness and pining for his lost love. Malachi poured some water into a small wooden cup and passed it to the glum prisoner.

"Here, it might help."

"Thank you," replied the Riding Officer, weakly, as he accepted the cup.

"They've taken her to Lincolnshire," announced Malachi after a pause.

"I'm sorry?"

"Your wife," Malachi said. "The sinister looking hunchback said they were taking her back to Lincolnshire."

"How do you know?"

"I witnessed it all," Malachi explained. "I was on the dockside when that Lockwood fellow cut the deal with the captain. He offered the captain a lot of money, and the captain accepted."

"Everywhere I go, there seems to be corruption!" said the Riding Officer, softly.

"They dragged your body on board while you were unconscious," Malachi continued. "Before the captain summoned me, I heard Lockwood tell some purple-faced freak that it was time to take his fiancée and head back to Lincolnshire where they would wait confirmation of your death."

"But how would they get that?"

"The captain was going to produce a fake letter which he would have sent to Lockwood when we stopped off at Cobh,"

Malachi informed him. "It was going to say that you embarked as a passenger alone and died during the crossing before we got to Ireland."

The Riding Officer grimaced. "The swine!" he growled. "I must get back to Lincolnshire now!"

"You'll be lucky," Malachi said. "Apparently, once you are announced as deceased, old piggy is going to marry your wife."

* * *

His nausea began to take hold even more strongly. The Riding Officer tried to regulate his breathing as the ship's swaying got more severe. He stared bleakly into the hold of the ship. Barrels and crates were all he could see. He rested his thumbs on his belt and sighed. *Is it going to end this way? After all I have been through with Anna?*

Suddenly he realised that the small leather purse he kept his money in was still tucked inside his belt! It contained some money he had put aside from his flying man escapades, and he had a revelation – he could escape once the vessel was docked in Ireland.

"Malachi!" called the Riding Officer as he struggled to his feet.

"What do you want?" asked the storekeeper. He stood quite calmly as if the ship wasn't rolling around at all.

"I want you to let me escape," the Riding Officer said, confidently. His fingers rested on his belt. Greed was a powerful tool, after all.

Malachi laughed. "Are you having me on?"

"I want you to let me out at Cobh."

"Why would I do that?" Malachi asked with a wry grin. "The captain would have my guts for garters if I let you go!"

"I'll make it worth your while," the Riding Officer answered, firmly.

"What do you mean?"

"Five sovereigns!" the Riding Officer told him.

Malachi stroked his chin as he pondered the Riding Officer. "Let's see your money..."

The Riding Officer reached under his belt and into the purse. He took out five gold sovereign coins. "There you go!"

Malachi frowned as he looked at two months' wages. "Deal!" he said after a minute. "Give it here!"

"No," the Riding Officer said. "Not until I'm out of here and on the deck."

* * *

Anna felt a splitting pain in her head as she regained consciousness. She heard the distinctive clip clop of horses' hooves on the turnpike. As she slowly and carefully looked around without moving her head she realised she was in a carriage.

"You're awake then, my darling?" said Lockwood in an oily voice. He smiled a smug, twisted smirk down at her.

"Where is my husband?" Anna asked. "Where is the Riding Officer?"

"The coward you refer to as your husband has headed to America ... without you!"

"My husband is not a coward," Anna replied. She swept her long darks locks away from her eyes as she sat up and faced her tormentor.

Lockwood laughed. His breath licked at her skin, and the smell of his halitosis made Anna feel like vomiting. "You don't know, do you, sweet Anna?"

"Know what?" She tried to hide the concern in her voice. *Don't let him get to you*, she told herself.

"Well, after you were inadvertently knocked unconscious by my associates, he fled like a coward. Yes – he ran off and abandoned you," Lockwood informed her, sweeping away some non-existent fluff from his jacket. "We tried to chase him but we learnt he fled England on a packet bound for America. How tragic."

"My husband would never do that," replied an incensed Anna, slapping the palm of her hand against the floor of the carriage, knowing Lockwood's account to be completely false. She could *never* believe him. "Your thugs knocked him out before me! I saw them do it!"

Lockwood's twisted smile suddenly turned to an angry frown. "Stop the coach," he bellowed. Anna was thrown forward as the coach halted abruptly. As she scrabbled to sit up once more, Lockwood said, "Now let me remind you, Miss Kitching, that you are *my* fiancée and you must do everything I say!"

"And let me remind you, Lockwood, that *I* am married to a real man," Anna replied, sitting up straight and remembering how confident her husband could be. *Oh, if she had an ounce of his courage,* she thought.

Lockwood was still frowning. "When we return to Lockwood Hall in Upperbridge, you will be spreading your legs for me, like you did as that man's whore!"

"I would sooner be my husband's whore than your wife!" Now the coach was stationary, she was able to haul herself up onto the seat opposite Lockwood. "I would sooner die than have intercourse with you!"

The hunchback growled, his eyes wild, and he slapped Anna hard across the face.

In spite of the sting, Anna was not scared. She did not try to rub the sting on her face away with her hand. She refused to show any sign of fear to Lockwood. Anna knew that despite all the accusations he threw at her husband, it was Lockwood who was the real coward. She glared back at him, defiantly.

Lockwood began breathing heavily. "Eustace!"

The door to the carriage tore open, to reveal Hogg. "Yes, Mr

Lockwood?"

"Bound and gag this whore. She has been insolent to me for the last time. Here we are trying to catch one of the most violent and dangerous men in England, and she will not assist. I fear that criminal has corrupted her mind against me, the man she loves: the man we know as Silas Palmer!"

Anna was stunned. *Where had this announcement come from?* "Who are you talking about? Who has corrupted my mind?"

"Your so-called husband, Silas Palmer, who fled like a coward," Lockwood informed her, his smile small and tight. His eyes blinked rapidly and he rubbed his hands together with pleasure. "He's a wrecker and a murderer. He killed not only Joseph Bell and our beloved Member of Parliament, Adam Grantham, but I also hear he murdered the rector in Clay Cross!"

Before Anna could reply, Hogg climbed into the carriage. He wrapped a cloth around her mouth, gagging her, then began to bind her feet and hands behind her back. Anna was disturbed by Hogg's heavy breathing as he seemed to get some perverted pleasure from tying her up. She was glad he did not discover her letter to the Earl of Lincoln and her husband's flying man money under her dress.

"Where to now, Mr Lockwood?" the gargoyle asked, his right eyelid batting away.

"To that farmer's place; that Dick Heskett," Lockwood announced. "He failed to co-operate with us the other day, so I suggest we burn down his property. It will teach him a deserved lesson and send a message to this whore about what happens when you fail to co-operate with me."

Anna said nothing. She slid from the seat to lie down on the floor of the carriage. She hoped that Heskett was safe, and that he had found the message they had left for him. She tried to regulate her breathing around the gag, but it was hard. The rotten fabric pressed hard against her mouth. She couldn't believe that Lockwood had ordered the murder of the elderly rector at Clay

Cross – most likely at the hands of Hogg. The rector had seemed a gentle soul, unlike the grim faced corrupt hypocrites Lockwood and her father would make her listen to every Sunday, where they would rant about low morals, greed and decadence. She knew they were in on the smuggling and spent most of the church collections on ladies of low moral fibre at Mrs Higgins' *guesthouse*. Anna felt for the elderly rector but he had failed to heed the message of warning they left for him on his pulpit.

* * *

The two men clung to the walls of the vessel as they ascended the ladders to the deck. "I could get shot for this!" Malachi shouted.

"You'll get your money!" the Riding Officer shouted back. "Just help me into a barrel and I'll make a break over the side."

"What I do for money," moaned Malachi.

"It is human nature!" The Riding Officer smiled to himself. He knew how money could change a situation – he had lived in Upperbridge, after all.

"How am I going to explain your disappearance?" Malachi asked, uncomfortably.

"I'm sure you'll think of something."

They forced the door open and made their way onto the deck. The wind was howling, the rain was lashing and the deck lurched up and down violently. Suddenly there was a growl of thunder followed by a flash of lightning.

"Here!" bellowed the Riding Officer.

"What?"

"Five sovereigns!"

"Thank you..." said Malachi, somewhat touched by the Riding Officer's honesty. He had half-expected the Riding Officer to disappear without paying him.

Why does this happen to me? thought the Riding Officer. *Two of the worst storms in recent years, in the space of a few months and I get caught in both of them!*

The two men stared at each other respectfully for a moment. Then they grabbed an upturned tub on the deck and began to drag it, against the wind and the rain, to the side of the ship. There was a clap of thunder and the whole ship was suddenly lit up by another flash of lightning. Eventually, the two men were able to drag the tub to the side of the ship.

"All the best, then!" shouted Malachi.

"What?" The Riding Officer was unable to hear him over the sounds of the storm.

"All the best!" Malachi shouted at the top of his voice.

"Oh right!" the Riding Officer replied, still unsure at what Malachi had said to him.

"Hey?" Malachi asked, unable himself to hear what the Riding Officer had replied.

The Riding Officer extended his hand to Malachi, and the two men shook hands. There was another flash of lightning and the sky was lit up.

"Take care!" the Riding Officer said to Malachi.

"You too!" replied Malachi.

Suddenly there was an ear-splitting crash, not of the thunder but of another ship crashing into their vessel. In the storm, a ship had been dragged off course and into the path of the Wandering Star. The ship's mast came crashing down across the deck, and the force of the collision caused the decking to buckle. The two men were thrown, sprawling, into the sea. The ice cold water felt like a thousand steel knives being rammed into the Riding Officer's torso as he hit it. A wave dragged him under momentarily and as he resurfaced he grabbed wildly. He was able to grasp hold of some debris and turn onto his back; but he couldn't see Malachi anywhere. There was a clap of thunder and the subsequent lightning lit up the sky once more. As the Riding Officer looked back at the briefly brightened sky he could see the two vessels, illuminated, beginning to sink then becoming engulfed by the waves on their way to the bottom of the waves where they would not be seen by mankind for generations to come.

The sea pounded relentlessly into the Riding Officer's face. "This is going to be a very long night!" he spluttered as he received a mouthful of seawater.

* * *

The storm engulfed the British Isles all night, tearing through the countryside. The Parish Gaol at Upperbridge was cold and wet but that was the least of Anna's worries. The wind and rain had howled all night, and she had not slept a wink.

She had only a rough idea where her man was. She hoped and prayed that he was safe and well. In the back of her mind, she knew if Lockwood had anything to do with it, he would be anything but safe and well. She wrapped her arms round her waist. Under her clothes she held her husband's letter to the Earl of Lincoln and the remaining money they had from her husband's Flying Man escapades, which was all in notes.

A single tear rolled down Anna's cheek and dropped into a pile of dust in the barren cell. She sat huddled in the corner, gently rocking back and forward, continuously whispering her husband's name. A spider crawled over her hand, but she barely noticed; a mouse squeaked, yet she did not hear. All she could think was, *Why am I here?*

At about seven o'clock the gaol house door opened, and in walked Hogg, an arrogant yet cruel smile upon his face.

"You can go now, Warne!" he told the deputy who had kept guard through the night.

"Very good, constable!" He picked up his jacket and left.

As the gaol house door closed, she heard the heavy breathing of the repellent-faced constable.

Anna stood up quickly, her eyes not leaving the form of Hogg.

She fell back against the wall as she tried to gain her balance. She covered her chest, her eyes darting left then right, longing to see something – anything – she could use as a weapon.

Nothing.

The key scraped in the lock, and Anna's heart began to pound. She felt an intense pain in her stomach as Hogg smiled menacingly. He cracked his knuckles as he entered. Anna bolted for the door but he grabbed her arm. He slammed her limb to the cell wall, pinning her so she could not move. Anna closed her eyes and swallowed as she felt his foul breath against her cheek.

"What do you want?" she whispered, her bottom lip trembling.

Hogg took his filthy hand, the nail clogged with dirt, and ran it from her chin along her neck towards her bosom. "You're a pretty girl!" he hissed.

"Stay away!" Anna said, as she looked away. She couldn't bear to see him.

"I want you to do something for me," he said, his sticky, grubby fingers stroking her face and making her skin crawl.

"No!" said Anna. She was petrified by the violent psychopath.

"I could have you killed," he whispered, "just like that half-witted simpleton, that Bell boy! He was a stupid bastard, wasn't he?"

"You killed Joseph?" The revelation shocked her and she stiffened.

"Oh yes!" hissed Hogg gleefully. She thought that he almost seemed proud at what he had done to Joseph. "Who did that retard think he was, telling me where I could and couldn't hunt, the stupid bastard! So I shot him!"

"What do you want?" she asked. Fear threatened to overwhelm her.

"You!" he hissed, clutching a handful of her skirts.

"I'm married to someone else," she told him, firmly, trying to keep her voice steady.

"I know, but your soon-to-be-late husband will be dead, just like his father!"

"What do you know about my husband's father?"

"I had him killed!" announced Hogg, a hideous smile of demented pleasure now spread across his face. "Did it with my own bare hands!"

"I thought it was Silas Palmer who killed him?"

"It was!" shouted Hogg. "Do I excite you?"

Anna turned her head from him but he grabbed her by the chin, his putrid fingernails driving into her soft skin. He wrenched her head so she had to look at him. She stared into his heartless eyes and felt the bile rise as he smiled, his teeth reminiscent of the monoliths at Stonehenge.

"Lockwood," she gasped, his grip leaving her struggling to breathe.

"I can kill him," Hogg hissed. "Like I did Grantham! Bang! Bang!"

Suddenly, the gaol house door opened again. Hogg leapt away from Anna. Anna peered over the door and history was made. For the first and only time in her life, she was actually glad to see Lockwood.

"My fiancée, Hogg," began the hunchback. "I'm ready to take her back to Lockwood Hall. I think she's learnt her lesson for her insolence last night."

A few minutes later, Anna was being forced out of the gaol house, away from one monster and into Lockwood's coach, into the company of another monster. Peering out of the window of the coach, Anna noticed the wind and rain had completely subsided. The sky was grey like the seals she had seen swimming off the coast during the summer. As the coach began to pull off in the direction of Lockwood's new residence, a ray of sunlight broke through the cloud and she could see a small section of blue sky. It was at that point that she knew her husband, the man she loved, was alive.

Chapter Nine

Welcome to Ireland

"Hey, Eamonn!" The voice had a strong Irish accent. The Riding Officer was slowly regaining consciousness. "I've found another one!"

The speaker tapped him with a boot on his head, and the Riding Officer began to cough and splutter.

"Hold on, Eamonn!" the voice continued. "Get Paddy; this one's alive!"

The Riding Officer began to clear his eyes and face. He looked up and saw a soldier towering over him. He was wrapped on to the remains of a mast and sails of the ship which had been washed ashore. The beach was barren apart from the debris of the ships that were wrecked the previous night, already washing ashore.

"Where am I?" he asked, hoarsely.

"The beach," the soldier told him.

"I can see that, but a beach where?"

"We are a couple of miles south of Cobh."

"Cobh?" said the Riding Officer, feeling somewhat bemused. "Am I in Ireland?"

"Yes, you are! Welcome to Ireland!" the soldier informed him, cheerfully. "Now we will get you in the cart and down to the infirmary to be checked out."

"Who are you?"

"The name's Christy McDermott," the soldier told him. "I'm a corporal with the army."

"I was on a ship..."

"I know," Corporal McDermott replied. "Horrible, horrible collision out there. They sent us down to find bodies."

"You mean survivors?"

The soldier nodded his head. "Those, too!" he admitted, cheerfully. "We're mostly picking up the deceased as that is all we tend to get after a vessel sinks. Especially after a terrible storm like we had last night."

"Charming," said the Riding Officer, bluntly. He slowly pulled himself into a sitting position.

"Eamonn's on his third wagonload!" chirped Corporal McDermott.

"Good for Eamonn," replied a somewhat stunned Riding Officer. He couldn't believe how the corporal made light of such a gruesome task.

"Paddy, on the other hand, hasn't even completed one!" the corporal added, grinning from ear to ear.

"Shame on Paddy!"

"Shame on Paddy indeed," answered the corporal, the sarcasm of the Riding Officer's comment going completely over his head. "If we don't get the bodies cleared up, they make a hell of a mess on the beach."

The Riding Officer simply sat and stared at the corporal. He had witnessed wrecks in the South of England and off the coast of Lincolnshire but the aftermath never failed to shock him. "Do you like your job, corporal?" he asked.

The Riding Officer sighed deeply. His muscles and joints felt sore and stiff, and the ordeal had begun to catch up with him. He looked out to sea. The sky was grey, as was the sea, and the shoreline was occasionally punctuated by a rolling wave, making it impossible for the Riding Officer to imagine how vicious the sea had been the previous night.

"Winstanley failed to negotiate worse..." he said, softly, as he rubbed some sand off his cheek.

"Let's get you on the cart!" the corporal said, helping the Riding Officer to his feet. "I didn't think we're going to have any more today; shame, that!"

"A *shame*?" asked the Riding Officer with alarm. A shame for not finding any bodies was the last thing he could think of when it came to not finding dead bodies.

"Yes," replied the corporal with a slight sigh.

The Riding Officer shuffled towards the cart, his drenched feet hurting with every step, his boots chafing and his soaked clothing clinging to his frame. "What will happen to the bodies you don't pick up?" he asked, thinking with compassion about the souls who had lost their lives.

"God knows!" said the corporal, flippantly. "Washed to shore, out to sea, picked up by a boat; who knows!"

As they approached the cart, the Riding Officer noticed two men in the back of it. "Not many survivors then, Paddy!" the corporal said to the wagon driver.

"There's a body down there, Christy," said Paddy pointing to a corpse on the deck of the cart. "He croaked about ten minutes ago."

The corporal helped the Riding Officer onto the back of the cart. He peered at the other two survivors. As he stared at them, they stared back, and he knew just how they felt – cold, wet, exhausted but relieved to have survived the whole ordeal.

"Move him over," said Paddy to the Riding Officer.

"Move who over?" he asked.

"The corpse," said Paddy with a jeer. "He won't mind!"

The Riding Officer pushed the corpse over and sat down. The corporal climbed onto the wagon, and said, "That's us, Paddy!"

"Walk on!" called the driver to the horse and the wagon pulled off.

The coast was calm. Occasionally they would pass a local who would stare at them with morbid curiosity. The wagon would pass a simple croft run by a simple crofter who again would look at the small party with sinister interest. They were the few. They were the lucky ones. They had managed to survive a horrendous disaster.

"Do you have any tobacco?" the Riding Officer asked

Corporal McDermott after a while.

"Here you go, lad," said the corporal as he reached into his pocket. He passed a pipe and a pouch of tobacco across.

"Thank you."

He puffed away on the pipe as the cart followed the winding road down to Cobh, past the staring locals, and he began to think of the one thing that truly mattered to him – Anna. Somehow he needed to get message to his beloved that he was safe, and that following his horrific journey on that ship, he intended to swear revenge on Hubert Lockwood.

* * *

At the infirmary, the Riding Officer and the other men were led from the cart. They were stripped, their clothes were burned, and they had a quick check for lice and vermin, then were sent to a bed with a nightshirt. The Riding Officer climbed into bed. They had been provided with a simple meal of stew and soda bread, and realising there was nothing he could do at the current time, he lay down, placing his purse under the pillow. He thought of his beloved Anna before drifting into a deep, troubled sleep.

As the Riding Officer slept, he dreamt of the events of the past few days – the lynching, the elopement, the marriage, Widnes as a flying man, his kidnap, and the shipwreck. Suddenly he found himself in Lincolnshire in the parish church, where he was stuck in a cage in the rafters peering down on the congregation below, watching a wedding taking place.

As the Riding Officer looked closer, he could see it was Anna, dressed in a black wedding dress symbolising her as a widow. Her expression was one of misery, and she was being forced to marry the despicable Lockwood. The Riding Officer looked down in horror. He began to shout and cry, he banged the bars on the cage, and he stamped his feet, anything he could do to let Anna know he was there. But the wedding proceeded. When the grim, grey faced rector asked if anyone knew of any reason why the wedding should not proceed, Anna began to look around the church in the vain hope that somebody would save her. The Riding Officer bellowed that she was married to him and he was alive and well. Alas, they exchanged their vows and walked down the aisle, man and wife. Anna's face was the epitome of misery. The Riding Officer screamed in horror. There was an evil laugh, the Riding Officer looked down and saw the vile face of Eustace Hogg. Hogg laughed as he pulled a lever that sent the Riding Officer's cage crashing to the floor.

The Riding Officer awoke and sat bolt upright in bed. There was sweat pouring down his forehead and he was breathing heavily. His head dropped to the pillow as he realised that it was just an extremely unpleasant nightmare. He began to regulate his breathing, and using the cuff of his nightshirt he mopped his brow. It was the middle of the night, and he gazed around the ward. There were pathetic souls lying in the beds near him; some asleep, some awake, some looked as if they were merely waiting to die.

The Riding Officer realised he had so much more to live for. For the first time in many a year he felt like there was some genuine meaning in his life. It was no longer one long game of cards he would never win or a long drawn out case of hurt and rejection. He no longer had to proceed in a job he hated – he had a reason to live. He knew he had to get word to Anna that he was safe, and he had to get back to England. If he didn't, Anna could be in the hands of the vile Hubert Lockwood. Or just as bad, or possibly even worse, the depraved grasp of Eustace Hogg.

* * *

It was mid-morning when the Riding Officer woke once more. Bird song was in the air and the sun was shining in through the windows of the infirmary. The Riding Officer found it hard to believe that only a day and half earlier he had been in the Irish Sea during the middle of a horrific storm.

The Riding Officer tried not to dwell on the storm. He had only one agenda, which was how would he get back to England? He had no clothes and the money he had would just about cover his new clothing. It was imperative that he got back to England, but how?

A man he vaguely recognised walked into the ward wearing a nightshirt. "Funny the people you bump into in these places!"

"Malachi?" said the Riding Officer in surprise. "I thought you drowned!"

"No," Malachi told him. "I was pulled out of the drink yesterday morning by some soldiers."

"Me, too."

"I'm looking forward to this," said Malachi cheerfully as he took the bed to the right of the Riding Officer.

"What? Stuck in an infirmary away from home?" The Riding Officer was completely amazed by Malachi's lackadaisical attitude. "You could have died!"

"I'll have a couple of days' rest and relaxation, some new clobber, and then back to Birkenhead," Malachi told him as he stretched out on his bed.

The Riding Officer propped himself up on his right elbow. "How are you getting home?"

"The firm's insurance company will pay for it," Malachi said with a grin. "Act of God, wasn't it?"

"Thank God for that!" exclaimed the Riding Officer with a massive sigh of relief. "A free ticket!"

Malachi laughed and grinned again. He shook his head and looked away from the Riding Officer. "Not for you," he told the Riding Officer. His voice had softened.

"What?"

"Only the passengers and crew get a free ticket."

"I was on that ship, though," the Riding Officer said angrily, incensed by another impending injustice.

"You were neither a passenger nor crew. You held neither a ticket nor held employment," Malachi advised. "At the best you were a stowaway and could find yourself at his Majesty's pleasure if you're not careful."

* * *

Four days had passed since the storm. Anna was sitting at the dinner table when she heard the news. She was devastated. It had torn through her like a sharp knife through thin paper.

"The Wandering Star was wrecked off the coast of southern Ireland during the recent storm following a collision with another vessel!" Lockwood said cruelly as he read from the newspaper. "That was the ship the man you call your husband fled on when he so cowardly abandoned you in Liverpool, and I came so heroically to your rescue!"

"Were there any survivors?" Anna asked, softly, readily expecting the answer, with tears beginning to well in her eyes as she waited for the worst scenario.

"Three men survived," Lockwood told her, his face hard and cruel, "and they were all crewmen!"

"Are you sure?" Anna asked, though she knew it was in vain hope.

"The paper says three crewmen – James Fuller, Isaac Johnson and Malachi Brooke!" Lockwood announced with glee. He thrust the paper turned to the page featuring the report in front of her. He knew his words were crippling Anna inside and soon she would be in his grasp. "No mention of *Silas Palmer*..."

"Excuse me!" said Anna. She grabbed a handkerchief and ran to the window. She turned her back to Lockwood and the hideous smile he had upon his face. She could hear him drumming his long digits on the table as he began to laugh. He was enjoying this too much, and she did not want him see her face. *Be strong,* she thought, *be just like your husband*. Anna wept.

"We might be hearing wedding bells soon!" said Lockwood, with his usual sinister smile. "The wedding of the year between the Merry Widow and the Humble Fishmonger! It is like something from the volumes of the bard, William Shakespeare himself."

The tears poured down Anna's cheeks from the eyes her husband had described so many times in their brief marriage as more beautiful than any precious stone. She peered out onto the coast. That was where she used to see him, the enigmatic yet romantic figure he cut against the rolling grey sea. The sea was flat and calm, and as Anna stared intensely upon the sea she noticed a small boat in the bay.

"Just think, my dear Anna," Lockwood started, "You'll be a *whore* no more..." He began to cackle once more. It was a familiar sound he had made the previous morning when he beat the cook for not preparing him breakfast to an acceptable standard, saying, "I don't *care* if your son is sick! I want my breakfast prepared correctly!"

Lockwood began to cram some kidneys into his gullet as he feasted on an ample breakfast. Anna could hear every mouthful and he mushed it around in his mouth as he chewed with his mouth open. Anna shuddered. Every morning her cruel captor would indulge in a gluttonous meal whilst she would be forced to dine on a small bowl of porridge. It was disgusting stuff that she had been forced to eat for years by her father, now it was the degrading Lockwood who made her suffer at meal times.

Anna was now stuck at Lockwood (formerly Grantham) Hall with the despicable Lockwood. If she had tried to escape Lockwood's lair Anna knew that she would be captured before she had left the grounds of the estate and would most likely be beaten. She was slapped regularly should she dare mention her husband; effectively she was a prisoner in all but name. Anna heard the door to the dining room open and an individual entered with a slow heavy tread.

"Mr Kitching is here to see you, Mr Lockwood," said the skeletal butler in a cold, expressionless voice.

"Excellent, Sykes! The latest contraband is here!"

All alone, she gazed out to the coast, looking through the haze to the small vessel in the bay. She thought of her husband mounted on top of his trusty mare. She thought him both powerless yet heroic as he undertook a job he hated. Anna smiled as she recalled the night he became the most popular man in the village when he tried to save the vessel that Lockwood and his cohorts had managed to wreck in such a cowardly manner, and she recalled him in the inn as he stood up to Lockwood and his bully mentality. Her tears began to subside. Anna knew that despite Lockwood's comments, her husband had not abandoned her, he wasn't a coward, he was not dead and, most importantly, he would be back to rescue her from Lockwood. And he certainly was not Silas Palmer!

Anna stood back from the window. She raised her head high and proud as she thought of the Riding Officer, who was certainly ten times the man Lockwood would ever be, to say the least. With a confident smile she knew that she would be happy to call the Riding Officer her husband. Suddenly she realised that there were no guards outside the house, and there were hardly any male staff present. She noticed through the window that Sykes and Lockwood were walking up the path to meet her father. She realised that there were only female staff present and she was the only non-employee in the house.

She quickly moved upstairs to her chamber, where she began to search for the letter her husband had provided for her to show to the Earl of Lincoln. She also collected the money her husband had earned as a flying man in Widnes. Just as she located it she saw Lockwood's entourage return to the hall; her escape was foiled but, very importantly, the first part of a plan was forming in her mind.

* * *

The four days following the shipwreck had been difficult for the Riding Officer. For those four days, hardly a minute had passed without him thinking of Anna. He knew she had now fallen back into the hands of the despicable Lockwood and his psychopathic henchman Hogg, and it was now essential that he returned to England and head back to Upperbridge to liberate her. The Riding Officer struggled to cope with the irony of the situation. A week earlier he had vowed he would never go back to Upperbridge but now he was being forced to return. The Riding Officer had bought some clothing from a tailor who had visited the infirmary; a pair of britches, a shirt and an overcoat plus a new pair of boots. He moved into a low-priced inn and slowly plotted his plan to return to England and have his one true love back in his arms. He knew he needed a pistol, a flask, a change of clothes and a boat ticket to England.

After checking the prices back to England he found the cheapest journey would be to Bristol. But he barely had half the money. There was one course of action he could take. He could rob a bank or become a highwayman but, no, not him. He was a man of honour now; he no longer gambled or fought duels, and the only honest course of action for the Riding Officer to do was get a job.

But how could he get a job? He knew no one. On the whole of the Emerald Isle he knew one person – Malachi – and even then he would be heading back to Birkenhead where he would be assigned to another vessel which would most likely sink.

Peering out of the room in the inn he had a revelation – he did know someone else. He had a name he could possibly go to who might be able to help him. As he gazed out onto the busy high street he saw a column of soldiers march past. The Riding Officer grabbed his overcoat and made his way to the door.

In a little over half an hour later, he found himself at the army barracks. He made his way up to the sentry.

"What can I do for you?" the sentry asked.

"I want to see Corporal McDermott," the Riding Officer replied in his calm, confident voice.

"He's off duty downtown," the sentry told him. "Try the Ship Tavern, full of cheap whores and no fixed stake card games; it's where all the soldiers go when they are off duty!"

* * *

A depressing hovel with a low ceiling were the terms the Riding Officer felt adequately described the Ship Tavern. When he entered, he ordered a pint of stout and observed the clientele. The sentry had been correct: it was full of cheap whores – cheap, unattractive whores. He knew their type. They were wretched women who were either widowed or their husbands were bedridden or possibly in gaol. They would ply their trade around the low-key inns, taverns and gin shops of London, offering a bang for the price of a measure of gin and no refunds if they gave you a dose of venereal disease.

When a pretty unpleasant specimen sauntered up to him and smiled, he simply said he was married and the woman smiled back with her mouth open displaying her rotten teeth and her foul-smelling breath. An overweight woman with no attractive qualities forced herself against him and again he said no. He had learned many years before the mistake of a liaison with women like this. When he was a younger man, the Riding Officer had made such an error; it left a man dead following a duel and the Riding Officer gained an unpleasant rash. It was the type of incident he had dared not tell his wife about. He gazed away from the whores and located the corporal, who was failing to impress a woman of very loose moral virtues.

The Riding Officer walked over and sat down next to him, saying, "Remember me?"

The corporal looked at him with a distant expression. "No..." he replied in a confused tone.

"You do," the Riding Officer informed him. "You stood on my head on the beach four days ago."

"That was you?" said the corporal with surprise. "I didn't recognise you stood up."

"Yes, and I need your help."

"What kind of help?" The corporal seemed suspicious of him.

The Riding Officer placed his elbows on the table with his hands raised. He locked his fingers together and rested his chin upon them. "I need a job."

"I can't do that! I'm a soldier," said the corporal, nervously, having jumped to the wrong conclusion.

"I mean employment," the Riding Officer confirmed. "Money for labour."

"Did you?"

"Yes. What did you think I meant?"

"I thought you wanted me to do something to you of a sexual nature," the corporal replied uncomfortably, the pitch of his voice having risen significantly.

"I don't," said the Riding Officer, clearly insulted. "Who did you think I was?"

"Well, there was a politician from Lincolnshire who tried that once in here," the corporal confirmed with an uncomfortable shrug of his shoulders. "He was not a nice man; he had a chap with no chin with him."

"I'm a married man," the Riding Officer explained. "I certainly don't want to do that with you."

"Oh!" said McDermott with relief. "I can get you a job as a civilian at the barracks."

"Good, good!" said the Riding Officer. "Now, I need another favour."

Corporal McDermott began to look uncomfortable again. "And what's that, then?" he asked tentatively, the pitch of his voice raising a few octaves.

"It's all right," the Riding Officer said with sarcastic reassurance. "I'm not making a pass at you."

"Oh, thank God for that," said the corporal with more relief.

"That politician has really affected you," said the Riding Officer in amazement.

"I looked at him and smiled politely then he tried to force me into a stable," the corporal recalled, rolling his eyes in disgust. "I nearly crapped my pants."

"What was his name?"

"Adam something..."

"Sounds like a familiar person," whispered the Riding Officer under his breath, knowing full well who the corporal was talking about. The late Member of Parliament for Upperbridge seemed to get about. *This is ridiculous!* the Riding Officer thought, *Grantham here in Ireland? Making a pass at this man I am talking to?*

"What's this favour you're wanting, then?" asked the corporal before he took a mouthful of stout.

"I need you to write me a letter."

The corporal laughed. "Don't tell me you're some big idiot who can't read or write?"

The Riding Officer recoiled in his chair, and he folded his arms across his chest. "I'll ignore that comment!"

"You are, you big idiot!" The Corporal gave the Riding Officer a friendly pat on the shoulder. "And you English call we Irish *thick*."

The Riding Officer stared at him with a look of discontent. "No," he said coldly. "I have had several volumes of poetry published and my work can be found in the British Library."

"Then why do you want me to write it?" asked the confused corporal, as he scratched his head. "Do you think I'm an idiot? Do you think I need to be watched over like some little boy at school?" He lifted his hands up and around his chest and moved back in his seat.

The Riding Officer sighed. "Will you calm down?" he told the flustered corporal. "Now, it's a long story..."

The Riding Officer proceeded to tell Corporal McDermott the events that led to him being in Ireland, concluding with, "...so as you can see, I can't risk my handwriting being recognised!"

* * *

It was a cold sharp morning as the Riding Officer made his way down to the dock.

"Which is the ship to Liverpool?" he asked a grizzled looking stevedore.

"That's the one!" grunted the stevedore.

The Riding Officer strutted over to the ship. He saw Malachi heading up the gangplank. "How do, Malachi!" he said to the Birkenhead native.

"Come to see me off?" asked Malachi with a smirk.

"I have, actually."

"Oh!" said Malachi taken aback by the Riding Officer's confession. "Why are you doing that?"

"I need a favour," said the Riding Officer. "I need a letter delivering to Lincolnshire."

"Lincolnshire? You want me to go to Lincolnshire?" said Malachi with a stunned expression on his face. "What's in it for me?" he asked, human nature beginning to take hold.

"Two sovereigns."

"Two sovereigns?" said Malachi, somewhat insulted by the Riding Officer's offer.

"And this!" said the Riding Officer, presenting him with a second letter. "It's a letter of recommendation to the Earl of Lincoln – you'll never have to work at sea again."

Malachi looked at the letter. "Deal!" said Malachi, offering a handshake.

The Riding Officer shook Malachi's hand. "Here's the letter," the Riding Officer informed him, passing it over with two sovereigns. "There's directions how to get there and a ruse to deliver the letter. It is of paramount importance that this letter gets to my wife."

Chapter Ten

Malachi's Little Journey

Malachi couldn't remember having walked so far in his whole life. He was a native of Birkenhead, the son of a shipwright. He was a man who had spent his whole life at sea. After over a week of travelling he was about two miles from his intended destination and was thoroughly exhausted. He sat down on a rock by the side of the road to remove a stone from his shoe. *Why have I bought those shoes?* They were rubbish and the soles were far too thin. *Why am I doing this?* he thought. Here was someone he barely knew and he had agreed to traipse all the way to Lincolnshire with a letter and the promise of a new job. At least he wouldn't have to work on the ocean anymore once his journey was completed.

Malachi had been in countless storms. He had been shipwrecked four times, been on two ships that had run aground, two vessels that had capsized and had been in three collisions involving ships in addition to having been bashed across the head and all his money stolen on numerous occasions. He'd never have to fear impressment as he knew the press gangs liked to target sailors. A safe, dry job on land with a member of the nobility would do him a treat. That was if there even was a job on offer. Or if there was an Earl of Lincoln. How did he know that the Riding Officer wasn't playing him for a fool? Was the Riding Officer who he said he was? He didn't even know the man's name until he read the letter of recommendation to the Earl of Lincoln.

It was a good half an hour before Malachi moved on, still wondering why on earth he was here on a dusty road in Lincolnshire with the potential that England's most wanted man was allegedly operating in the area, as a favour to somebody he barely knew. He had left his job, travelled across the country and for what? Something, someone and somewhere that might not exist.

Eventually Malachi decided to walk on and he was relieved a few minutes later when he saw a stone road marker informing him that Upperbridge was just two miles away. He reached the outskirts of the village about an hour later. His feet were blistering and his body parched. Before going to the building known as Grantham Hall, Malachi decided to refresh with a drink at the fountain which stood opposite the inn before he went to an inn for a tankard of mild ale and a meat and potato pie.

* * *

The mild ale seemed decent enough but Malachi wasn't particularly enthusiastic about the pie, and he sat at a table in the inn with a severely uncomfortable bloated feeling about him. On top of that he was being annoyed by a group of local men who kept peering across at him as if he was some kind of circus attraction, a poor unfortunate soul who bore a deformity or had been ravaged by a cruel medical condition before being dragged around the country by some heartless showman who wished to make a quick penny at the expense of another poor soul's misfortunate or hardship. He had been told of an inn in Birkenhead where the locals would stare at strangers in an unwelcoming manner, a place in Rock Ferry by all accounts.

Heading to Grantham Hall and then onto Lincoln that evening would not be wise. Malachi was tired and he didn't fancy this area after dark, having witnessed a few of the locals. He was also taking heed of a warning in the Riding Officer's letter about a notorious criminal who could be operating in the area. He decided that he would stay the night in the inn. Malachi located the landlord, a big nervous-looking man who seemed to be far more concerned about somebody's forthcoming presence.

"A room?" he muttered to Malachi when he enquired.

"I would like a room for the night," Malachi confirmed to him.

"Fair enough," the landlord muttered. "A shilling per night!"

"That's fine by me," answered Malachi, unimpressed by the host's lack of interest in his customer.

Malachi returned to his table to finish his mild ale. As he poured himself another cup he suddenly became aware of why the landlord was so preoccupied. The door opened and a familiar pig-faced man entered the inn, accompanied by a sycophantic entourage that consisted of a revolting little man with rotten teeth, a thin dour-looking man and the hideous-looking man he had seen with Lockwood at Liverpool.

Lockwood sat back in his chair, a smile on his face, and his arms across his chest with the fingers on each hand interlocking.

"Have an ale, Mr Lockwood," said one man, pouring him a tankard of beer from a jug and offering it to him.

"Some roast beef for you, Mr Lockwood," added another man, placing a plate of food in front of him. "It's on me."

"I bought you a brandy to celebrate, Mr Lockwood," said another man, holding a goblet out for the hunchback to take.

Lockwood's head rocked as he unleashed a booming laugh and slapped his thigh with his hand.

The landlord would occasionally glance over at the entourage. He rubbed his hands together nervously and puffed his cheeks. He was a big man who could easily handle himself in a fight but he seemed very uncomfortable.

Occasionally, a raddled-looking old woman would emerge from the kitchen, her face reminding Malachi of a lump of iron ore. She would stare over in awe at Lockwood and his associates. She would fiddle with the strings on her apron and lean in their direction, almost as if she wished to be part of their group. Malachi ordered some more mild ale and sat quietly, listening to the man he was quickly learning to despise. Lockwood was holding court, boasting with the purple-faced man of their exploits, particularly of how they had finally finished off an individual who they referred to as "that damned riding officer" – so that the path was clear for the hunchback to marry a local girl named Anna, who Malachi deduced was the Riding Officer's wife.

Malachi covered his mouth with his handkerchief as he smirked. He knew the truth about "the damned riding officer" and his plans.

"He was a murderer!" said an old man with grey hair. The revolting individual stood up causing a chair to crash backwards. "He killed Grantham, that rector, and Simple Joe!"

This must be Samuel, thought Malachi, stroking his chin.

"Calm down!" said the man Malachi believed to be Hogg. He grabbed Samuel by his shirt. There was a severe frown on the purple man's face.

"That Riding Officer was a murderer!" said Samuel, shaking his fist. "I bet he was really a highwayman."

Hogg twisted tight on Samuel's shirt and drew him closer so he could stare into his face. "Calm down or *I – will – break – your – face.*"

"Gutless murderer!" said Samuel, flailing an arm. "The gutless murder of a simpleton, kind Mr Grantham and a man of God! You'd have to be a complete coward to do that!"

Hogg jammed his forehead against that of Samuel's. Malachi could see Hogg's lips moving but he could not hear what he said. He let go of Samuel who recoiled, holding his hands up as if he was mimicking surrender.

Malachi placed his right elbow on the table and used his hand to cover his eye-line. He had drunk in public houses and inns across the British Isles and America, never make eye contact with a violent thug. They are intolerant people who don't want people sticking their noses in.

His stomach rumbled as he had a sip of ale. *Damn that pie!* he thought. He had been concerned for the last part of his journey, as a notorious criminal was apparently present in the area. The last thing Malachi needed was some crook to bash him over the head and steal every penny he had. It wouldn't be the first time. It had happened countless times to Malachi.

"Well, I know I would never do that," he said to himself as he sat back in his chair, folding his arms across his chest.

"Not from around here, are you?" asked a rude voice. The tall, thin, dour man was standing by Malachi's table. His arms hung loosely by his sides, but his hands were twitching into fists.

"No, I'm from Birkenhead," Malachi responded without hesitation. *So this must be Dixon.*

"What are you laughing at?" probed Dixon, his fists now tight balls.

"I'm not laughing," Malachi said as he casually took a mouthful of mild ale.

"You were, before!" snapped the man.

"Was I?" Malachi shrugged.

"What are you doing in Upperbridge?"

"I'm passing through on business," Malachi answered, calmly.

"It better be business," Dixon told him, "because if I catch you in here again, you are a dead man!"

* * *

It was about two o'clock in the morning. Malachi lay in his bed unable to sleep. He was thoroughly exhausted following his journey and he knew he must rest up well for the next stage of the trip. There was one problem though; that meat and potato pie had not settled well at all, leaving him with terrible indigestion. A bit of peppermint oil was what would usually do the trick when he was at sea but alas he had none. What *had* that raddled woman put in that pie? He rubbed his tender stomach, hoping that whoever had eaten the food from the inn within Lockwood's party was suffering as much as he was. Before heading up to bed he had watched Lockwood's entourage fawn pathetically over the old woman who he had gathered was the cook after the hunchback had praised her cooking while leading a toast. *Food that bad,* thought Malachi, *does not need praising, it needs condemning! Preferably condemning to the nearest cesspit...*

It was no good. Malachi had to do something about the indigestion. He climbed out of bed and slipped out of the room, deciding to head downstairs to the kitchen and see if he could find something to help his stomach. He was glad he had heeded The Riding Officer's warning and avoided the fish.

As he descended the staircase, hoping that the old cook had retired for the evening, he became aware of an intense heat from the kitchen. The closer he got to the kitchen door, the more intense it became. *Was the inn on fire?* But there was no smoke. Malachi glanced at the bottom of the door and could see a bright orange glow. With great trepidation he pushed the door open.

"Fire!" shouted Malachi, frantically. "There's a fire!"

Malachi had been greeted by a shocking sight – on an old chair in front of the fire sat the burning carcass of Mrs Wood, the inn's cook.

* * *

Malachi desperately wanted to leave the inn as soon as possible the next morning. After discovering the fire, the inn had been evacuated and the local authorities called for. The constabulary had re-entered the inn to confirm the fire had burned itself out. Bizarrely, apart from some scorching on the chair and a small section of the floor by her chair, no other part of the inn had been burnt. It seemed to be a case of spontaneous human combustion. The combination of the heat in the kitchen and Mrs Wood's apparent enthusiasm for gin had led to her rundown old carcass bursting into flames. All that remained of her were a few skull fragments and a couple of charred vertebrae.

All concerned seemed to find this a satisfactory explanation. Mrs Wood was an old woman with a dependence on gin, she ate little and when she did it was usually the food she served at the inn. She would fall asleep whilst in a drunken stupor in front of the fire on a regular basis which no doubt dried out her body, and all were happy to accept this explanation of her demise with the exception of Samuel who seemed to insist it was the work of the Riding Officer and would only desist in his accusations when Lockwood barked at the revolting old man that the Riding Officer was deceased and had an airtight alibi for once before proceeding to strike the obnoxious man about the head as if he was a schoolboy. Malachi returned to his room for a few short hours of sleep, vowing to get out of Upperbridge as soon as humanly possible the following day.

* * *

As he left the inn, Malachi met the white-haired old man known as Samuel.

"Excuse me," Malachi began, "could you direct me to Grantham Hall?"

"Lockwood Hall!" snapped the old man, stamping his foot.

"I'm sorry!" said Malachi. He didn't like the old man's tone. Malachi was a seaman, and he had witnessed many a fight and brawl over very little, particularly if someone happened to look at someone else in the wrong way. He wasn't about to be intimidated by a man with three teeth in his head.

"It's Lockwood Hall!" the old man barked again.

"Could you direct me there?"

"Over there!" snapped the unpleasant man.

"Thank you," replied Malachi. He covered his face with his hand. *This man is impossible,* he thought. Then across the cobbles, a boy of barely fifteen rode past in a riding officer's uniform, his head high in the air with arrogance and a look of superiority on his face.

"He's young," said Malachi in an offhanded way.

"Scum!" screamed the old man in a shockingly aggressive manner before spitting at the horse's hooves.

* * *

Just over a fortnight had passed since Anna had been separated from her husband. How she longed to see him, his kind smile and enigmatic soul. Anna was sitting in the drawing room trying to read. Amazingly, she had found a volume of poetry by the enigmatic Peter Lloyd in Grantham's old library, and it seemed to give her hope as she longed for the word that her husband was safe. She *knew* he was safe. She read the poetry in an attempt to understand the soul of a poet; even though they were married there was still so little that she knew about him.

In the same room, the nauseating Lockwood was sitting in the company of the Justice of the Peace. They were drinking contraband sherry, and sitting where the portrait of Grantham's mother once hung. Now, in its place, hung a picture of a handsome young man in regal robes with the title plate on it is frame that read 'King Hubert I – King of Britain and Ireland'. They were laughing at the expenses of others, namely the former cook at the inn.

"I have to admit, Augustus, that I have no sympathy for that raddled old bag!" announced Lockwood, slapping his thigh.

"I consulted books on the phenomenon, Hubert, and spontaneous human combustion has the habit of striking gin-soaked old women," the Justice of the Peace replied.

Lockwood laughed, heartlessly. "She was a simple individual to amuse," he said. "All you had to do was praise her beauty and cooking, which made her putty in your hand."

The Justice of the Peace looked shocked. "The wretched woman was neither beautiful nor competent as a cook!"

Once again Lockwood let out a booming laugh. "I know that, Augustus! But she was a useful ally at times. She regularly let me know *who* was being disloyal."

Anna sat up straight, lifting her back from the chair. She rolled her shoulders and gently sat back. She could not see Lockwood's eyes but knew that following his comment and the emphasis on the word "who" that they were burning through her.

"How did you learn of the wretched woman's fate?" the Justice of the Peace asked.

"Hogg roused me," Lockwood informed him. "A traveller staying at the inn discovered the fire and raised the alarm. My ever-loyal parish constable rode here, because he was concerned it could be sabotage."

The Justice of the Peace laughed as he straightened the lapels on his jacket, stroking away a few particles of fluff as he went. "Why would anyone sabotage the inn?" he asked Lockwood in a bemused tone.

"We meet there," Lockwood explained. "There are elements sympathetic to the former interference known as the Riding Officer. That Timms family comes to mind…"

"Well, at least we know he couldn't have done it." The Justice of the Peace laughed hideously.

"On a similar note, I must commend you, Augustus," Lockwood said, tapping his pipe on the corner of the desk, letting debris fall to the floor. "The new riding officer seems ideal."

"He's perfect. Very young, very naïve. He feels that he is doing it for both King and country, so he'll be easy to wrap around my finger."

"I can't see him posing a threat to anyone." Lockwood laughed. "Very full of himself, I must say! The little upstart even tried to tell Hogg how to do his job. Might be worth warning him that dear Eustace has something of a temper."

"Very handsome, too. He looked very fetching in his uniform," said the justice. "I can see me and him having a *good* relationship."

"Is that true, Augustus?" Lockwood said, condescendingly. He twisted his unsightly features to his left hand side as he stared at the Justice of the Peace with his right eye. "Is it a case of when you say jump, he jumps; when you say bend, he bends; and when you say drop your britches, he does?"

There was a twinkle in the Justice of the Peace's eye as he smiled. His large hooked nose pointed into the air. "Let's just say he was very willing!" he told Lockwood. "I think we should make my new friend a hero for the day, dear Hubert; I know a couple of actors who have fallen on hard times. They could play a pair of ne'er do wells and my young friend could arrest them; it would be most amusing! They work the inns playing the parts of arguing fools in order to get by. They argue over the ownership of a hat in order to gain free food, drink and clothing for their silence or should they not get that, they stage a brawl so they can have a free night in the gaol and a breakfast in the morning."

Lockwood laughed cruelly. "Well, at least we don't have to worry about our new riding officer running off with a serving wench! You know, some common *whore*."

Anna turned a page and grimaced as a page of the poetry book ripped. The hideous comments unsettled her. She looked down at her right hand as it trembled, her palm swimming with sweat.

"Speaking of *whores*, Hubert," the Justice of the Peace said, "when will you be getting married?"

"Once we have confirmation that our friend the former Riding Officer is deceased," Lockwood informed him. "We can also put Grantham's murder to bed at the same time along with the identity of Silas Palmer! And I think possibly along with another that happened in London shortly before our friend moved to this community. Patricide is the most horrific of crimes, don't you think?"

The Justice of the Peace straightened his face. "I would like to know who it was who pulled the trigger that killed Adam."

"And why is that, my dear Augustus?" the hunchback inquired cautiously. He grasped the arms of his chair as he leaned back in the seat. The Justice of the Peace had been a lifelong friend of the late Adam Grantham.

"I owe him a drink!" the Justice of the Peace replied with a cruel smile. "When Adam was killed, I was able to cash in a life insurance bond from Lloyd's of London. We agreed to it as business partners and by *agreed* I found someone to forge his signature and to pretend to be him. As a result I am now considerably wealthier!"

Lockwood's laugh cut through Anna. He seemed delighted to realise the Justice of the Peace was on a similar mental wave length to himself. "I'll let our esteemed constable know."

"The constable?"

"Eustace Hogg employed the man who pulled the trigger," Lockwood explained. "A business associate of his was disguised as a riding officer, and some of the fools in the village will forever be convinced our friend did it; the perfect crime!"

The two began to laugh in sinister fashion. Anna covered her mouth then reached for a cup of water as she felt she could vomit. She emptied the cup and stared with the ferocity of a naked flame through gunpowder. She knew that with his confession in her presence that Lockwood had made another step up the ladder at Newgate Gaol. He had two left feet but she knew the Tyburn Jig was a dance that even her captor could master. The drawing room door opened slowly with a grating creak which made Anna cover her ears. Sykes, the skeletal butler, entered, his face cold and dour.

"There is a Mr Samuel here to see you, Mr Lockwood," Sykes

informed the master of the house.

"And what does he want, Sykes?"

"Mr Samuel advises there is a stranger in the village looking for Grantham Hall," Sykes said, his face like that of a stone carving with no emotion or movement attached.

Lockwood grimaced. "It's *Lockwood* Hall."

"Apparently, Mr Samuel did advise the stranger of that matter," Sykes said, his skeletal features unchanged and his voice unemotional. "Unfortunately, the man's accent was that of a Cheshire port on the Mersey River giving the effect that he has a blocked nasal passage, so he is most likely to be a thief after some of your valuables, Mr Samuel advises."

"Very well, Sykes," Lockwood replied, drumming his fingers on his thigh. "Give him some bread and cheese from the kitchen."

"Very good, sir," replied Sykes.

"And give him a bath and some of Grantham's old clothes," Lockwood said. "Samuel stinks to high heaven," he added, "I can't stand it when a person begins to neglect their personal hygiene to that level!"

Anna bit her lip and covered her mouth to stop herself from laughing at the hunchback's completely hypocritical comment.

* * *

The Justice of the Peace had not long left Lockwood Hall when the skeletal butler returned to the drawing room.

"There is a Mr Brooke from the Monarch Packet Company in Liverpool," Sykes informed those present.

"What does he want?" Lockwood asked, with a glimmer of evil in his eye, realising this was the news of the information he was awaiting.

"He wishes to speak to Miss Kitching," Sykes explained.

"Send him in!"

Malachi peered around the door, trying to assess who was in

the room. He walked in slowly, clasping a letter in his hand, his grip so tight it creased the envelope. "I wish to speak to Anna Kitching!"

"She is there," Lockwood told him, rudely, whilst his eyes glistered wickedly as he waited for the news the bearer had brought. "She is *my* fiancée and what you can say in front of her, you can say in front of me."

Malachi walked over to Anna, and he passed her the letter Corporal McDermott had written for the Riding Officer. "Miss Kitching, I've been sent by the Monarch Packet Company to regretfully inform you that your husband passed away in Cobh infirmary the day following the wreck of the Wandering Star."

Anna's heart sank, her chin began to tremble, and she could feel her soul shattering like cheap porcelain being struck with a blacksmith's hammer. "Excuse me!" she said, turning to the nearest window as the tears began to stream down her cheeks. She wished to run out of the room but she knew Lockwood would prevent her from doing so.

Lockwood clapped his hands together loudly as he began to laugh. Every sound was like a bullet being fired into Anna's soul.

"In the envelope you'll find your husband's death certificate and a letter from the head surgeon at Cobh infirmary confirming his death," Malachi advised, unnerved by the hunchback's antics.

Lockwood took a grey, stained handkerchief from his pocket as his laughter subsided. He wiped his face, sniggering with delight.

"I think I need to be excused myself!" said the twisted man. "If I laugh anymore, I'll give myself a hernia." He exited the drawing room, and his laughter could still be heard outside as it echoed down the hallway.

Anna stared bleakly out of the window. She was shocked and her heart was broken. She could never have believed that this would happen. Ever since they had exchanged vows in that small Derbyshire church, she had believed they would never be parted until they were both grey and old. She had believed so strongly that he would return to rescue her. Malachi walked over to join Anna.

"Are you still here, Mr Brooke?" a grief-stricken Anna asked through her tears, longing to be left alone so she could grieve in peace and quiet.

Malachi carefully checked no one was present, not the hunchback, nor the skeletal butler, before saying softly, "Your husband is not dead, Anna! That was a ruse he told me to use to fool Lockwood. His letter explains this further."

Anna was amazed by this sudden revelation. "He's alive?" she asked, in complete shock as she took the letter from Malachi. Her emotions had rocketed from one extreme to the other.

Malachi nodded. He reached out and, gently grabbed Anna's arm. "He's in Ireland and trying to get back to England," he explained. "Please read the letter."

* * *

As Malachi was leaving the drawing room, Lockwood began to descend the staircase into the hallway.

"Where do I know you from?" Lockwood asked, bluntly.

"I don't know..." said Malachi with great caution, hoping Lockwood would not recognise him as a mere crewman from the Wandering Star. "I was at the inn last night and I was the one who discovered the remains of the cook."

"Where are you from?" Lockwood inquired, the pitch of his voice considerably lower. "I feel I know you from elsewhere."

"Birkenhead," Malachi replied.

Lockwood peered at him. He pulled a pocketknife out of his trousers and unfolded the blade, running his thumb along it. "Are you the man I had kill young Heskett a few years ago?" he accused.

"No!" said Malachi, shocked at the allegation.

"Are you sure?"

"Yes!" replied Malachi. "I must be going. I need to get back to Liverpool."

Lockwood smiled. It was supposed to be a kind smile, but like his predecessor Grantham, Lockwood looked like he had haemorrhoids. "Quite correct! *That* man was from Leatherhead!"

Malachi smiled nervously and hurried to the main door. His shoes scuffed in the gravel as he walked hurriedly down the main drive, and once out of the gates he sprinted for what felt like a mile in the direction of Lincoln, walking until sunset and falling asleep in a ditch. He finally reached Lincoln a day and a half later.

* * *

That night, by candlelight, Anna read the letter she had received from her husband via Malachi. Even though it was in Corporal McDermott's handwriting, she felt the connection. It told her the Riding Officer was safe and well, he was living in Ireland and was trying to raise the funds to return. He advised her not to send the money to him, as Lockwood might become suspicious and rumble his plan. He had revenge to heap on Lockwood and it had to come as an extremely unpleasant shock to him.

The door to her bedroom chamber opened and Anna became aware of the foul smell that signalled the presence of Lockwood.

"Anna, my dear!" he began. He took his pocketknife out and began to bore the wall with its blade as he spoke. "I've decided that now you are a widow, we will be getting married in two weeks."

"Will we?" asked Anna, sarcastically, the contempt in her eyes burning through Lockwood.

"Oh yes!" replied Lockwood in his oily voice. "I have plans for you..."

"Such as?"

"Firstly, I simply can't wait to feel your lovely bare naked bosoms for the first time," Lockwood told her with a sinister glint in his eye, "but you'll also be the perfect whore to entertain my business contacts. Captains of industry, financial masterminds, heads of states, rich Arabians, Kings and Queens of Europe; you'll serve their sexual needs perfectly."

Anna frowned. She said nothing and simply waited for the disgusting man to leave; she told herself she would *never* be his whore and would soon be back in the arms of her husband. When Lockwood finally did leave, it was there and then that Anna began to formulate the remainder of her plan to escape the hellish life that seemed to lie ahead of her.

Chapter Eleven

An Unwanted Admirer

Nearly four weeks had passed since the storm in which the Wandering Star had been wrecked. The Riding Officer had heard no news from his beloved Anna. He kept telling himself it would be all right, it would take a while for his message to get to her in Lincolnshire, and he did advise Anna in his letter to only contact him once she was safe in Lincoln and out of the grasp of Lockwood. But in the back of his mind he could only wonder if the message had reached Anna. Had Malachi delivered it to Anna? Had Malachi been able to reach Liverpool safely, let alone reach Lincolnshire? Was Anna safe? And, indeed, was Anna even in Lincolnshire?

There wasn't much he could do. He just had to keep working away until he had the funds to return to England and await news. He had been working at the barracks as a civilian for the past two weeks. He painted, he cleaned, he fetched, he carried and did countless menial jobs to earn what he could but no matter how hard he worked he was still struggling to raise funds. He had made his own bed as this was the only way he was willing to earn the money. He decided that he would never risk his life as a flying man again and in an age when impressment was still in place he, as a strong, physically fit man, did not want to risk working on a ship.

The Riding Officer sat outside the civilian quarters smoking his pipe one evening, wondering if he would ever see his wife again. As he gazed up into the skies above Ireland he became aware of a companion. He slowly looked to his left and saw a young woman.

Her name was Kirsten and she was the sergeant's daughter. Since the arrival of the mystery man from England, she had been captivated by him. *Who was this man,* she asked herself. Kirsten approached him slowly before sitting down next to him.

"Hello," she said softly with a smile.

"Hello to you," he replied with a smile of his own.

"I've seen you around the barracks," Kirsten said to him. "I think you're very handsome."

The stranger smiled, obviously flattered. "Thank you."

"What brings you to Ireland?" she asked.

"I was shipwrecked," the Riding Officer explained. "I'm trying to earn enough money to return to England."

"Why do you want to go back to England? Do you not like Ireland?"

"Ireland is fine. I really like Ireland, the people are great," he replied, "but I need to go back to England."

"Why's that?" Kirsten probed.

"I just do."

"Tell me!" She began to play with her hair.

"I need to get back to my wife," he told her at last.

"You are married?" She sounded disappointed.

"Yes," the Riding Officer replied. He teased her, saying, "I knew you would be disappointed!"

"I'm not disappointed." She blinked slowly whilst looking into his eyes.

"You are!" He was amused at her bluster.

"How long have you been married?" Kirsten asked.

"Five weeks."

"Only five weeks?" Kirsten pulled her neckline down.

"Yes."

"Why are you here while she's in England?"

"We got separated," he advised, "and it's a long story."

"Is it?" Kirsten swept back her hair. "Tell me about it..."

"I'd rather not." The Riding Officer attempted to move away.

"Don't go." Kirsten grabbed at his arm. "Tell me about it."

"No." He smiled, politely, saying, "I don't even know your

name."

"It's Kirsten."

"*You* are Kirsten, then?" The Riding Officer stepped back.

"Yes, why ask?" She leaned forward, her bosoms heaving as she did so.

"No real reason..." The Riding Officer looked away from her. "What's your name?"

"Well, you might be surprised to know it's..."

Before the Riding Officer could answer, the figure of Christy McDermott appeared. "A game of cards in the mess," he told the Riding Officer. "Are you in?"

"No," replied the Riding Officer. "I'm going to get my head down."

* * *

The Riding Officer had begun to traipse back to his quarters when he felt a hand grab his right arm. It was a man's hand and when he looked to his right he saw Corporal McDermott bearing a serious expression on his face. During his time in Ireland he had seen the corporal as something of a jovial fool, a good-hearted individual who was not overly blessed with brains. The look on the corporal's face was extremely serious though, and it was an expression he had not seen on his Irish friend's face before.

"Stay away from her!" he warned the Riding Officer in a low voice.

"Stay away from who?"

"Stay away from Kirsten!" the corporal advised. "She's trouble."

"Why is that, Christy?"

"That girl is one of the biggest tarts in town."

"I've heard all the rumours about her. I know how to deal with girls like that and I already know a lot about them," the

Riding Officer said. "I used to live in London."

The corporal looked him in the eye, his face still deadly serious. "She's a daddy's girl."

"Which means?"

The corporal's usual smile was absent. He looked left then right checking that he could speak in confidence. "She's the apple of her father's eye," the corporal said at last, dragging his hand across his chin. "Her father is Sergeant Brady."

"And who is Sergeant Brady?"

"The bald-headed man with the ginger moustache," the corporal told him. "As far as he is concerned, his daughter is the perfect picture of purity touched by no man!"

"I gather she is anything but pure," the Riding Officer answered, recalling the earlier behaviour of the sergeant's daughter.

"Indeed!" Corporal McDermott confirmed. "She has been to bed with countless men; enough to form at least two regiments of soldiers."

"Does the sergeant not approve of this then, Christy?" the Riding Officer asked.

"He doesn't know."

"And has he ever caught anyone with her?" The Riding Officer leant back against a nearby wall. He pulled his pipe and tobacco from his pocket and began to pack the pipe.

"Not as such," the corporal said. "But he has heard the rumours and fought both duels and fistfights against those who have attempted to spoil his beloved daughter's purity."

The Riding Officer kicked away a small stone. "Likes a scrap, does he?"

"Yes, he has a tremendous temper."

"He doesn't scare me, regardless whether I touch his daughter or not," the Riding Officer stated, holding his head up.

"Just be careful," the corporal warned. "I've seen what Brady can do with both his fists and a gun."

"I'll be fine. I won't give in to temptation."

The corporal looked the Riding Officer in the eye. "Just stay away, is all I can say. There is a saying about a woman scorned."

"What about it?"

"That girl is at her most dangerous when she is rejected," he told the Riding Officer.

"What are you on about?"

"When somebody rejects her, she makes their life hell!" the corporal explained. "She'll set her father on them. There was a lad who rejected her – scorned, she told her father that he tried to rape her – the sergeant shot him dead in a duel!"

"I'll be fine..." said the Riding Officer, softly. "I can handle myself."

"Just be careful..." the corporal explained. He looked down at the ground then up at the Riding Officer. "Trust me, I know from experience."

* * *

The Riding Officer lay on his bunk puffing away on his pipe for a few hours. His head was full of thoughts – mostly of Anna, but other themes cropped up. Money and travel were two, and Kirsten's proposition was another. Should he have rejected her proposition, could he accept her proposition, would he accept her proposition, or should he listen to Christy's advice? One particular thought kept cropping up, though. The game of cards Corporal McDermott had told him about that was taking place in the mess. Many times the Riding Officer had seen hundreds of pounds won on a game of cards by professional gamblers and card sharks. He knew the men at the barracks were amateurs trying to occupy their time, and he could really make this work in his favour. If he played his cards right, he would be able to win enough to buy a pistol and return to England.

* * *

With only a couple of days till her enforced marriage to the revolting Lockwood, Anna knew she had to act fast and find a window of opportunity in order for her to escape to Lincoln where she would have safety with the Earl and Countess of Lincoln.

She already had a plan, and over the past few days she had been pulling it together. She had found some of Grantham's old clothes which could be worn, she found a small bag into which she placed the letter to the Earl of Lincoln, the letter from her husband and the money he earned from being a flying man, and in one of the rooms she found Grantham's collection of guns. Anna helped herself to a pistol and all she needed now was for her chance to open. She stashed the items into an old trunk in her chamber which could easily be accessed. It was easy to hide the items from Lockwood as he hardly went in her chamber. There was something reassuring yet still nauseating about his threat to wait until their wedding night because he was a "fine Christian citizen". He reminded her of that lie on a daily basis, in a weak attempt to look like a man of strong moral fibre.

Fate would have it that on the penultimate day before the wedding, Anna got that opportunity. She awoke to find a sea mist had rolled into land. The buzz of "Herring!" told Anna that some contraband was about to be delivered to Upperbridge and the Justice of the Peace would be occupying the time of the new riding officer. The guards who usually patrolled the manor house headed off to the coast to help with the contraband. Anna realised that apart from Sykes and a few other servants, there was no one else in the house; even those preparing for the wedding had headed for the beach. This was Anna's time and she had to make the most of it.

Anna had been sitting at the dining table as Lockwood shovelled ham and eggs into his mouth. She was unable to finish the simple fare she had in front of her. Lockwood stopped to wipe the sweat from his brow as egg dribbled from his chin onto his shirt. She turned her head so she did not have to witness this barbaric spectacle. *I do believe I have found a new form of torture,* she thought as she was forced to listen to every mouthful. Anna rolled her eyes back and covered her mouth with a napkin as she recalled him eating a bowl of soup a day earlier that left her suffering from nightmares.

There was a cry of "Herring!" and Lockwood sat bolt upright almost as if his ears pricked up. He stood up, knocking his chair over before lumbering off, egg yolk streaming down his chin, without the decency to say goodbye. Anna dropped her napkin. She stood up and slowly walked to the door. She gently opened it and peered out into the hallway. It was clear. There was not a servant in sight.

Anna hurried up the stairs, but she slipped and pitched forward, falling to the floor. She pulled herself up as her heart raced. She swept some dust off her clothing, took a deep breath, and calmly walked to her chamber. She undressed and donned her disguise, throwing her clothing into a cloth bag and placing the gun at her side in a holster. She looked at her face in a mirror. *I look too feminine,* she thought. She cut some of her hair away and fixed it to her face in the shape of a beard and moustache. *Now,* she thought.

Anna felt her heart racing. She opened the door to her chamber and crept along the corridor hoping not to make a sound or any unnecessary movements. Any moment she expected her heart to charge up her chest and out of her mouth. She headed down a staircase.

Suddenly she stopped. Ahead of her was a maid dusting, who looked across and saw her. She froze on the spot as she stared at Anna. Did she recognise her? Anna recognised the maid. Lockwood threw hot tea in the poor girl's face when she did not curtsy when she caught him wearing his ermine robes. The maid said nothing and continued to dust allowing Anna to slink down the servants' stairwell at the rear of the house.

There was a servants' exit at the rear of the building, out of sight of the public. Anna gently opened the old wooden door hoping that it did not creak. It did not but she suddenly found herself rooted to the spot. In front of her was Samuel, standing with his back to her, obviously placed there to guard the property. Or maybe it was to keep him out of the way. She held her breath and without thinking she struck the scavenger over the head. He fell to the floor unconsciously. He wasn't expecting the blow and to Anna's relief had no time to call out, plus the impact had rendered him unconscious so he could not raise an alarm.

Anna's stomach fluttered as she carefully walked across the lawn of the estate. She looked back, hoping that no one would see her from the house. As she reached the perimeter of the estate she began to sprint. *So much easier in trousers,* she thought as she made it to a low fence and vaulted over it into the village.

* * *

Anna's feet pounded along the cobbles as she ran towards the Parish Gaol. If she stood any chance of getting to Lincoln then she would need a horse and knew exactly where there was one. As she headed to the stable at the rear of the building, she paused. Anna noticed that the door to the main building was open. She crept up to the opening and peeped in. Nobody.

She slipped in, careful not to make a sound. *Incredible,* she thought, *not a person in sight.*

Walking up to the cell she noticed the forlorn figure of Gregory. He looked weak, his clothes were filthy and he struggled to stand.

"Stand back!" she said to him. "Away from the lock."

"Miss Anna?" he gasped.

Anna pulled out her pistol, stepped back and fired at the lock. The bullet exploded loudly. Her second shot broke the lock. She pulled the door open and tried to help Gregory out of the cell. He was a big man and she couldn't move him. He struggled to his feet and shuffled to the door.

"Leave me, Miss Anna," he instructed her, "Please make haste."

Anna was reluctant to leave him. "I have to get a horse. I will take you with me."

"No, I will just hinder you." He smiled. "I can go outside and buy you some time, though."

Anna ran outside and into the stable of the gaol. She smiled as she saw another hideous caricature of Lockwood etched on the wooden walls. She grabbed a saddle and bridle and as quickly as she could, she saddled her mount. Anna tried to lead her out of the stable quietly but she was rumbled.

"Oi!" There was one of Lockwood's lackeys standing in the street. "What do you think you are playing at?"

Anna said nothing. She quickly mounted and rode away, kicking the lackey as she passed.

"There's a thief!" He tried to pull himself off the floor. "Someone's stealing from Mr Lockwood!"

Suddenly, Anna was aware that half the male population of the village were after her. She glanced over her shoulder as she saw the unmistakable figure of Lockwood shaking his fist. "Who is *he*?"

Anna put her head down as the horse galloped towards the woods. The main road would not be safe so she knew this was her best option. She approached a small lane at the rear of the hall that led to the coverage of the greenery. As she neared a small hut with an open five bar gate, a gun somewhere in the village went off. A man emerged from the little hut laughing maniacally as he pulled the gate shut. Anna squeezed the horse gently with her legs and she galloped on.

She leaned forward as the gallant mare leapt the obstacle and she was sure to lean back as they grounded. "Good girl!"

She looked back and saw the manic watchman pull the gate open as two horses thundered through, hot on her trail. Anna pulled the reins gently to the left as she encouraged the horse to head through the woods. The mare complied.

Anna dodged low-hanging branches as her mount weaved through the trees and cleared fallen trunks. She cast a glance back again, and saw the two men were gaining. Her horse crashed through a river spraying water everywhere.

She ducked a low branch as her horse almost ground to a halt. "On!"

The two men were gaining as she weaved around one tree then another, fortunate to duck a branch just in time.

There was a dramatic cry as one of her pursuers hit the same branch. Anna hoped that the loud crack she heard was his neck breaking. She smiled as it looked like the second man had been held up by the incident. Anna's glee was short lived.

A giant fallen tree lay in her path. As her mount left the ground she felt her foot slip from the stirrup. When the animal returned to terra firma she was jolted from the saddle and hit the ground with force. Winded, Anna grabbed for her pistol. Her pursuer cleared the log and came to a halt.

"Well, well, well." He rubbed his hands together and dismounted. "A little dandy!"

"Well, well, well," Anna mocked, careful to shield her weapon. "A big oaf!"

The man rubbed his hands together once more. "I *hate* dandies!" He locked his fingers together and cracked them. "I am going to enjoy this!"

"And I hate oafs." Anna pulled her weapon. "I am going to enjoy this!"

She fired, hitting the brute in the arm. He clutched at his limb as he fell to the ground, the sleeve of his jacket turning a scarlet colour. Anna reloaded the gun as he lay prone on the floor. "I know you," she said as she peered down at him. "You raped a twelve year old girl behind the inn two summers ago!"

"I..." The man gasped, his hand now covered in blood as he clutched at his wound.

"I *could* leave you here to bleed to death." Anna pointed the gun towards the man. "But I am not that cruel. I'll slay you like the beast you are."

"No..." uttered the man. "Help me...!"

Anna laughed. "Go to hell!" she said. She cocked the pistol as if to fire at his head. "*Wait.* That would be too *easy!*"

Anna changed the direction of the firearm and pointing towards his groin. There was a bloodcurdling scream as the weapon discharged into his genitals. Anna calmly walked to her horse and remounted. "On!" she said, gently squeezing the horse as she trotted through the forest and towards the turnpike.

As she found her way onto the road, Anna reached for her bag of belongings. She pulled out the telescope once owned by her husband and peered back towards Upperbridge. She laughed as she noticed Lockwood's coach on its side, in a ditch. The wheel had fallen off and there were two men trying to pull her former captor from the ditch, failing to do so.

"So that's what Gregory meant about buying me some time."

* * *

A bird cried as Anna approached a country inn. She was hungry and tired. A room for the night was what she needed. There was a man sitting outside at a table with a platter in front of him. In his right hand he clasped a joint of gammon. He took a huge bite out of the meat and chewed with his mouth open as he stared at Anna.

"Poof!" he snorted, and a chunk of meat flew from his mouth.

"I'm sorry?" said Anna as she dismounted.

"You look like a poof."

"Thank you." Anna scowled. "Where is the landlord?"

"Inside." The man picked up a jug of ale with his left hand and began drinking directly from the receptacle.

As Anna walked to the door, it opened. "Roger!" called an uncouth voice. A woman exited the hostelry. She stopped and smiled at Anna, saying, "Hello, handsome."

Anna smiled, uncomfortable at her words. She backed away from the unprepossessing woman.

"That you, May?" shouted the man at the table.

"Yes, Roger dear." She smiled at Anna and winked, rubbing her tongue around her lips. Anna's jaw dropped. *She's in for a shock...*

A little while later, Anna found herself outside drinking a bitter ale and mopping up the remnants of a rabbit stew with a crust of bread. The woman known as May strutted over.

"Hello, my lovely," she said, sitting down on Anna's lap.

"Hello," said Anna, almost falling back.

"What's your name then, lovely?"

"Ann... Andrew." Anna looked uncomfortably into the wench's eyes.

"What a lovely name! I'm May." Anna cringed as the woman kissed her cheek.

"What are you doing with that poof?" Anna looked up and saw the thug who had been eating the gammon joint.

"He's not a poof! He's lovely."

"Am I?" Anna's eyes grew wide as she squirmed, trying to shift May from her aching legs.

May tried to feel for something that Anna did not have, and frowned. "What's wrong? Do you not like me?"

"I said he was a poof." Roger thumped his fist onto the table causing the platter and bitter ale to be jumped off.

"He's not a poof, he's just shy, aren't you, lovely?"

"Erm..." Anna looked away, hoping for a distraction.

Suddenly, Roger's face was an inch from her own. "You ever been with a woman?"

"Not to speak of..." said Anna.

May cooed. "Oh, here, no wonder he is shy – he's a virgin!"

Roger laughed, slapping his hands across table causing it to jolt once more. "That or he's a pansy! I bet he would prefer it if you had a dick, May!"

"Leave him alone." May looked into Anna's eyes. "Want me to make a man of you?"

Anna rolled her eyes as her jaw dropped again. "No, thank you..."

"Why *not?*" Roger was red about the face, the veins on his neck standing out. "My wife not good enough for *you* then?"

"Because I don't." Anna looked him in the eye and shoved May from her lap and she fell onto the ground.

"Here!" she shrieked, "he threw me on the floor!"

Roger grabbed at Anna, pulling her up from her seat. Anna tightened her arm and released a mighty elbow powerfully into his gut. Roger doubled over and Anna kicked him into the head, the loud crack ringing out. She noticed a flow of blood running down his head onto his cheek. She turned to May.

"Do you know what, May?" Anna folded her arms. "*If* I ever decided to sleep with a woman then she would have to be a much prettier sight than rotten old tart like you!"

* * *

Anna descended the staircase of the inn dressed as a woman the following morning. A small trap had been secured to the Riding Officer's horse, who pawed the ground with her hoof as she snorted. People could be extremely understanding once the situation was explained particularly when Anna knew that the landlord of this inn was a former resident of Upperbridge. "Any enemy of Hubert Lockwood is a friend of mine!" he had told her.

Anna patted her husband's faithful mare. "I'll arrange for the trap to be returned from Lincoln."

"Very good, miss," replied the landlord with a cheery smile.

"Well, well, look at Lady Muck," said a voice. Anna turned round to see May the trollop sitting at the table outside.

"Nice to see you upright, May." Anna threw a bag of personal items onto the back of the trap.

May screwed up her face. "How do you know who I am?"

"Everyone knows the local tart." Anna wiped some dirt from the seat of the trap. "It's rich of you to call me muck when you are the local tramp."

May looked offended. "I am no tramp."

Anna laughed. "That is like saying that Dick Turpin was not a criminal."

"If you were a man I would set my husband on you."

Anna climbed into the seat of the trap. "Where is your husband? Is he that brute who was cramming a joint of gammon down his gullet?"

"Well, he's ran away…"

Anna leant forward. "And why was that?"

"He got beaten up… by some poofter…"

Anna laughed loudly and slapped her thigh. "No, he didn't."

"He did. The filthy beast kicked my Roger in the face."

"I don't think so."

"What do you know anyway?" shouted May, spitting at Anna.

Anna smiled. "I know a lot." She gripped the reins. "I know that you made a pass at the person you were calling a poofter."

"I did not." May turned her back to Anna.

"Oh yes you did."

May turned back to face Anna. "How do you know? You weren't there."

"Oh I was," said Anna, "because it was *me* you made the pass at!"

* * *

As Anna reached the city of Lincoln she wondered if Lockwood had realised she had escaped and she had been the person they were pursuing out of Upperbridge. She knew she had to send help back to Upperbridge to free Gregory. The poor man would not last much longer unless he was saved. He could become just another victim of the Hubert Lockwood regime. The horse and trap drifted though the Bailgate area of Lincoln, where an overweight man was trying to sell less than impressive vegetables to passers-by. He gasped as he saw Anna driving the trap and ranted how it was not a woman's thing to do and how they should know their places.

"Shut up, you bloated pig," she had shouted.

The man's face went bright red as he hurled an apple which had turned brown and soft at her. "Don't speak to me like that, whore!"

Anna reached into a small bag at her side. She took out a round bullet and threw it at the vendor, and he squealed mightily as it hit and ripped his skin.

"Some fat bags of wind should know their places!" Anna laughed. *Men, will they ever learn?*

Eventually, Anna arrived at the residence of the Earl of Lincoln. It was a fine looking building, the outside walls recently painted, with the windows and their frames clean and respectable. What a change this place made from the shabby home known as Grantham and, later, Lockwood Hall. Then again, the current owner and his predecessor were not people who could be accused of being clean. The lowest point of Lockwood's month had to be his bath. Best described as a being in a petulant tantrum, he would send his lackeys to fetch water from the stream and they would return it to his home where he would sit in the far from fresh fluid in a small wooden tub with a scowl upon his face complaining of how bathing "takes away one's dignity". Incredibly, Lockwood seemed to be the only person Anna had ever met who was capable of smelling worse after a bath then he did before it.

The doorbell rang, sounding heavy and old. Anna began to worry as no one answered. She rang again, and after what felt like an age, a grey-haired butler dressed in black with great bags under his eyes answered the door.

"Yes?" he said, sounding cold and uncaring.

"I am here to see the Earl of Lincoln. My husband sent me."

The butler looked down his nose at her. "Do you have an appointment?"

"No, but I have a letter, if I could just..."

"No appointment then you cannot see his grace."

Anna sighed. "How do I get an appointment?"

"You must write a letter and mail it." His eyes blinked, and Anna felt a chill run the length of her spine. "Then we decide if you are fit to visit him."

Anna tried to remain calm. "How long will this take?"

"Around three to four weeks."

"What?"

"You will then have to wait three to four weeks and we will notify you by post. Good day." The butler attempted to shut the door.

"Don't you dare close this door on me," said Anna as she fought to keep it open.

"Please leave," he said. "Or I will get the guards."

"What's going on?" asked a familiar voice.

Anna looked up to see Malachi descending the staircase. "You're the man from the Monarch Packet Company."

"I was." Malachi reached the bottom of the staircase and tried to open the door.

"You know this person, Brooke?" The butler glared at Malachi.

"I do. This is Miss Kitching. We've been waiting for her."

"A likely story!" The butler shoved Malachi in the chest. "Some confidence trickster out to rob the Earl most likely!"

"I am Miss Kitching. I have a letter." Anna reached into her bag of belongings and passed the document over. The butler ignored it.

"Leave." He tried to close the door but Malachi prevented him. They began to argue loudly.

"What is all this noise about? My wife is trying to rest!" Malachi and the butler stopped as the Earl of Lincoln made his presence felt.

"I have a letter," said Anna, she passed it to the Earl.

The nobleman cast an eye across it and smiled warmly. "Please come in, Anna, we've been waiting for you." He turned to Malachi, saying, "Brooke, take her trap around to the stables." He turned to the butler to add, "And you, you old fool, take her belongings to the guest chamber."

* * *

The guest chamber at the residence of the Earl of Lincoln was warm and comfortable. The bed linen was fresh and the floors were clean, and Anna felt safe and secure for the first time since she had been parted from her husband. She was away from Lockwood who planned to treat her like a common whore and Hogg who attempted to force himself on her. That night Anna wrote to her husband. By the flicker of the candle she informed him that she was safe and well, she was with the Earl of Lincoln and was waiting for him. In her letter she explained how she had escaped the village in Lincoln.

She knew that the letter would be off to Ireland and soon her husband would be returning. She longed to see him once more. She had missed him dearly since they were so cruelly torn apart. Even though she had received word from him, Anna couldn't help but wonder if her husband would really be coming back.

* * *

The air was tight and the Riding Officer was unable to sleep. In his instructions to Malachi he had failed to tell Malachi to send a message back whether or not the letter had been delivered. This mistake made him worry.

He had had an interesting day. He had risen early and gone fishing off the coast where he had caught two mackerel. Whilst staring into the Irish Sea that morning as the sun reflected off its beautiful blue colour in a way that reminded him of his wife's beautiful captivating eyes he became overcome with the feeling that she was no longer in harm's way. There were times that he felt he had an almost psychic bond with his wife.

On returning to the barracks he had found Kirsten in his quarters. She made a tenuous excuse for being there before she left. For the rest of the day, whenever the Riding Officer turned around, Kirsten would be there; whatever job he was doing, she would be nearby. All day long he felt her eyes burning into him with pure lust.

He thought about that game of cards in the mess. With the air so close and his head filled with complicated thoughts, there was no wonder that he could not sleep. He kept thinking of his wife in Lincolnshire and how he longed to just simply hold her in his arms. The Riding Officer had a great knowledge of card games and he knew this could help him if he wanted to win money. But did he really want to descend into his old ways? He remembered London; he remembered his gambling addiction.

Oh, how he had wasted countless hours, evenings and pounds on cards. How he had desperately trying to chance his hand at roulette. The cock and dog fights he attended, betting despite the fact they disgusted him; the ridiculous bets he would undertake; the duels he had fought over a few words muttered in the heat of the moment. Did he really want to return to that way of life? Of course he didn't. He had been exiled to hell, a man handpicked to fail at a job he would detest by a corrupt and conniving man.

The Riding Officer began to think deeper. He had earned money on the side from his poetry and art. Why had he not used any of that to pay off Grantham? He had kept it telling himself he would keep it for food, fuel and anything he felt was truly essential. But the truth, he concluded, was Grantham was not keeping him in Lincolnshire – the only person who was keeping him in Lincolnshire was himself.

He was in Lincolnshire for reasons brought on him by himself. He had been devastated at his father's death. Earlier on that fateful day he had spoken with his father who had learnt of his son's debt with Grantham. In a brief and hostile exchange, his father told him he was in no fit situation to inherit his company. The Riding Officer didn't want to go back to London as much as he had not wanted to stay in Lincolnshire.

Being in love with Anna had made him stay. When he looked back at it, he had fallen in love with her at first sight when he saw her sitting outside the inn late one summer evening. The Riding Officer didn't know how many people there were on the face of the planet from the frozen North of America, through the jungles of the Amazon, the deserts of North Africa and Arabia to the lands of the East and the Southern Lands discovered only a couple of decades earlier by James Cook, but one thing he did know was that of all those people, Anna was the most beautiful.

For the first time the Riding Officer truly began to play back the actions of that fateful day in London in his head. The company building was being renovated and as he left angry and disgusted with himself, he recalled the stare of a builder on the scaffold. Suddenly, the Riding Officer sat bolt upright on his bunk. The builder, he recalled, was a hideous, purple faced gargoyle. Just like Eustace Hogg. Exactly like Eustace Hogg! That is where he knew him from originally!

When a Lincolnshire Member of Parliament by the name of Adam Grantham approached him, a major event was about to occur. Grantham had a business rival who he needed to be finished off. It was his son's rival, who was in debt to him, but if he was out of the way, then Grantham could take over his rival's business interest. He had a plan for the son but his rival needed removing first, so Hogg arranged for a man named Silas Palmer to do the job. Palmer, posing as a builder, had entered the building, crept into the man's office then strangled him. Grantham was able to remove the man's son via blackmail to Lincolnshire and purchase his rival's business. Palmer apparently took immense pleasure from threatening the dead man's widow; she sold off her late husband's business to Grantham very quickly whilst her son was exiled to the coast. The notoriety of Palmer would increase, leading to him being wanted in six counties for theft, assault, rape and murder.

It all began to fall into place. Grantham had sown the seeds of doubt in the Riding Officer's father's head, his father had disowned him, Hogg had killed his father, Grantham had exiled him to Lincolnshire, Grantham had brought Hogg to Lincolnshire – and Hogg was the man who killed Joe Bell. And, most likely, Hogg had murdered Grantham himself.

The Riding Officer realised he must return to Lincolnshire as soon as possible. It was ironic as he realised that if he had gone to America he might never have got to the bottom of his father's death. As far as he was concerned, Eustace Hogg must die. But there was one thing that bugged him – where did Silas Palmer fit into the whole equation?

* * *

"So what did you do as a job in England?" asked a soldier, a little while later in the mess. The soldier shuffled a deck of playing cards and began to deal them out. The Riding Officer was sitting with four other men including the corporal. They had been provided with a fine meal of fish and potatoes.

The Riding Officer reached across to a platter and picked up a last crust of bread, taking a bite. He chewed slowly and swallowed. "I was a riding officer," he informed them with a large degree of discomfort.

The soldiers groaned at the information. A soldier picked up a jug of ale and topped up his tankard before passing it to the corporal. "Why would you want to do that?" Corporal McDermott asked. "It's a terrible job to do!"

"It's a complicated story..." started the Riding Officer. He felt unable to make eye contact. He hated to talk about his former occupation. "I'm sure I've explained my past to you, Christy."

"That was the job you hated?" asked the corporal with his bottom lip drooping.

The Riding Officer rolled his eyes. "Yes..." He sighed.

"We used to have a riding officer around this area," the corporal explained. "Frank was his name."

"Was he any use?"

"Useless," replied Eamonn the Wagoner. He turned his head and spat onto the floor. "He spent most of his time falling in the sea or chasing the wrong person! He was very easily led and manipulated, hell, I can't remember him ever making an arrest."

"Did everyone hate him?" asked the Riding Officer with a slight snort.

"No, we liked Frank," the corporal replied, gazing into space. "He was useless and rather stupid but genuinely harmless. He liked to think the best of people."

"Whatever happened to Frank?" asked another soldier.

"Died of constipation!" the corporal told them. He threw his hand of cards onto the table.

"He died of constipation? How did he do that?" asked the Riding Officer, as he laid his winning hand on the table for all to see.

"He was trying to pass a motion whilst being a bit bunged up and had heart failure! Poor bastard."

"Did the authorities try to replace him?" asked the Riding Officer. He scooped up his winnings.

"No," replied the corporal. "No one wants the job – you don't want it, do you?"

"Christ, no!" exclaimed the Riding Officer. He sorted the money into piles. "Why would I want to take that job?"

"You would be the perfect man," advised a soldier who gathered up the cards to deal once more, "with the experience you've had and all that."

"Two problems," the Riding Officer said. "One is I need to get back to my wife in England, and the other is that the last job I'd ever take would be that of a much maligned riding officer –not again!"

* * *

Of the money he had won that night, the Riding Officer now had enough funds to buy himself a new pistol, a water flask and still have enough stakes for the rest of the week. His opponents were amateurs, and he decided he would milk them for the rest of the week. He wouldn't get too greedy, and if he avoided showing too much prowess then hopefully within seven days he would be on the next boat back to England. He was not a bad cards player – his fatal flaw had been not knowing when to walk away. He often ended up blowing the majority of his money.

It would not be important to let Anna know he was gambling again. Anna didn't know him when he gambled and she wouldn't have wanted to. What happened in Ireland would stay in Ireland. An interesting thought that was. He had felt Kirsten's gaze bearing into him all night; he was intrigued by the interest she had shown in him. Would she simply be something that would happen in Ireland and would stay in Ireland?

* * *

"I want a pistol that *works*," said the Riding Officer, beginning to lose his composure. The Riding Officer had spent two hours trying to find a gunsmith in Cobh and now that he had, the man in question was being uncooperative. The shop sat on a small backstreet and no matter where he asked nobody seemed to know where it was. Only by chance did he wander past.

There were rows of unloaded quality guns lining the walls. One look at the Riding Officer and the gunsmith had concluded he would want to purchase a cheap weapon. After a simple test fire the gun had fired awkwardly, burning the Riding Officer's hand.

"That's the cheapest I have now after you destroyed the other gun," said the gunsmith, rudely, pointing to the trunks packed with low quality inefficient weapons that blocked the floor. "We *might* be able to find a nice cheap weapon in here..."

"I don't want cheap. I want *efficient.*" He slapped his hand onto the counter with force. The Riding Officer saw a candle flicker in the backroom.

The gunsmith clasped his hands together. "Why didn't you say?" said the gunsmith with sudden false charm.

"That's what I have been trying to tell you!"

"Why not try this one?" said the gunsmith, handing him a gun. He had suddenly realised his customer wanted to spend money on a decent weapon.

The Riding Officer checked the barrel and the grip on the trigger. The butt felt good in his hand. "We'll give it a test shot," he said to the gunsmith. The Riding Officer looked across to the window and could see two boys peering in, obviously fascinated by the firearms.

The gunsmith led the Riding Officer to the rear of the premises, and there was a patter of feet as the two boys ran around to follow them. A gull flew over the yard and into the distance before perching on the roof of a building.

"How far away is that gull?" he asked the gunsmith.

"I would hazard a guess of about a hundred yards."

The Riding Officer smiled. He raised the gun and fired it; the gull shrieked as it tumbled to the ground. The two boys gasped in amazement and awe.

"That'll do perfectly!" he said. "I'll take it to go," he added, "no need to wrap it in a bow!"

* * *

After a few more days, the Riding Officer had enough funds for a ticket to Bristol. He had milked the soldiers and civilians in the barracks gently, not displaying too much of his prowess, setting himself a stake and a limit, knowing when to walk away – all as he had planned. If only he had done that in London. Then he thought if he had, he could have been betrothed to an awkward, melodramatic actress.

She had been the first woman he was ever intimate with. He was nineteen whilst on semester from university following his first year. He met her at a summer ball. Their eyes met across the dance floor, and they danced away all night before they retired to his residence and made love into the small hours. Their relationship was on and off for years until the Riding Officer became crippled with debt. She found herself a member of the nobility and the Riding Officer became just another memory to her.

But had he not learned to walk away from his vices, then he would never have met his beloved Anna. And had it not been for the inspiration of an amazing woman and the rolling sea off the coast of Lincolnshire, he would never had have created some of the greatest artistic work of his life.

That night he made his way back to his quarters, knowing he had finally enough money for a ticket home to England and it would only be a few days before he was finally reunited with his beloved Anna, and his torment would be over. He had sent a message to her that he would be back in England soon and they would be together again. Anna's letter to him confirming she was safe in Lincoln had arrived the day he went to buy the pistol; the relief was an enormity to him.

The Riding Officer knew he required just one more night of cards to secure some travelling funds. He was fully aware of the threat of highwaymen and other vagabonds. He knew how to look after himself, as he had dealt successfully with a few lowlifes over the years.

As he returned to his quarters, the Riding Officer noticed something was afoot. The door was not quite shut. The Riding Officer was pedantic about doors being shut so straight away he knew there was an intruder. With great trepidation he entered the quarters.

"Hello!" said a soft, lustful voice.

"Hello, Kirsten."

"I heard you're going back to England," said the sergeant's daughter with a look of lust in her eyes.

"I am," said the Riding Officer. "Why are you here?" He spoke harshly. He knew what Kirsten wanted but he was a man, and he had urges like any other.

"This could be our last chance to be together." She ran her fingers through her long blonde hair, blinking slowly and sighing deeply so her bosoms heaved. Kirsten reached down and lifted her skirts, flexing a leg in the direction of the object of her desires.

"It's not going to happen!" the Riding Officer told her, pointing a finger at the young woman.

"I love you!" Kirsten declared suddenly. She reached up and tried to pull the Riding Officer onto the bed.

"And I love my wife," replied the Riding Officer. As he pulled back he realised that he was not tempted in the slightest by his admirer. She didn't love him, and she didn't know him. "I would appreciate it if you left."

Kirsten got up from the bed. There was a spiteful look in her eyes, for she did not like being rejected. "Tell me this, Englishman," she said, scornfully, "why are you in Ireland and she's in England?"

"Fate!" replied the Riding Officer, "and fate will take me back."

"Fate brought you here to me. This was supposed to happen!" Kirsten shouted, stamping her foot and swinging her arm at him. "If you wanted to go back to England you would have gone."

"Don't tell me what I do and don't want," snapped the Riding Officer, insulted by her insinuations. "I realised something," he added, his voice softening as he spoke. "I stayed in a community I hated for three years because of my wife. I've been here in a community I've liked but ever since I've got here I've wanted to get back to her, in the community I truly hate. I love Anna and nothing will stop me from being reunited with her."

Kirsten's eyes glistened. Though scorned, she was full of fire. "There's a little saying around here," she said. "What happens in Ireland, stays in Ireland."

"You don't get it," the Riding Officer replied. "The only thing staying in Ireland is *you*."

"I'll be here. You'll be there. Your wife doesn't need to know," Kirsten hissed sensually. She reached out grabbing the Riding Officer's shirt and attempted to kiss him.

"I'll know," the Riding Officer answered, pushing the harlot away. "My wife means the world to me and I wouldn't jeopardise what I have with her for anything. Not for the Queen of Sheba and certainly not for some cheap whore like you."

* * *

The Riding Officer fell into a difficult sleep not long after he retired. Once his unwelcome guest had departed he dreamt he was trying to return to England by sea but every time the vessel he was travelling on approached the coast a great mighty hand would reach down and move the vessel miles out to sea. The closer he seemed to get to his one true love, the further he was moved away and he had to repeat the long hard slog to be by her side once more.

It was around three o'clock in the morning when the Riding Officer was awakened. The door to his quarters was almost ripped off its hinges as an irate figure entered. With a roar, the figure tore the blankets from the Riding Officer and turned him out of his bunk.

"What is going on?" protested the Riding Officer, scrambling to his feet in fury.

"You've been with my daughter!" bellowed the figure. "What have you done to her?"

By the moonlight shining in through the open door and window, the Riding Officer began to make out the stocky but powerful frame of Sergeant Brady, father of Kirsten.

"I've not been with your daughter..." the Riding Officer began.

"She came back to my home in tears, saying that you forced yourself upon her!" the sergeant raged.

The Riding Officer laughed. "Your daughter tried to force herself upon me!"

The sergeant pushed the Riding Officer. "Who do you think you are, Englishman?"

The Riding Officer grabbed the sergeant's tunic, and said calmly, "I am someone who does not like being accused of something he didn't do."

"You piece of shit!" The sergeant swung to punch the Riding Officer but the Riding Officer grabbed his arm. The two men tumbled to the floor and began to scuffle.

"What's going on here?" shouted a voice at the doorway. A group of soldiers piled into the room and split the two men apart. The Riding Officer found the room was lit up by a lamp held by Corporal McDermott.

"What in the name of God is going on here?" he asked, staring at the Riding Officer and then at Sergeant Brady.

Blood dripped from the sergeant's nose. He wiped it away as his chest heaved. "This lowlife Englishman has violated my precious daughter!"

"I've done nothing with your not-so-precious daughter."

"I demand satisfaction," the sergeant barked. "I challenge you to a duel!"

"No. Not for me!"

"Then I will gun you down, you coward!" the sergeant said as he made a grab for the Riding Officer. "You better watch your back!"

"I'm no coward..." replied the Riding Officer, narrowing his eyes to a slit as he remembered his past.

"Then duel with me or I will gun you down," the sergeant responded. "The only thing worse than an Englishman is a cowardly Englishman!"

The Riding Officer felt his fists begin to ball and his teeth clench shut. "You're on!" he hissed at last.

The sergeant smiled maliciously. "Then it will be pistols at dawn," he advised. "The only good Englishman is a dead one!"

* * *

There was a light haze as dawn began to break a few hours later over Cobh. The Riding Officer began to stride towards the agreed meeting place quickly.

"Do you think this is wise?" Corporal McDermott said as he fiddled with the buttons on his uniform.

"No, I don't," replied the Riding Officer. He began to take his pipe from his pocket.

"Then why are you doing this?" The corporal sounded almost hysterical.

"Because I know I'll win," he informed his Irish friend as he packed tobacco into his pipe.

"How do you know you will win?"

The Riding Officer stopped and smirked. "This isn't my first duel. I was once the most feared shot in the whole of London."

The corporal didn't seem to be impressed. His faced trembled as he said, "Brady is one of the finest shots in the whole of Ireland. He'll massacre you! Trust me, I know."

The Riding Officer shook his head and laughed. "I don't duel anymore."

"Which means he'll massacre you!" the corporal repeated.

"When I did duel, I was one of the finest shots in London," the Riding Officer advised the corporal, and they continued towards the chosen spot.

* * *

A little over fifteen minutes later, the Riding Officer found himself back to back with Sergeant Brady on a small beach around the back of the main headland. *A great spot for landing contraband,* the Riding Officer thought as he surveyed the lie of the land. There was debris lining the beach that had been washed ashore. He heard a seagull shriek. *A warning shot,* he thought, as he raised his pistol and fired. There was a plume of feathers as the bird dropped to the beach, flying no more. He looked over his shoulder and saw Brady staring; his eyes wide and his mouth tight, he could hear the sergeant's breath increasing rapidly. He noticed the gun shaking in Brady's hand.

The Riding Officer smiled and turned away. "I guess you've heard of me."

He laughed as he stared at the look of fear on Corporal McDermott's face.

"You will now take ten paces and then when the handkerchief drops you will turn and fire!" called the referee.

The Riding Officer took his ten paces. He was relaxed and focused unlike the sergeant who he heard stumble on the rocks. The handkerchief dropped to the floor, the Riding Officer spread low – and fired.

There was a loud explosive bang as the Riding Officer's shot hit the barrel of the sergeant's gun. The gun barrel shattered as the sergeant screamed in agony as it was forced from his hand and it dropped to the ground. His face turned bright red as he clutched his wrist and fell to his knees in agony; the bystanders, referee and his second ran to the sergeant, while the corporal ran over to the Riding Officer. "I have to check on him..."

The Riding Officer nodded. As the corporal ran to aid his senior officer, the Riding Officer dropped his pistol. He followed the corporal over towards the fallen sergeant.

"My mother was an apothecary," he said. "I can check your wrist for you, sergeant."

The Riding Officer dabbed some paste on the back of the sergeant's hand and then onto his wrist.

"It just seems like a burn and maybe a slight sprain," he advised the sergeant. "The force of the shot must have pulled it back."

"I feel like a fool!" the sergeant muttered.

The Riding Officer grinned wryly. "That's what duelling does to people," he said. "It makes fools out of people."

"That was a hell of a shot," the sergeant said. "I've never seen a shot hit a gun before."

"It's a trick I picked up in London," the Riding Officer said and smiled. "I never try to kill anyone, I just try to disarm them."

The Riding Officer began to wrap a gauze bandage around the sergeant's wrist. "How long do I need to keep this on for?" he asked the Riding Officer.

"About a week or so."

The sergeant paused and looked at the Riding Officer. "So, did you?" he asked the Riding Officer at last.

"Did I what?"

"Violate my daughter!"

The Riding Officer grinned wryly. "Do you think I would be treating your hand if I had?"

"I wouldn't think so, because once it healed, it would be heading straight for your jaw if you had!" the sergeant answered.

"Exactly," the Riding Officer replied. "From what I've heard, your daughter isn't so precious."

The sergeant sighed. "I think I'm overdue a talk with that girl."

* * *

At ten o'clock that morning, the Riding Officer headed towards the docks, with a ticket for the next ship to Bristol sitting in his pocket. The Riding Officer knew he would have some fond memories of Ireland. He had enjoyed the majority of his time on the Emerald Isle, which was surprising considering the manner he had reached Ireland – not to mention the fact that only a few hours earlier there had been a man wanting to shoot him dead.

As the Riding Officer prepared to board the ship to Bristol, he sighted the familiar figure of Christy McDermott walking towards him.

"What brings you here?" the Riding Officer asked.

"I've come to see you off." There was a smile upon his face and bounce in his walk.

"I'm glad you have," the Riding Officer told him. "You've been a good friend to me, Christy."

"And you've been a good friend to me," replied the corporal. "I just want to wish you all the best and hope you see your wife soon."

The Riding Officer nodded. "What's happened to Kirsten?"

"Her father sent her away," the corporal responded. "From what I heard, he packed her bags and sent her to the convent to let the nuns straighten her out."

"So what did you do, Christy? How did you earn the wrath of Sergeant Brady?"

The corporal placed his hands on his hips, he looked away then back at the Riding Officer again. "I was one of those fools who slept with his daughter," the corporal admitted, rubbing the tip of his nose. "And when I didn't want to go back, she told her father I had forced myself on her."

"What happened from there?" an intrigued Riding Officer inquired.

"He proceeded to knock out three of my teeth!" He grinned, showing his teeth to his friend.

"They look fine to me."

The corporal laughed. "These are dentures!" he told the Riding Officer. "They are solid walrus ivory," he added. "If I knew how much they were going to cost me, I would never have touched her!"

Chapter Twelve

The Highwayman and the Sea Serpent

Motion sickness was something the Riding Officer just could not adjust to. All the way from Ireland he had suffered, finding the best way to pass the journey was to stand on the deck watching the horizon. It might have been summer and the sea calm, but he was far too sensitive to the rocking of the ship. He stared at his second inspiration as he thought of his first. *Not long,* he thought, *and I will be back with my beloved Anna wrapped in my arms.*

In Ireland he had truly realised how strong his feelings were for his wife. There had been times in those few days of marriage after they eloped where he had wondered if he had made the correct decision; to elope with someone he didn't really know, to make a commitment with that person to spend the rest of his life with. When the local trollop made a pass at him in Cobh he knew his feelings ran deep and he cared so strongly for Anna. It was her that he loved and it confirmed to him that he had made the correct decision to elope with her.

For such a poor traveller as the Riding Officer, the journey had been rough from start to finish and there were times when the Riding Officer suspected he would be reacquainted with his previous meal. He sipped water from his flask and was relieved as the vessel drew into the Bristol Channel. A smile spread on his face when he peered over the starboard side and saw the green and pleasant land of England.

It was as he stared at the coast line of South Wales on the port side of the vessel a little while later, that he sighted the most unusual sight. At first he had thought he had seen a seal but on second glance he realised it was too big; a whale, perhaps? No, the long undulating grey shape was serpentine! A long neck with a horse-like head emerged from the sea.

"Did you see that?" shouted the Riding Officer in amazement.

"See what?" asked a female passenger.

"That, there!" said the Riding Officer, his outstretched shaking finger pointing to the unknown creature as he nearly broke into a fit of hysterics. He had never seen such a thing before; he'd never believed in something he regarded as far-fetched fantasy and to see it up close was a complete shock.

Slowly more passengers and crew congregated at the side of the ship, all in awe of the unfamiliar beast. One slightly hysterical passenger blithered that they should return below before the ship capsized. There was a buzz of conversation and speculation from the ship's patrons as to what this bizarre creature was. Something intrigued the creature about its viewers, and it continued to follow alongside the vessel in view of its new-found friends. It was equally as fascinated in its observers as they were with it. It followed the ship towards Bristol and as the sun set it swam around the vessel until it vanished as nightfall drew close. For the rest of the trip, the ship was full of a buzz about the mysterious travelling companion.

* * *

The Riding Officer spent an uncomfortable night in a dilapidated inn near the Bristol docks. The bed on which he had attempted to sleep was small, hard and uncomfortable, there was a musty smell and it sounded like an all-night orgy was going on downstairs. When he arrived at the inn, he was surprised at the amount of voluptuous women of loose moral virtues who seemed to frequent the establishment and within minutes he had been propositioned by a woman named Molly who promised to show him a good time. The Riding Officer thought it would be best to decline and proceeded to his room for a few difficult hours of sleep.

He rose early, no longer wishing to stay in the bad-smelling room. After making his way through the inn which was decorated with half-eaten food, discarded clothing, spilt ale and a couple of comatose regulars, he paid his bill and slipped off through the cool quiet streets of Bristol in the direction of Lincoln, and away from the alleged good time Molly had promised him. The sun was low and the streets were quiet. The Riding Officer knew he could cover plenty of ground much more quickly in these conditions. Shortly after leaving the inn, the Riding Officer made a personal vow to himself that he would never travel by boat again – he had realised he had no sea legs at all, and they were only fit for dry land. A little while later he took his legs and he strode into the country roads of the shire of Gloucester.

It was evening as he headed towards Cheltenham. His feet felt sore and the meal he had eaten at a country inn a few hours earlier had not settled. He had clashed with a few patrons, one of whom had recognised his name from his past in London and his queries into anyone carrying knowledge of the infamous Silas Palmer had caused further friction. As he approached a wooded area he heard a sudden cry.

"Stand and deliver! Your money or your life!"

The Riding Officer placed his hand slowly on his pistol. "I have no money!" the Riding Officer claimed, falsely.

"You must have!" said the voice. "You're my first."

Realising he was up against a novice the Riding Officer slowly turned around to face his challenger. Twenty feet behind him he saw a masked highwayman, a lad of barely nineteen. His eyes were full of fear as the gun he was carrying sat uncomfortably in his trembling hand. The Riding Officer could see the fear in his eyes at what he was doing. He was standing a distance away, his pistol looked uncomfortable in his hand and he could hear the would-be highwayman's voice trembling.

"You had better shoot me then," he said to the young highwayman.

"I have no bullets..." said the young man, sheepishly.

The Riding Officer drew his pistol. "You daft lad," he said, coldly, as he shook his head and cocked his weapon.

The would-be highwayman fumbled his pistol and it fell clumsily to the ground, lodging barrel first into the soft ground. "Are you going to shoot me?" the young man cried in terror, pulling an old handkerchief he had tied around his face as a mask away. His clothes were tattered and he had a mangy old drape around his neck to act as a cloak but it struck the Riding Officer as being more of a hindrance. It looked like a costume a child might don to play a game of make-believe.

"No," sighed the Riding Officer. "You're just a lad and clearly don't know what you're doing."

The young man thought about reaching for the pistol but realised that he would be open to a shot. "What are you going to do?" the lad asked nervously. "I've got no money so you can't rob me."

"Tell you what, lad, I'll share a meal with you," the Riding Officer told him. "That dead pheasant – we will roast it."

"What dead pheasant?" the bemused young highwayman asked.

"That one in the field," the Riding Officer said, looking the young man in the eye. "That one there," he added, pointing his pistol in the direction of a pheasant strutting around in the field.

"That pheasant isn't dead!" stated the young man.

The Riding Officer smiled, his pistol still remained pointed in the direction of the field and whilst still looking the young man in the eye he fired. "It's dead now!" he said as there was a sudden explosion of feathers, and the Riding Officer knew he had an evening meal.

* * *

A camp fire snapped, flickered and crackled away, a makeshift spit sitting over it where the pheasant had been roasted. The Riding Officer sat against an old log as he took out his pipe. He looked at the young man who was sitting on his cloak. He noticed a woodlouse scurrying across it and scooped it up and gently placed an arm's reach away so it would not get trodden on or run into the fire. The young lad reached out and grabbed the last piece of their fare. He took a mighty bite which he quickly chewed then swallowed, wiped his mouth with his sleeve and turned to the Riding Officer.

"You're all right," the young man said to the Riding Officer as he gnawed away at a piece of the roasted pheasant's leg. "You've been good to me; people usually treat me like dirt!"

"Why did you do it?" asked the Riding Officer as he packed tobacco into his pipe. "Why did you try to hold me up?"

"Don't know," the lad shrugged as he dropped his head.

"What's your name?"

"George," said the lad. "George Williamson."

"Nice to meet you, George." He shook the young man's hand.

"What about you?" George asked. "Who are you?"

"I used to be a riding officer," he began, lighting his pipe. "I was framed for a crime I didn't commit. I eloped with the world's most beautiful woman who agreed to be my wife, became a flying man in Widnes, but then my wife was kidnapped whilst I was thrown on a boat to America to be murdered. I was shipwrecked off Ireland before it was too late and I returned to England last night, and right now I'm on my way to Lincolnshire to settle some scores. Plus I watched a sea serpent off the coast of Wales last evening! It's all been like something off the pages of a Jonathan Swift novel."

There was a silence. "Why did you do it, George?" the Riding Officer repeated. "Why did you hold me up?"

George shrugged. "I guess it was because I needed money," he said, glumly. "I've never been good at reading or writing."

"So you tried to hold me up?"

"I was desperate!" George replied. He reached for some twigs nearby him and threw them onto the fire.

"You didn't know what you were doing, did you, George?" the Riding Officer probed.

George's head dropped down. "No," he answered, sadly. "I thought it would be so easy. I've heard other people talking about how easy it is to rob someone and how they had done it, like this man in an inn about a mile up the road the other day. Anyway, how did you know I was a novice?"

"First of all, you announced your presence away from me," the Riding Officer explained. "You should have crept up on me and placed your gun to the small of my back. That way, I couldn't have turned around and challenged you." The Riding Officer drew from his pipe. "Even if your gun wasn't loaded, you could have scared me. Made me throw my purse away then make me lie face down as you gathered it up."

"That makes sense!" said George, sadly. "How do you know about these things?"

"I've had a few scrapes with highwaymen," the Riding Officer said. "Vicious men who couldn't care about anyone but themselves; not like you, George, you would never have shot me."

"My gun wasn't loaded..." George admitted with a foolish grin on his face.

"You wouldn't have shot me, regardless," the Riding Officer stated.

"Why's that?"

"Your heart is not in it," deduced the Riding Officer. "You didn't want to harm anybody. So, what's the deal with you, George?"

George paused, wondering if he should tell his new friend his tale of woe. "I'm from London originally," George started eventually. "My father was a chandler in London, and I was his apprentice...until he was shot."

"Your father was shot?" asked the Riding Officer. "My father was murdered, too..."

George nodded sadly. "A man named Silas Palmer shot him. He was a really ugly man, they said he was the ugliest man in England. He was an ex-Bow Street Runner with a bald head! A horrid scar on his face, too."

The Riding Officer's eyes grew wide. *Another one?* he thought. *Why do I keep running into those who have fallen afoul of my enemies? First the farmer, then the corporal and now George!* Another piece of the puzzle had slipped into place. "Why did this Silas Palmer do that?" he asked George with intense curiosity. He began to wonder; this seemed to be too much of a coincidence.

George shrugged. "I'm not sure really. He just looked at Palmer the wrong way. This Palmer character had this pear-shaped head and when he got angry his whole head would turn purple, it looked quite funny. Palmer burst into our shop bawling and shouting at my father. Something had upset Palmer in the street and his face was purple – he looked hideous, just like a gargoyle. My father just stared at him, trying not to laugh! Then Palmer shot him in the face from about a foot away. He told me to get out of London or he would kill me. So I did!"

"How would you like to confront Palmer, George?" said the Riding Officer as he drummed his fingers against his own leg.

"Yes!" said George, a look of fire suddenly on his face. "But how would I be able to do that? I don't even know where he is!"

"Then come with me to Lincoln!" said the Riding Officer. "I might have a surprise for you. I didn't realise it but Silas Palmer had been under my nose for a considerable time..."

* * *

The road to Lincoln was long, hard and uneventful. The Riding Officer and his companion survived by shooting fowl and rabbit. Occasionally they would stop at an inn for further refreshment.

The most eventful moment of their trip was a fight between two drunks at an inn near Loughborough. The Riding Officer had been sitting with George as they drank some mild ale and ate some locally produced porkpies. Two drunks who could be best described as gentlemen of the road had been standing near the bar, sharing a jug of ale and telling a loud, somewhat theatrical, tale of their recent journeys. The Riding Officer surmised them to be actors who had fallen on hard times and were in need of a bit of attention.

They suddenly began to dispute the ownership of a well-worn hat that was sitting on the bar; it was a three-cornered, battered article full of holes and falling apart at the edges. Its use as an item of headwear was near its end but to the two gentlemen of the road it was extremely valuable, as they stated that a true gentleman would never be seen in public without a hat.

The larger man grasped the left lapel of his jacket with his left hand and jabbed the smaller man with the finger on his other hand. The smaller man recoiled with a melodramatic look of shock on his face. The larger man puffed out his chest and looked down at his smaller companion. The Riding Officer covered his mouth. He could not hear a word but he knew what was happening.

A slowly mouthed word saw the smaller man's nostrils flair and they traded insults back and forward until the smaller man pushed up on the tips of his toes and slapped the larger man.

He reeled back, covering his face. His mouth wide open, he used a rude word to describe his companion before slapping the smaller man.

"*You...*" said the smaller man, shaking his fist.

The bigger man very slowly drew back his fist, but the smaller man pounced at him, gripping his waist like a grappler. With a flurry of shouting and flailing limbs, they spilt out of the inn door and out into the street onto the ground, careful to avoid a muddy puddle.

The patrons of the inn piled out of the door, keen to watch the brawl unfold. George, too, got to his feet. He sucked in his stomach, puffed out his chest and stood tall. He began to march forward but a strong arm reached out and held him back.

"Not our place, George," said the Riding Officer, looking the young man in the eye. "Let these two queens put on their performance." Eventually the local constabulary arrived and the two men – still disputing the ownership of the item of headwear – were taken away to the Parish Gaol.

"Why did you stop me?" George later inquired.

"Quite easy," the Riding Officer said. "They were actors. They didn't draw any blood when they brawled or cause any bruises – their performances were theatrical!"

"But why did they do that?" asked a confused George.

"Once again that is easy," the Riding Officer answered. "They were short of money. The argument they began was in order to be given a free hat or a free jug of ale in order to be kept quiet. The brawl was staged in hope of pity giving them a free meal or board from someone who felt sorry for them, but when that didn't work they continued to brawl because they would get a night in the Parish Gaol – there's a grey cloud on the horizon, George, they want to be inside and not outside tonight. It's not a bad idea, I've got a few coins so we'll stay here tonight. When the rain comes, I want to be in a nice warm room and not freezing to death outside!"

* * *

On the way to Lincoln they spoke a little. The Riding Officer told George he believed he knew who Silas Palmer was. George, in return, explained to the Riding Officer that after he fled London and the wrath of Palmer, he had struggled to find work. His lack of educational skills let him down and he failed to hold down a manual job. He had moved to rural Gloucestershire and tried to work as a farm labourer which was disastrous. As a result, he had turned to crime in a desperate bid to earn money. The Riding Officer understood.

George felt himself very lucky to have fallen in with the Riding Officer. This man could easily have killed him a few days earlier on the road outside of Cheltenham but he had chosen not to. He had, instead, taken the young man under his wing and promised him a modicum of revenge on the man who had destroyed his life – Silas Palmer. He had quickly come to realise the mistake he had made attempting to hold up a man and the ramifications it could have had. The Riding Officer was stunned that fate had had him and George cross paths. Was this really a coincidence? He'd stopped at an inn the afternoon they had met. He had heard two patrons discussing the rumour that a man once known as the most feared shot in London had died. The Riding Officer took it on himself to correct them and advise that rumours of his passing were greatly exaggerated. A few hostile words saw him fire a bullet or two to prove his point, telling the awestruck patrons that his biggest regret was he never got a crack at Silas Palmer. Perhaps George had sought him out after witnessing the incident. Could he be wishing to try and even the score with the scourge known as Palmer? Following the shot at the pheasant, George was completely in awe of the Riding Officer's gunmanship. Perhaps the young man had tried to earn his respect and display to him that he was up to the task of tackling Palmer.

He was enthralled by the Riding Officer's tales. Not just the amazing journey he had made from Lincolnshire and back via Ireland but the tales he told him of when he lived in London and later Upperbridge. George had come to idolise the man who had quickly become his friend. They were on the final stretch of their journey and had stopped to camp overnight before they concluded their trip to Lincoln.

"Tell me about Widnes again," George said to the Riding

Officer as they began to bed down.

"What about Widnes?" the Riding Officer asked, tiredly. His mind was far away. He was exhausted but knew he had to push on to be alongside his beloved Anna once more.

"Tell me about when you were a flying man!" George replied, enthusiastically.

The Riding Officer sighed. He was tired and his young travelling companion had been near-enough obsessed with his recollection of his exploits in Widnes a few weeks earlier. "I slid about two hundred feet down a rope and earned a lot of money," he said to George. "I would rather you asked me about the sea serpent I saw off Wales. I enjoyed that much more."

"What was it like?" George inquired. "What was it like being a flying man?"

"There's no experience like it," the Riding Officer informed him. "It's very hard to explain it."

"How did you feel?" George asked, not aware that his friend didn't wish to talk about it.

"I have never been so scared in my life," admitted the Riding Officer. "I was petrified I would leave my wife a widow after less than a week of marriage."

George smiled. "It must have been amazing!" he chirped.

"No, George," the Riding Officer advised him. "It wasn't, it was absolutely terrifying, and I would never do it again, not even for all the money in the Bank of England."

"Where is the money you earned? How much did you get?" George continued to probe.

"My wife has it, I earned a lot of money," the Riding Officer answered in an unenthusiastic tone.

"Why's it with your wife?"

The Riding Officer let out an exhausted sigh. "George," he said, "it is late, I'm tired and tomorrow I will be reunited with my amazing wife in Lincoln. We need to rest."

The Riding Officer closed his eyes as he attempted to drift

into sleep.

"I want to be a Flying Man!" George proclaimed. "Just to earn that money for doing so little. I could be a professional, just like that Anthony bloke you were telling me about! I wouldn't have to work again."

The Riding Officer shook his head gently. "No, you don't, George," he advised the young man. "It would be more of a foolish mistake than the one made when you attempted to rob me."

"I'm going to be a Flying Man," murmured George. "I'm going to be a success."

"Well, good luck!" said the Riding Officer. "You'll need it."

He glanced across and noticed that his young companion had drifted off to sleep. The Riding Officer sighed. Tomorrow would be a long day.

* * *

The day started early and after avoiding a highwayman who they noticed prowling in the bushes ahead of them, the two men proceeded to Lincoln via a different route. The Riding Officer heard nothing all day from George except for his plans to be a Flying Man and become the foremost showman in Britain. According to George, his legend would be one that would last for centuries leading to countless books and plays being written about his life, performed on a weekly basis by a great heroic actor of the age. The Riding Officer sighed. George was not a bad lad but he had no grip on reality. Still he would rather George asked him about the sea serpent.

They passed through an area of the town known as Bailgate. It had narrow winding roads that led to the market lined by small charming little buildings, two down two up in nature. The market was bustling as traders brought commodities to be bought and sold. As they passed a large orange-bricked building people bumped into them right, left and centre.

"Now then..." started a man who had walked accidently into the Riding Officer and caused a heavy collision. He stopped before he had started and then gasped, "Palmer!"

The Riding Officer frowned. As they continued along the winding road they attempted to gain directions to the Earl of Lincoln's residence but no one seemed willing to do so. Instead they would murmur the name "Palmer" or hiss "Grantham". A rotting turnip sat at the side of a street under a Tudor building and the Riding Officer kicked the spoilt vegetable hard against the structure, leaving an unsightly stain on the white walls as it exploded on contact, spreading the remains of the brassica across the street.

The Riding Officer felt a tug on his shirt. He turned to George who was frantically pointing to a poster on the wall of an inn that sat on the corner of a road.

"What does it say?" George asked, uncomfortably embarrassed at his lack of reading skills.

"It says *Wanted for Murder - Silas Palmer, reward £50.*" The Riding Officer was kicking the remains of the turnip again.

"But that's not Palmer in the picture," said George, "that's you!"

"I know!" the Riding Officer released a mighty punch against the wall. Pain flared in his knuckles, returning him to his senses. He stared again at the portrait. "Grantham had that 'commissioned' months ago. Made me sit for an artist whilst the contraband was landed. I could never fully work out why... until now!"

Lockwood must have found this! he thought, slamming the palm of his hand against the wall. *This was his plan all along when he tried to frame me.*

"Who's Grantham?" asked George. "Did you kill him or something?"

"Nothing to worry about, lad!" the Riding Officer replied,

reclaiming his nonchalant air. "Our friend Silas Palmer knows more about that."

He did not care what the people said; he just longed to see his beloved Anna.

* * *

Placing herself strategically near a window, Anna watched, hoping to see her husband approach. She wanted to be the first person to greet him. For two days she sat, hoping and waiting, longing for the man she loved to return to her life. She knew he was coming – she had the same feeling she had had the day the Wandering Star was wrecked and she had stared at the clouds over Upperbridge on the way back from the Parish Gaol.

A little after five o'clock in the afternoon, Anna saw a familiar figure, albeit a worn and wearily looking one, walking towards the Earl of Lincoln's residence. Anna quickly got to her feet. Her heart was pounding as she ran downstairs to the door. She burst along the corridor and ran as fast she could into the street. She flung her arms wide open and ran straight into the arms of the Riding Officer.

He embraced her tightly, never wishing to let go; they held each other for what seemed like an eternity, two star-crossed lovers finally reunited after being so cruelly torn apart.

"I never want to be separated from you again!" the Riding Officer uttered to Anna, overcome with emotion.

"And I never want to be separated from you, too!" Anna whispered to the Riding Officer, tears of happiness beginning to well in her eyes. They stared deep into each other's eyes and kissed. It was a kiss that could and would have sparked a thousand love affairs. So perfect, so beautiful.

* * *

"I have hoped for this for so long," the Riding Officer said softly to his wife, as they lay cuddled up together in bed that evening.

"So have I!" Anna replied, her head resting on his chest as he stroked her long black hair. She smiled. For the first time in as long as she could remember Anna felt safe. She no longer felt a need to look over her shoulder. She could hear her husband's calm heart, and she smiled again as it soothed her.

"You are still as beautiful as the first time I ever saw you," the Riding Officer said to Anna as he gazed into her captivating, inspiring eyes and recalled that evening outside the inn. Anna smiled, the picture of enchanting beauty. They kissed passionately.

"I should have listened to you. We should have come here from the start!" said the Riding Officer, reflectively. "We would have been safe, secure and away from our foes in Upperbridge! I should never have dragged you across England. I would have solved my father's murder much more quickly."

"No, you thought we were doing the right thing," Anna replied. "Besides we had some fortune on the way," she added. "I still have our money from your flying man escapades – we can still go to America! I know for a fact Lockwood hates sailing and will not get on a boat for any reason, as he has a fear of the sea."

The Riding Officer shuddered and rolled his eyes. "Unfortunately, the only way to get to America is sailing and I've had enough of boats to last a lifetime," he told her. "I would like to move away from Upperbridge though. Maybe somewhere tranquil and inspiring. What about Cornwall?"

"What about Cornwall?"

"Let's go and live there!" the Riding Officer suggested. "You and me. Let's make a fresh start."

"All right," replied Anna. "We'll go tomorrow!"

The Riding Officer shook his head. "No," he replied to Anna, softly. "I have to head back to the village and back to Upperbridge."

"Why do you want to go back there?" asked Anna. "We'll

never need to head back to that god-awful place again."

"I need to close a turbulent chapter of my life. I don't want to spend my whole life looking over my shoulder," he explained. "I'm going to speak to the Earl tomorrow. It's time to finish off both Hubert Lockwood and Eustace Hogg once and for all!"

* * *

The tea tasted good as the Riding Officer sipped it out of a bone china cup. He was sitting with the Earl of Lincoln in his drawing room. Sun shone through the spacious windows into the room. The walls were covered in a pleasant cream wallpaper augmented by portraits of the noble's illustrious family. The furniture was new and comfortable unlike the creaking wrecks that had sat in the drawing room of Grantham Hall.

"As I say," the Riding Officer told the Earl, "I need the regiment to follow later."

"Very good," said the Earl, lifting his cup from its saucer, "settle what you need to first. If we can apprehend these men then it is all the better, especially as you believe one of them happens to be one of the country's most notorious outlaws."

"And you say you have witnesses who will testify?" asked the Riding Officer.

The noble took a sip of his tea. "Absolutely! We caught a poacher by the name of Binns a fortnight ago. As part of a plea bargain he's ready to tell all about Lockwood and his empire."

"Well, if the man who is known as Eustace Hogg is who I think he is, we might be able to solve a few crimes," the Riding Officer explained.

"Indeed," replied the Earl, sadly. "When news broke of Grantham's murder, it was your name that was accused. I tried to send some men up to Upperbridge to help you but you had left. I was able to bail Mr Gregory from the Parish Gaol though, and he is also willing to testify against Lockwood."

"I'm glad to see Gregory was freed, captured twice. Anna told me she would never have made it without his help by sabotaging Lockwood's coach. There is one other thing. I am *still* the one accused of Grantham's murder. It's not necessarily under my own name but those posters have a certain *likeness*. Should we successfully apprehend Hogg then maybe I will be able to clear my own name. I heard the murmuring yesterday as we walked through the streets of Lincoln."

"Not anymore. I'll have them pulled down as the reward was claimed," the Earl advised. He took another sip of tea. "You've been declared legally dead as a stowaway on the Wandering Star; I wouldn't be surprised if that loathsome Justice of the Peace, Augustus Stewart, has pocketed the reward money."

"I did notice the reward was high," said the Riding Officer.

"I've been watching Stewart and I believe he is embezzling money," the Earl declared.

"It might be worth paying Mr Stewart a visit in the morning," the Riding Officer informed the Earl. "Anna told me that he has a more than a professional relationship with his new riding officer! In all honesty, I have nothing against people who lead that lifestyle, but Augustus Stewart is such a vile man. I want to press as many charges as possible against my foes so I need as many allies as possible; I want them to get exactly what they deserve."

"Agreed," the Earl said. "There are three men willing to accompany you to Upperbridge and I believe you know them all."

"Do I? Who are they?"

"They are my footman, Brooke," the Earl said. "Mr Gregory, the blacksmith, and a farmer by the name of Heskett who heeded your warning and came here."

"I would like to take the young lad George along with me, too," said the Riding Officer. "He could be useful. He can identify a certain individual for me."

"Agreed," said the Earl. "We'll provide a cart and some provisions."

"There's a family I can reply on for support in the village," the Riding Officer told the Earl. "The Timms family."

"Very good!"

"Was Anna all right when she arrived?" the Riding Officer inquired.

"She was tired but otherwise fine. I was somewhat sceptical at first, but once I saw your letter and Brooke was able to verify who she was, I was able to believe her."

"It was good of you to look after her," replied the Riding Officer. "She means the world to me."

"Your father told me to look after you," the Earl informed him. "And that must include your wife!"

"You knew my father?" The Riding Officer was stunned by the announcement.

"We were dear friends," the Earl explained. "We met many years earlier when your father rescued me from drowning and I was forever in his debt. We lost touch before you were born." The Earl picked up his cup and saucer and took a sip of tea. "He turned to me for help not long before his death. Last time I spoke to him, he was very concerned about you. You seemed distant and troubled and he was being bothered by Grantham about a merger, too!"

"I didn't know that!" exclaimed the Riding Officer, as another piece of the jigsaw fitted into place.

"I spent a considerable time trying to trace you as you vanished from the face of the planet. It was when I had a chance meeting with a publisher that I learnt exactly who you were and where you were. I was on my way there to prise you out of Grantham's grasp when that storm struck."

The Riding Officer nodded. "I appreciate that … father was always guilty of caring too much."

"And he was being hassled by England's most wanted man,

Silas Palmer, too, by all accounts," the Earl informed him, placing his cup and saucer back onto the table. "His name was floating about following your father's death. He had been seen around the Houses of Parliament with Grantham, up to and after your father's death."

"It all makes perfect sense..." said the Riding Officer.

"I heard you had left London to be a riding officer," the Earl continued, "and when Timms came to me with your tale of heroics on the night of the wrecking, I knew it was you."

The Riding Officer's gaze became distant as piece by piece it all began to come together.

Chapter Thirteen

Return to Upperbridge

It was a mission of all or nothing for the Riding Officer and his cohorts. He would either return to Anna with their nemeses vanquished or he would return to her in a box whilst Anna would be continually watching over her shoulder for a despicable hunchback and a hideous gargoyle.

The five men were sombre. They spoke little in the cart as they headed to the village of Upperbridge. They took turns to control the cart, ate a little, drank only water, slept and played cards. Only George really spoke. He told of his plans to become a flying man and how he would become the most famous man in England. How the Riding Officer wished for once George had asked about the sea serpent. He would have liked to have talked about the sea serpent. For the first time in a long, long time he had something to talk about that did not revolve around Grantham, Lockwood, his former job or smuggling. He had been completely fascinated by the incident because it was so different but alas when he did mention it no one seemed interested.

One of the few events of the trip that the Riding Officer remembered was the face of a man of whom they passed on the way to Upperbridge. The man looked familiar – too familiar, his face overcome by shock, as if he had seen a ghost. He bolted to a nearby horse and mounted it, riding the beast off into the distance in the direction of Upperbridge. The Riding Officer smirked when he realised where he remembered the man from and he wouldn't have been surprised by where the man was heading.

The Riding Officer said least of all. He serviced his pistol, ate a little roast beef and mostly he thought of Anna. *This is it!* he said to himself as he gazed at the small portrait of Anna he had sketched of her the night they had been reunited. *Revenge!*

Mr Timms almost fainted when he saw the Riding Officer at the farmhouse door. "I thought you were dead, lad!" he exclaimed.

"No," replied the Riding Officer. "Just having a break. Reports of my demise were wildly inaccurate."

It did not take much persuading to encourage Mr Timms and his sons to join them on their mission. But there was one final act for the Riding Officer to undertake before he would stare fate in the eyes once more.

* * *

The landlord of the inn could hardly believe his eyes and ears at times. He shook his head as he listened to Lockwood and Hogg toast and boast to their latest felony in the middle of a public place.

"Good work, Hogg!" Lockwood laughed, cruelly, slapping the palm of his hand on the table. "Poor old Kitching, though!"

"Poor indeed!" cackled the gargoyle.

"But he was of no use to us any longer," Lockwood explained. "His daughter, my fiancée, has fled, so he was completely useless! That damned Riding Officer may be deceased but the corruption of my fiancée's mind against me by him has been done. Whatever I do, I must get her back."

"But where is she?" Hogg muttered. "I went to that Timms family and tore the place apart looking for her, but she wasn't there. She has no other allies; that Gregory fellow was bailed out by the Earl of Lincoln and all charges were dropped."

"I don't care, I must have her back," the hunchback barked. "She is vital to my plans for my empire. I need her to strengthen my power, in the hope that one day I will become the ruler of Britain! I could become King, Eustace, parliament, the lords, the throne ... it all seems so correct to me ... it's my destiny ... I will be the most powerful man in the world..."

Hogg frowned as he heard Lockwood's delusional statement but the frown soon turned to a smile. He knew if he stuck close to Lockwood, becoming his most loyal and trusted aide, he would be able to eventually overthrow Lockwood and the fortune, the empire and the throne would all be his – *rather a nice bit of irony*. But there was something he needed to let Lockwood know, something that had been niggling away at him all day.

"I heard a rumour today..." he began.

"What was that?" the hunchback asked, rudely. He drew out his pocket knife.

"A certain person was sighted, heading this way!"

"Who is that and who told you?" Lockwood slowly unfolded the blade.

"Someone who is supposed to be dead," Hogg said. "An agent told me this afternoon."

"Which agent?" asked Lockwood, driving the point of knife into the table.

"It was Perkins, the actor who fell on lean times!"

Lockwood laughed nervously before slapping his hand across Hogg's shoulder. "He's pulling your leg, Eustace, he's an actor! That person we are referring to *is* dead and I heard it confirmed."

"What if it's not true?" Hogg probed as he scratched his chin. "Perkins was white as a ghost, and he told me all about when he lied for you in court when they tried those smugglers."

"Which smugglers are you talking about?" Lockwood asked, looking at his long claw like fingers with their yellow nails clogged in dirt. "Smugglers around here are like cows in a pasture!"

"They were the ones with the tea. Our men said it was The Grand Old Duke of York case," Hogg said. "They said they were fishermen. Perkins said he was a humble fisherman and claimed the Riding Officer was unfairly harassing him. The men got off the charge."

"You were not in Upperbridge at the time of that trial, Eustace," Lockwood informed Hogg. "You have absolutely no idea what you are drivelling on about."

"But Perkins told me all about it," Hogg replied. "Perkins was convinced it was him."

"There's more chance of Kitching – who we buried this very morning – of being alive than that simple, foolish Riding Officer!" Lockwood lifted his arms and rested them behind his head, lifted a leg and draped it across a stool. Hogg stared at him. He didn't like this nonchalant attitude. He picked up his tankard and emptied it.

"More ale, landlord," he snapped to the publican. "*Now*."

The landlord was sitting at a nearby table. Curiosity had finally got the better of him and he was reading a volume of the works of Peter Lloyd. A rumour had begun to spread around Britain that the man himself had recently perished. Lockwood caught sight of his reading material which had recently become exceedingly sparse within the parish, and quickly pulled his thin leg from the stool and stood up. He strutted over to the landlord and ripped the volume from his hands.

"I do *not* think that is appropriate reading material, you useless man!" Lockwood flung the book onto the fire. "It is far more use *there*! Just be careful, you know what happens to useless people. You only have to look at Kitching."

The landlord felt nauseous and it was not just because of Lockwood's lack of personal hygiene. Jeremiah Kitching had been found dead. Suicide was the verdict but murder was the truth. Two witnesses claimed to have seen him commit suicide and Lockwood had said he was depressed after his daughter left the village in strange circumstances. The villagers were terrified of Lockwood, and they knew they could never be safe with him about. A by-election was looming and Lockwood was set to stand as a candidate. The eligible voters had already agreed to vote for him; some willing with the right incentive, and the rest too scared not to. Once in the Houses of Parliament he would have the whole community at his peril and would be able to expand his evil empire across rural Lincolnshire.

As the landlord shuddered at the thought of Lockwood standing for parliament, there was an explosive crash. The door to the inn was kicked off its hinges, spreading splinters and dust. Whoever had kicked the door open began to whistle the tune to *"The Grand Old Duke of York"* very slowly and methodically. As the dust settled, both Lockwood and Hogg sat aghast, mouths wide open as a living ghost, a man supposedly dead, strode into the inn with a hint of arrogance. His face was cold, focused and fearless.

He ground his balled right hand into the palm of his left. "Hello, Mr Lockwood," said the Riding Officer.

"I thought you were dead!" stammered Lockwood in a state of growing shock.

"Not pleased to see me, Hubert?" asked the Riding Officer, as he grabbed a tankard of ale from under Lockwood's nose, downing the remainder of the drink. The drops that were left he threw over his foe's repugnant face. "You made a fatal flaw in your plan to kill me off. It was the captain of the ship who would send confirmation of my death and not a surgeon at an infirmary!"

His expression changed as he saw genuine fear in his nemesis's face. Then he turned to Hogg, saying, "Eustace Hogg! Or should I say – Silas Palmer!"

Hogg drove his hands onto the table as he lifted himself up, the tips of his fingers turning white. He swept some empty tankards from the table. "You're under arrest!" he said, spit flying from his foul mouth.

"Arrest for what?"

"Murder!" barked the gargoyle.

"For whose murder, Palmer?" the Riding Officer asked, an incensed look in his eye. "Would that be Joseph Bell, whom you shot, or Adam Grantham, whom you also shot?"

The violent constable froze, his right eye beginning to twitch. He opened his mouth to speak but nothing came out. As his right eye continued to twitch he turned his head in order to look at the Riding Officer with his left eye. "Don't know what you mean…" he said eventually as he rolled the heel of his boot on the floor. "Why are you calling me Palmer?"

"You know exactly why I am calling you Palmer, you hideous man! *You* are Silas Palmer!" shouted the Riding Officer as he stood tall with his hands on his hips. "*You* are the most wanted man in England! You've brought disrespect on me and my family! I demand satisfaction. I challenge you to a duel!"

* * *

Lockwood was a crimson colour as he stomped through the grass, his boots becoming soaked by the dew. He glared at the constable as they made their way to the green. Lockwood scowled. He shook his head and picked up a stone which he hurled at a cow in a field. It missed its target. He swung a kick at a plant, knocking its head clean off. "This is not a wise move, Eustace!" he told Hogg. "Not only are you about to take on this man – a fine shot I must add – in a duel but we have to *walk* here!"

"You should have let me finish him off last night," growled Hogg, picking up a stick and snapping it across his cocked knee.

"Do you mean in the night with that mob of misfits against just you and me?" Lockwood asked Hogg, sarcastically. "That is how the likes of him win, when it is an uneven playing field – unlike a sportsman such as me! We will take care of him after the duel. Provided you can incapacitate him this time."

"I didn't recognise any of his lot," said Dixon, who was trailing at the back.

"I only knew that fat oaf Gregory and the Timms family,"

answered Johnson. He was carrying a chair for the benefit of Lockwood.

"The old white-haired man was a farmer between here and Clay Cross," Lockwood informed them. "There was a man who claimed to be from the Monarch Packet Company with them. His name was Brooke or something, from Leatherhead or somewhere as uniquely pointless."

"Who was that young lad, Mr Lockwood?" Dixon asked.

"I have no idea, Dixon."

"He had a run-in with Silas a couple of years back," Hogg suddenly announced. "Silas shot his father."

"Are you sure it was Silas?" Lockwood asked with a twisted curiosity.

"What are trying to say?" barked Hogg, aggressively.

Lockwood stopped suddenly causing his associates to crash into him, knocking him to the floor. Johnson dropped the chair as he ran to help Lockwood up. He pushed Johnson away.

"Are you sure it was Silas?" he asked, his chest bumping against that of Hogg's.

"What are you trying to say?" asked Hogg, raising a fist. Johnson, who was standing nearest to him, dragged his hand across his face and backed away.

Lockwood looked at his hands which were covered in mud from where he had fallen. "Our friend the Riding Officer made a pretty strong allegation against you, Eustace," he said. "Or should that be Silas?"

Hogg laughed, startling a crow in a nearby hedge that flew up and away. "I'm not Palmer!" he told everyone whilst staring into space. "If anyone is Palmer it's him, the Riding Officer!"

Lockwood grabbed hold of Edwards and proceeded to wipe his dirty hands on the man's jacket. "How can you prove that?"

"Once I've shot him and he can't run away, we'll stitch him up," Hogg said. "We'll tell everyone that he is Palmer! We get our agents to provide evidence, blackmail that young lad to say it was him, and job done! Anybody want to argue about that?" Hogg cracked the knuckles of his right hand into his left palm.

Lockwood stroked his gruesome chin, "I like the way you think, Eustace."

Dixon made his way through from the back. "What is his name?" he asked. "The Riding Officer, what actually is his name?"

Hogg reached out with a gigantic hand and grabbed Dixon by his shirt. "All you need to know is that it's Silas Palmer," he said as he lifted the Herring Caller off the ground, "and he's the most wanted man in England!"

Lockwood's porcine features lit up as Hogg dropped Dixon. "Do you hear that, Samuel?" he said, rubbing his hands together. "The Riding Officer is, in fact, Silas Palmer!"

The face of the horrible man began to contort. "Palmer? *He's* Palmer?" He flailed an arm. "Kill Palmer!"

Suddenly, Hogg's head snapped around, his face has turned a hideous shade of purple. "What did you say?"

"Kill Palmer!" reiterated Samuel, thrashing his arms around chaotically. "Kill Silas Palmer."

Hogg foamed at the mouth. His brutal hand reached out once more and grabbed Samuel violently by the throat. "Don't let me hear you say that!"

The scavenger gasped and spluttered as his faced turned a powerful shade of blue.

"What's the matter?" Eustace asked Lockwood, folding his arms effeminately. "Silas Palmer waits for us on the green, if you remember."

"So he does," hissed the constable in a soft voice before he threw Samuel to the ground.

* * *

It had been over three years since the Riding Officer had fought a duel in England, when he had wounded a man at dawn on Muswell Hill. He had not slept the night before that duel. Just the same as this duel, the adrenaline pumped through his veins. At dawn, he would have a chance for revenge. He remembered that last duel in London so distinctively.

Something petty had caused it. It had been an offhand comment which had escalated and soon the two men were pointing pistols at each other. His challenger had walked away with an arm wound and nothing of ill will was said between the two as they played cards later that night. A wry smile spread across the Riding Officer's face as he recalled the foolishness of it all; that and he was fighting his second duel within two weeks having supposedly given up duelling three years before. But that wry smile soon faded as he realised the gravity of this situation. This was not petty or foolish; this was serious – this was the man who had murdered his father. He now knew that Eustace Hogg and Silas Palmer were the same man and it explained how he managed to evade the authorities for as long as he had. The Riding Officer growled. It was a classic trick amongst felons. No less a figure than Dick Turpin had done it sixty years earlier.

"It's nearly dawn, officer!" said Gregory the blacksmith.

"Very good, Gregory!" replied the Riding Officer from where he sat under a tree.

"Thought he would be here by now," said Malachi. He looked down at the palms of his hands, drenched with sweat. He rubbed them against his trousers.

"He'll be here," replied the Riding Officer, taking his pipe from his pocket.

"Shall I fetch the wheelwright, lad?" asked Timms, who was leaning against another tree.

"Please, Mr Timms," said the Riding Officer. He began to pack his pipe with tobacco. "He'll be a valuable witness once this is over."

George's head peeped out from behind a tree. "Maybe this

Hogg chap won't come..." he said.

"He'll come, George," said the Riding Officer, coldly. "Eustace Hogg, or Silas Palmer to give him his correct name, is a viciously violent, bloodthirsty man. He loves inflicting pain and misery on others – he wouldn't miss an opportunity like this for the world!"

The Riding Officer began to inspect his gun. "Won't the referee bring the duelling pistols?" asked Heskett.

"Yes, Mr Heskett, but I want you to remember the plan," he replied. "If we are to overthrow Lockwood and Hogg we must stick to it. I want to lull them into a false sense of security. Malachi is my second. Mr Heskett will be here, too, and I know Hogg will not come alone so keep your pistols hidden. George, Gregory and the Timms brothers are to hide in the undergrowth with the rifles until I give the word."

"Here they come!" said Malachi.

"Who has he got with him?" asked Heskett.

Gregory stood on his tiptoes. "There's Lockwood, Johnson, Edwards, Samuel and Dixon!" he confirmed.

The Riding Officer rose to his feet. "Places, men."

* * *

Lockwood looked over from his chair with a grimace and a scowl. He slurped some coffee from a cup, letting it dribble over his chin. The coffee itself was carried in a flask by Samuel. He was not happy. The first time he had seen the Riding Officer was in London, four years previously in a gambling den, and in his company had been a beautiful woman. Lockwood had gone to London to corrupt an official. A fishmonger had set up business in Upperbridge and was destroying Lockwood's trade. After toying with the idea of having him murdered, he feared people might empathise with the victim, although Lockwood saw himself as the real victim as his trade had suffered as a result of the man who offered cheaper, fresher fish.

The way to get rid of the competition was to have everyone against his rival, so he must make him a subject of hatred. Britain was at war with the French and any patriotic Briton would hate an agent of the enemy in their community. Lockwood visited a friend who, after a substantial payment, began to fabricate the evidence that Lockwood's rival was an agent of the Directory of France looking to use Upperbridge as a potential landing site for the French Navy should they decide to invade. The execution of the man was swift. The Minister for Justice sent a detachment of guards to Upperbridge and he was removed very quickly. Lockwood and his associate retired for an evening's gaming as a way to celebrate. It was then that he cast his pig-like eyes upon the Riding Officer for the first time.

The Riding Officer had gambled wildly, and he had lost heavily. But the main event of the evening had been provided by a man who stormed into the den demanding satisfaction; it emerged that the young woman in the Riding Officer's company was the Swedish Ambassador's daughter. She had been in England for three months and had begun to gamble to pass the time. It was there that she met the Riding Officer. She was taken by his almost instant natural charm and they began an affair. They used a small flat away from his residence and her father's home for their liaisons and she did not want her father to find out – but he did.

The man who stormed into the gambling den claimed to be the young woman's fiancé, even though she denied she knew him at all. The man began to taunt the Riding Officer who initially did not want to duel, but the man hit a nerve and the Riding Officer finally agreed. Lockwood and his associate headed to Muswell Hill early the next morning with a group of other intrigued spectators. The shot that settled the dispute was talked about for years to come. The Riding Officer had shot the gun clean out of his opponent's hand, leaving him with a sprained wrist. The

Riding Officer left his foe with the comment that he hoped the man had been paid him well to make the unsuccessful challenge.

It pained Lockwood to admit it to himself but he was impressed when the Riding Officer had arrived in Upperbridge. He had planned to corrupt him early and have the Riding Officer train him in the use of a pistol. As Lockwood drank more coffee, he speculated that if the Riding Officer had let himself be corrupted and had trained Lockwood to use a pistol like he should have, then Lockwood would have been able to take him out with a single shot from where he sat. Another black mark against the name of the Riding Officer. *Why does he insist on doing himself no favours?*

Hogg had insisted that they stuck to his plan. He would wound the Riding Officer and then Lockwood and his cohorts would take out the Riding Officer's entourage. The Riding Officer would be taken to the Parish Gaol where he would sign a confession admitting he was Silas Palmer and had committed the murders for which Hogg was responsible; then they could do away with him. Lockwood felt uncomfortable. He didn't like the overconfidence of Hogg, and in particular the way he presumed he would incapacitate him with ease in just one shot. Lockwood felt he must commend the Riding Officer on his foolishness, though. He had turned up with only the man he believed was from Leatherhead and the old farmer from the Nottingham Road who both seemed unarmed. At least they would be a pushover.

* * *

The Riding Officer's boots left a trail in the dew-soaked grass as he and Hogg took their paces.

"Kill the murderer!" snapped Samuel, in an attempt to distract the Riding Officer. The tactic failed. The referee's handkerchief dropped and both men's guns sounded almost simultaneously. Hogg's shot fired high but the Riding Officer spread low; he knew his target.

There was a bloodcurdling scream from Hogg as the Riding Officer's shot tore through Hogg's right knee. The gargoyle crumpled to the ground, his eyes rolling back as the pain cut through his body, and blood began to billow from his leg. His entourage instinctively ran to him, forgetting the plan that was made.

"Leave him!" bellowed the Riding Officer in a calm, confident voice. "Cover them, men!"

Malachi and Heskett drew their pistols and the others emerged with their rifles. They circled Hogg's entourage.

"What is going on?" said Lockwood. His head flailed back as he stood with legs wide apart and his hands on his hips.

"Gentlemen, in a little over half an hour the County of Lincoln regiment will be here to arrest you all!" the Riding Officer informed him.

Lockwood clasped his clammy hands together, his mouth drooping as he shuffled his feet. "On what basis will they arrest us?"

"First of all, there's wrecking," said the Riding Officer. "You tried to blame that on me. Then there's theft, namely of my horse; and kidnap, that would be my wife and myself; wrongful imprisonment, of myself and Gregory to name but two. Then bribery, there's countless there; and murder, Joe Bell, my father, Grantham, a village rector and Kitching as well."

From the corner of his eye he saw Hogg reaching for his dropped gun. The Riding Officer turned and kicked Hogg's arm. Hogg released another bloodcurdling scream as the force of the kick snapped his wrist, sending the gun out of harm's way. The Riding Officer knelt down on Hogg, his knee pinning the gargoyle's head to the ground.

"Is this the man who shot your father, George?" the Riding Officer asked George.

"Yes, it is!" replied George, a look of contempt burning

through Hogg. "That's Silas Palmer, that's the ugly devil who murdered my father in cold blood."

"When I heard Silas Palmer described as the ugliest man in England, I should have known it was you, Hogg," the Riding Officer proclaimed, driving his knee even harder into Hogg's head. "I found it hard to believe there was anyone uglier than *you* in the whole world."

"Here's Timms!" announced Malachi.

"He's got the wheelwright with him," added Gregory.

"That's the man who shot Joe Bell! Eustace Hogg did it," stated the wheelwright without being asked. "I was too scared to identify him..." he admitted, humbly. "I was afraid of Lockwood. I thought they might try to kill me if I spoke out. I remember Cutler..."

"Malachi, do you recognise anyone?" the Riding Officer asked.

"I recognise pig-face here," Malachi confirmed, pointing to Lockwood. "He was the one who paid to have you killed. He also referred to your wife as his fiancée."

"How about you, Mr Heskett?" the Riding Officer inquired of the farmer.

"His fish killed my brother," Heskett said, pointing his pistol at Lockwood.

"He also had your nephew killed," the Riding Officer added. "I know all about you, Lockwood. The way you took over another man's business and another's home, the corruption you've spread, the lives you have ruined and your demented delusions of grandeur. The game is now up - there will be *no* King Hubert the First."

"You know nothing, my friend," Lockwood said.

"I know a lot more than you realise. I can guarantee that you will be dancing the Tyburn Jig sometime in your pathetic future, courtesy of your brutal past."

Lockwood clasped his hands together, almost as if he was

pleading for mercy. "I'm just a simple fishmonger who has been unfortunately dragged into this embarrassing situation."

"I am no idiot, Lockwood, unlike you."

The Scotsman's jaw trembled before it hung open, and he swallowed. He had the air of a desperate man as his eyes widened and he dropped to his knees. "You can't hold me responsible for Mr Hogg's actions..."

"I can when you've instructed him, my dear Hubert!" the Riding Officer replied with an arrogant smile. He debated whether he should aim a kick at his grovelling foe but decided not to. "Your days in Upperbridge are numbered, Lockwood. Your empire is *over!*" Then the Riding Officer turned to his men, and said, coldly, "Someone bandage this freak of nature's leg. And the rest of you – may you all hang!"

* * *

The last of the summer was upon the village of Upperbridge, Lincolnshire. The sea was murky grey in colour and the waves were becoming more aggressive, tossing boats around as they travelled, and charging up the beach when they met the coast. The Riding Officer gazed into the body of water as he wrapped his arms around the waist of his beautiful Anna, who, too, was transfixed with the view of the North Sea. He slipped his hand into Anna's as he felt relief, knowing that in only a few weeks smuggling would be rife in the village but, for the first time it what felt like a lifetime, it would not be his responsibility.

"We can head to Cornwall tomorrow," said the Riding Officer. "There was a considerable reward on Hogg's head. I've split it with the men who helped me capture him."

"Very good!" said Anna softly, deep in thought.

The Riding Officer began to caress his wife's neck. "You smell nice!" he whispered in her ear.

"It is some scent the Countess of Lincoln gave to me. From the

Indies, apparently," Anna answered, still somewhat distant.

"What's wrong, Anna?"

"I don't feel sad about my father's death," admitted Anna.

"Why is that?"

"As far as I'm concerned, he stopped being my father many moons ago when greed and corruption took over him. But I hate myself for not caring."

"I know how you feel," the Riding Officer said. "Part of me hates myself for what I did to Hogg."

"Eustace Hogg is a violent brute," Anna replied. "If anyone deserved that, it was him."

"He's had to have a leg amputated," said the Riding Officer.

"Couldn't have happened to a better person." Anna ground the heel of her shoe into the ground.

"He is a human being..." the Riding Officer said, his head dropping.

Anna placed her hand on her husband's face and gently lifted it so he could look into her eyes. "Eustace Hogg isn't human," she said, "he is anything but! Do you know he tried to force himself on me?"

"No, I didn't..." said the Riding Officer, finding some justification in his actions. He slipped his hand into his wife's and squeezed tight. "Tomorrow we'll be away to our new life," he said, "to Cornwall!"

Excerpts from the Press

The following passages are adapted from contemporary accounts, pamphlets and newspapers in England, ranging from September 1797 to May 1798.

Eustace Hogg, also known as Silas Palmer, was found guilty of ten counts of murder spreading over five years and six counties. The former Bow Street Runner was hanged at Newgate Gaol on the 21st December 1797. Palmer was one of England's most wanted felons. There was a reward of thirty thousand pounds on his head which was claimed by a group of men in Lincolnshire. Amongst those he was found guilty of murdering were a Lincolnshire plough boy Joseph Bell, Lincolnshire draper Jeremiah Kitching, the rector of St George's Church in the Derbyshire village of Clay's Cross, and the former Member of Parliament for the Lincolnshire Borough of Upperbridge, Adam Grantham. A coachman who had formerly worked for Grantham gave testimony that Hogg had disguised himself as a riding officer in order to the murder the politician and frame a local man for the crime. At the time he was hanged Hogg was an amputee. His right leg had been removed from just above the knee as a result of a gunshot that led to his capture.

Born Silas Palmer, he had joined the Bow Street Runners at a young age. He quickly climbed the ranks but was later discharged for his conduct. He took the name of another ex-Runner who died of pneumonia in order to shield his true identity as he worked as a hired assassin.

Hubert Lockwood was found guilty of five counts of murder, two counts of kidnap and one count of wrecking with the intent to plunder and endangering life. Former employees of the fishmonger from the village of Upperbridge, Lincolnshire, gave evidence that Lockwood had ordered the murders of Bell, Kitching, Grantham, a former riding officer named Heskett and Heskett's father. He was hanged at Newgate Gaol on the 22nd December 1797, the day after Eustace Hogg's execution.

Hubert Lockwood had amassed an empire of crime that not only involved smuggling but extortion and murder. When an opponent to his empire had emerged, Lockwood would have it arranged for them to be eliminated. Lockwood was a Scotsman in origin and had fled Edinburgh twenty years earlier. A warrant had been issued for his arrest after he raped a woman from high society. Lockwood re-emerged in Upperbridge two years later as an apprentice fishmonger. He inherited the fishmonger's business when his employer died in mysterious circumstances. In addition, Lockwood inherited the entire estate of the former MP for Upperbridge, Adam Grantham, who had numerous criminal interests dating back many years.

When Lockwood's residence was searched, the parish constabulary uncovered many of Lockwood's criminal interests and documents linking him, the late Adam Grantham and Eustace Hogg to numerous crimes including an audacious plan to overthrow the government and a plan to assassinate the King of Great Britain before installing Lockwood himself as king. The documents also revealed Lockwood's plan to remove Grantham by assassination and the plan to frame a local man for the crime.

Gabriel Dixon, a former herring caller from Upperbridge in Lincolnshire, was the hangman at the execution of Hogg and Lockwood. When found guilty of the charges of murder and wrecking, Dixon entered a plea bargain to save his own life. As part of the bargain, he testified extensively against both Hogg and Lockwood on the crimes of murder and wrecking, focusing on their attempts to frame the local riding officer for two major crimes, neither of which he had committed.

Augustus Stewart was found guilty on multiple counts of bribery and corruption with one further count of sodomy. On the morning that both Lockwood and Hogg were arrested, a division of the County of Lincoln Regiment attended Stewart's home just outside the village of Upperbridge in the county of Lincolnshire where they found Stewart engaged in a lewd sexual act with a young man of fifteen years. Augustus Stewart was sentenced to death by hanging. He hanged on the 4th January 1798. His accomplice in the act of lewdness awaits trial.

Isaiah Samuel, a scavenger from Upperbridge in the shire of Lincoln, was found guilty of four counts of murder, one count of wrecking and multiple counts of perverting the course of justice. He denied all charges and attempted to blame them on a man formerly employed in his home village in the position of a riding officer. He was charged with multiple counts of contempt of court for his attitude in the dock. Whilst in custody, a male child of nine was found at Samuel's former residence in Upperbridge. The child, who had been kidnapped from a circus two years previously, was malnourished and had been routinely subjected to physical and sexual assault by Samuel who was found guilty of sodomy. In an old trunk at Samuel's residence the parish constable made the grim discovery of the skeletal remains of two other children. Samuel was tried and found guilty of two further counts of kidnap and sodomy. He awaits execution.

George Williamson, formerly of London, perished in an accident in Grimsby on the 17th November 1797. The nineteen year old former apprentice chandler had spoken prior to the accident of emulating a friend who had acted as a flying man in Widnes, Lancashire, a few months earlier. Witnesses stated that Williamson was doing it more for the thrill than any financial award. He had earned a substantial amount of money from a cut in the reward for helping to catch one of England's most wanted felons. Reports state the rope used was loose and Williamson fell, fatally fracturing his skull on impact with the ground. He had no next of kin.

Lawrence Timms, a farmer from Upperbridge, was announced as the new parish constable of the area. A new Justice of the Peace is yet to be appointed. Both positions were recently vacated during a series of high profile arrests in the Lincolnshire village. On his appointment, the Earl of Lincoln commented that the area had been blighted in recent times by a series of corrupt officials and deserved a man who could be trusted and respected.

Frederick Cheever was arrested by the Upperbridge constabulary on the evening of January the 3rd whilst drunk and incapable. Whilst in the custody of the constabulary, Mr Cheever suffered a fatal stroke and passed away. It later emerged that Mr Cheever was a local Member of Parliament and he was the second MP from the area to die within a year. Adam Grantham died a year earlier when he was murdered by the notorious Silas Palmer. An election is due to take place to fill the vacant seat, but a suitable candidate is yet to step forward.

On the 20th of November 1797 a thunderstorm hit the Lincolnshire coast. During the storm a bolt of lightning struck the woodlands on the outskirts of the village of Upperbridge. The woodland burned most of the night until the rain put out the fire. The fire burned away some deadwood and in the process it uncovered human remains. Witnesses who found the remains believe them to be of a Mr Cutler, a former citizen of Upperbridge, who vanished three years previously and was believed to be a victim of the empire of Hubert Lockwood. Those who discovered the remains identified a piece of jewellery that was a personal item of Mr Cutler.

The estate of Jeremiah Kitching, a draper from Upperbridge, Lincolnshire, was settled. His only living relative, his daughter, inherited his entire estate. She sold his draper's business and assets located in Upperbridge, Lincolnshire for a substantial sum and left the area. Her current whereabouts are unknown.

Chapter Fourteen

The Beginning?

England was in the last throes of summer as the young couple approached their new home in Cornwall. They had purchased a home in a small hamlet not far from the coast. They travelled cautiously, taking a week to make the journey, and still felt fresh as they closed in on what was to be their new home and their new life.

The Riding Officer sat behind Anna as they rode his trusted mare to their new home along the coastline. The sun was beginning to fade and the Riding Officer knew that winter was on its way. He felt content that he wouldn't have to spend hours in the cold, the rain, the sleet and the snow, patrolling for men who might never arrive and he would have absolutely no chance of ever arresting yet alone prosecuting; he was a riding officer no more. He was glad he was away from the vices of London. He was content that he could live comfortably and create his art freely. His arms wrapped firmly but gently around his beautiful wife's pleasing figure. Anna would be company enough for him on those cold, winter nights.

Anna felt her husband's hands around her waist. She felt safe and secure for the first time in her life. She was glad to be away from those endless propositions from the drunks in the inn and she was secure in knowing that the threat of a despairing marriage to Lockwood was no longer hanging over her. She felt relief that Hogg was no longer a presence and a fear she would not have to deal with. She gripped her husband's hand; she knew that now she was with him she would never have to be scared again.

They had passed through the South of England with a looming threat of highwaymen, vagabonds and other lowlife criminals. It didn't bother Anna as she knew she would be protected by her husband and if she could survive the soon-to-be-late Hubert Lockwood and his associates, then highwaymen and vagabonds were nothing to be feared in the slightest.

If someone had told her six months earlier that she would leave Upperbridge, married to the man she loved, she would have burst into hysterical laughter and would have most likely been incarcerated in the local asylum. But there she was, married to the great enigma; there was still a lot of mystery surrounding him but she knew she loved him. Anna had felt safe all the way from Upperbridge. Ever since she had learned that Lockwood and Hogg had been arrested she had been at peace with the world. Finally she was away from the corruption and greed of the Lincolnshire village. Her new community might have a few rogues but it would never be Upperbridge; to begin with, it wasn't a rotten borough like Upperbridge. An old chapter of her life had finally been completed and a new one was set to begin.

* * *

The cold began to set in as the daylight began to dwindle. As his faithful mare trotted on the Riding Officer smiled, realising a torrid period of his life was over. His vices cut off, his debt erased, he was free to be creative and earn money from his work. But the main thing was that it would be inspired by his one true love. The woman who had once saved his life.

"I never asked you, Anna," he began to his wife, "how were you able to save me that night I was lynched?"

Anna smiled. She had waited a long time to tell the tale to her husband. "When Binns and Edwards dragged me to Lockwood's residence, I waited till I was inside the house. Then I bit, clawed and kicked until I could steal a pistol in the house and escape," she explained. "A well-placed foot to a gentlemen's groin can do wonders!"

"How did you get to the green?" the Riding Officer asked.

"On your horse," Anna confirmed. "I went where the mob had been and I knew they had taken you to the green because that's where Lockwood instructed all the lynchings he arranged to take place."

"I wasn't the first?" the Riding Officer asked, quite shocked that it had been a regular occurrence.

"Oh no," said Anna, calmly. "There have been plenty of lynchings in that village. Some were riding officers, some innocent people, some who threatened Lockwood and his empire. How ironic it is that soon he will dance the Tyburn jig himself at Newgate."

"How did you get me down from the tree?"

"I shot the rope!" Anna replied. "I'm a crack shot with a pistol. I'm not a prissy city girl, you know."

The Riding Officer wrapped his arms around Anna once more. He placed his head on her shoulder and rested his cheek next to hers.

"If I ever stop loving you, I want you to throw me off the nearest cliff!" the Riding Officer said to Anna.

"It's a deal," replied Anna before she leant back and kissed him on the cheek.

"I don't know how many people there are on the face of the planet," he said, "but I'm damn sure I have married the most beautiful person on this planet."

"Tell me about Malin..." Anna said, softly.

"Why do you wish to know about her?" the Riding Officer asked, confused. How had his wife learned that name? "That was a long time ago..."

"When Lockwood was at his cruellest, when he was raging about how you were a coward and a criminal," Anna said, "to hurt me he would tell me that soon you would be heading back to Malin eventually; so who is she?"

The Riding Officer smiled. "She was the daughter of the

Swedish Ambassador," he explained. "She was also my former lover."

"What happened to her?" Anna asked.

"We met when I was on my downward spiral. We did everything to hide our affair from her father. When he found out he sent a man after me."

Anna looked at her husband. "What did this man do?"

"He challenged me to a duel," the Riding Officer replied. "I was able to disarm him during the duel. That was the last duel I fought until only a few weeks ago, when that brash Irishman in Cobh and the hideous freak known as Silas Palmer crossed my path."

"So where is she now?" Anna asked, still curious about this woman from her husband's past. "Where is Malin?"

"Her father sent her back to Sweden. She married a cousin of the king of Sweden."

"So she is gone from your life?"

"Gone for over three years," her husband confirmed. "I don't miss her. If she hadn't gone, I would never have met you!"

Anna turned so she was side saddle on the horse and facing her husband. She looked into his eyes and they kissed long and passionately.

* * *

They were about a quarter of a mile from their new home as the sun was setting. They had picked up a sack full of vegetables and chunk of beef which would contribute to the stew they would enjoy as their first meal in their new house. As they made their way along the coastline path, a figure on horseback approached them. He was a young man in his early to mid-twenties wearing a riding officer's uniform.

"Halt!" he said in an authoritarian manner. "Who are you?"

"We are the new owners of that property over there," the

Riding Officer advised him, his hand clutching the reins pointing in the building's direction. "We have the relative deeds if you don't believe us."

"I hope you are not smugglers," the local riding officer said.

"We are anything but," the Riding Officer replied with a laugh. "Are you a local?"

"Yes, I am!" the local replied, his nose rising up in the air as he tried to make himself look important.

"You don't sound it," the Riding Officer told him, using his duellist's instincts in an attempt to rile his arrogant challenger. "You sound about as Cornish as the late Maximillian Robespierre."

"My father is a local landowner," the man said, sneering. "I had a fine education at the finest public schools and universities!"

"So you became a riding officer after gaining all of that?" asked the Riding Officer. He couldn't help sounding condescending.

"Anything to serve my king and country before I inherit my title," replied the local riding officer, offering a salute. "I am a man of honour."

"I tried that, officer," the Riding Officer informed him. "It is the most unrewarding job in the world."

"You must be a fool, then," sneered the officer.

"I am no fool!" snapped the Riding Officer. "It is you who strikes me as the fool."

"I am an officer and gentleman and you will address me as a gentleman," the local officer demanded.

The Riding Officer smirked at the fool in front of him. "Who do you think are?" he asked the local officer, "The Duke of York?"

"My name is Simeon Brand and I am a servant of my king and country," the local man declared. "And I am a gentleman so you are to refer to me as *sir!*"

The Riding Officer smirked again at the pompous little man. "I don't know why you want to be a riding officer," he said. "The hours are lousy, nobody respects you, you are continuously threatened and the pay is certainly not worth it. You are best off getting yourself a proper job, lad!"

"And who are you to say that to me?" demanded the local officer, grabbing his pistol from his belt. "Who exactly are you?"

The Riding Officer sat up straight in his saddle and in his calm, clear, confident voice replied, "I am one of the most sought-after people in the land. I am a poet and *I* am a man of honour. My name, sir, is Peter Lloyd!"

**TOP HAT
BOOKS**

Historical fiction that lives.

We publish fiction that captures the contrasts, the achievements, the optimism and the radicalism of ordinary and extraordinary times across the world.

We're open to all time periods and we strive to go beyond the narrow, foggy slums of Victorian London. Where are the tales of the people of fifteenth century Australasia? The stories of eighth century India? The voices from Africa, Arabia, cities and forests, deserts and towns? Our books thrill, excite, delight and inspire.

The genres will be broad but clear. Whether we're publishing romance, thrillers, crime, or something else entirely, the unifying themes are timescale and enthusiasm. These books will be a celebration of the chaotic power of the human spirit in difficult times. The reader, when they finish, will snap the book closed with a satisfied smile.